A
LONG
WAY

A LONG WAY

Jay Bern

PENTLAND PRESS, INC.
UNITED STATES OF AMERICA

PUBLISHED BY PENTLAND PRESS, INC.
5124 Bur Oak Circle Raleigh 27612
United States of America
919-782-0281

ISBN 1-57197-121-1
Library of Congress Catalog Card Number 98-065641

Copyright ©1998 J.B. Homburg

Printed in the United States of America

Thanks to all who were very supportive by showing genuine interest in my writing endeavors during the challenging stages of this work, especially my wife and my editor.

Chapter One

Holland, 1940.

One calm and sunny Sunday morning, Ian Halls was on the beach with many other soldiers enjoying the nice weather along with villagers. Children were making sand castles and digging moats around them, while mothers kept an eye on their broods. Suddenly a caravan of cars stopped on the boulevard, discharging families who seemed agitated.

Doors slammed, there were loud voices, and children were crying. Everybody near the commotion looked up at the arrivals, who apparently were not from the area. The newcomers were soon surrounded by villagers and soldiers, who asked what was going on. They heard a story which sounded like it was from another world.

The group consisted of Jewish families who had escaped the pogroms in Germany and fled to Holland to seek freedom. Because they had been confronted with the rigors of Nazidom first hand, they had anxiously followed the news of the past weeks and again felt threatened, believing neutrality was wishful thinking. They told the bystanders that they had purchased an old but seaworthy lifeboat stationed in the village. They intended to cross the North Sea to England in that boat.

To the group around them it all sounded unbelievable and the situation was difficult for them to comprehend. However, it became very real when the doors to the boat shed were opened, horses were tied to the boat's undercarriage, and members of the coastal sea rescue brigade started to bring the boat out on the beach.

Everybody stared without moving, but when the wheels of the carriage began to bog down in the soft sand, some soldiers, Ian amongst them, jumped into action and helped push the heavy load toward the sea. The pandemonium was complete; the horses shied, the men of the brigade shouted, and the pushers huffed and puffed. Slowly the vehicle moved again and was kept going until the boat was in the water and lifted from the carriage.

Loud cheers went up from the spectators along the coast when the lifeboat floated and the Jewish group became even more excited and started moving their belongings to the edge of the water. There was hardly any surf on that blissful calm day and the women and children could get on board easily. Helping hands tossed their luggage over the gunwale, while some of the refugees handed bystanders notes with names and addresses of persons who would come and take their cars.

Ian noticed that there was food, water, and a tarpaulin on board and saw a full set of oars, but then his eyes fell on the pitifully small diesel engine and he wondered if these people would ever make it to England. He mentioned his doubts to the leader of the group, who looked at him. "Well, son," the leader said, "it is better to perish on our way to freedom than to come into the clutches of the Nazis. Good luck to all of you," and he turned around with tears in his eyes. After some cranking, the little engine sputtered and caught, and when soldiers gave the boat a last shove, the boat turned its bow to the sea and gradually began making slow speed. The occupants' waves were returned by the crowd on the beach.

Children had stopped playing, the mothers had left their knitting behind, and everybody stood on the beach staring at the disappearing boat, which looked quite tiny and vulnerable in the distance. Nobody spoke, each with their own thoughts on what they had just witnessed and its consequences. Long after the boat was just a little blip on the horizon, the crowd went slowly back to its previous spots, but there appeared to be little joy left.

Soon Ian went back to his temporary barracks, eagerly looking for his friends who hadn't been on the beach, and when he found them, told the story of what he had witnessed.

His friends were flabbergasted to learn that people were willing to risk their lives to flee from their safe country—or was the country not so safe? The stories they had heard and read about suddenly seemed real.

"These people know what is going on and we still live here like we're on an island, as if nothing will happen to us," Ian said with conviction.

"Well, what can we do more than what is being done already," answered Bob, the pragmatic.

"We should be better informed about the reality," said Dan, but then contradicted himself, "In that case, the whole population would be alarmed and chaos would result."

So the talk went on, with other soldiers listening in and giving their opinion, but no one had a solution. "Let's wait and see" was the conclusion and many realized that various countries, by taking just that approach, were being overrun by the German war machine.

As if to underline Sunday morning's happening, the roll call that evening it was announced:

- All furloughs were, as of that moment, canceled, and those on leave had to return to their bases immediately.
- The Geneva Convention rules had to be strictly followed.

- The antiaircraft gun battery, stationed around the nearby military airfield, was put on full alert.
- Emergency food rations would be issued.

On the early morning of May 10, 1940, the country was, without any declaration of war, invaded by German storm troops.

The country was at war.

Chapter Two

As Ian's captain had predicted, all hell broke loose for the country that had not experienced war for more than one hundred years.

In order to prevent bridges from being blown up, enemy troops, under cover of darkness the night before the attack began, had infiltrated the most eastern area over the border. The first day they quickly overran the eastern part of the country, which was not strongly fortified. They encountered strong resistance at the more hilly area in their push westward to the coast.

The Dutch government issued a strong protest against the barbaric move and by radio broadcast told the citizenry that the country had been invaded by an enemy which came like a thief in the night. Due to the German move, the Low Country asked for help from the Allies. The Dutch realized they would be no match against the German overwhelming manpower, equipment, air force, and war-experienced assault troops.

The entire Western European front line exploded into action. Britain, heavily occupied with many operations elsewhere, could only send some demolition troops on warships to the coast of Holland with orders to blow up refineries and other installations, while France, with its hands full on the Maginot line, could only share some infantry battalions, which arrived late in the southern part of the country.

Meanwhile, Ian, Bob, and Dan got first-hand experience in the fighting.

From the first moment of attack, the signal corps was flooded by a constant flow of messages and Iandid not have a chance to come to grips with what was actually happening. He soon realized that, being a key operator, he was not supposed to get a handle on what was going on, but was to send and receive messages as his primary duty.

When he returned to his room after an exhausting, long, first day, he could not tell others very much about the situation in the occupied eastern part of the country, since communications from that area were practically broken off. Only then did he remember that his family lived there. He jumped from his bunk, raced to a nearby public phone and had to wait in line. When it was finally his turn, he found that there was no contact.

There was little else to do but worry.

Bob, the so-called eagle-eyed gunner, was together with the others of the gun crews manning the four heavy anti-aircraft guns, protecting the airfield and the aircraft stationed there. It was still early in the morning. Soldiers hauled ammo and loaded guns, and the gun crew took their positions with instructions from each of the gun sergeants, who managed to calm everybody by acting as if it was a usual exercise.

This worked wonders. Bob sat in his chair from which he could swivel the gun in a horizontal plane according to coordinates given by the battery's central command via his earphones. He felt coolly determined to do his task. His colleague, doing the same in the vertical plane, also was fully prepared and ready.

They did not have long to wait until the first squadron of four German Stuka dive bombers was reported coming in from the sea, without much advance warning. The squadron first headed east and it looked as if it was heading inland for another target. But it came back and circled above the airfield. The control command post issued a stream of coordinates but the guns could not keep pace and pointed in all different directions. This was the favorite tactic of the Stukas. When flying in a circle above the target the coordinates changed every second, which made it difficult for anti-aircraft guns to follow.

The gunnery sergeant took over the command center, noticing immediately the problem his, and other, guns were having. He shouted for them to lay a barrage of fire at a given elevation ahead of the squadron. At any given point in the circle, the Stukas went into a straight dive with a loud, chilling scream, let their bombs drop, and at the last possible moment pulled out of their dive, using their machine guns to strafe the battery and its protective machine gun nests. It all seemed to last an eternity, but in reality took only a few minutes.

Aircraft scrambled to get in the air while under fire, and the few that succeeded were no match against the more maneuverable and faster enemy. Then it was over, leaving desolation behind. More than half of the twelve machines were on fire and exploded and two machine gun nests were silent, but all guns remained undamaged. Their crews were in shock and Bob remained in his seat as if in a trance until the sergeant bellowed them into action.

"Reload, move, move, damn it. Keep alert. Others might be back any moment. And be fast. There isn't a moment to lose."

With this sudden outburst, they all came to their senses. One crew member had to be replaced. He was crying and writhing his body. Bob, realizing this was his first encounter with a case of shell shock, gritted his teeth, cooled down from his rage, and shouted to his colleague in the other seat, "Next time, we'll get the bastards–shoot their balls off!"

The sergeant smiled encouragingly, "All right, men, on your posts and be fast and ready."

In an anti-climatic moment Bob noticed the wrecked planes, saw the fire fighting crews applying a foam cover, and noticed Red Cross soldiers carrying wounded and dead men toward waiting trucks. My God, who will it be next time, he wondered, but strangely enough felt kind of detached from the whole nightmare.

Suddenly, he heard a voice, "Bob, are you all right?" It was Dan with the food supply detail, looking at him questioningly. Bob turned around to him, "That was bloody scary and I still hear the screaming of the engines when they dove and pulled up over our heads. This makes our exercise on dummies towed by slowly flying planes in a straight line look like a terrible joke."

Nothing happened for many hours until suddenly the command post bursted into action, alerting gunners to incoming aircraft. This time everybody was ready. A machine gun started rattling, but was soon silenced by the order "Friendly craft." Two fast fighter planes with the national emblem on their wings flew over and disappeared.

"It would be nice if we had more of that type instead of the old slow ones we have here," somebody said in a tone full of envy.

The five remaining biplanes had been hauled out of their hangars and positioned on the airfield, ready for action to the best of their ability. Bob felt admiration for the pilots who, no doubt, were fully aware of their odds against a situation such as they had witnessed hours earlier. Ian received a coded message with instructions that the planes had to be diverted to a more inland airfield that offered more advance warning against approaching enemy aircraft and a better fighting chance. He passed the order to the command post and shortly thereafter the planes took off.

"Are we going to defend an empty airstrip, or what?" Bob asked the sarge.

"Hold your horses, son. Some wooden dummy craft are being trucked to us right now."

The gun crew looked at him, wondering how on earth the sergeant could know about that. He was correct, since some hours later the camouflaged dummies arrived on flatbed trucks, were quickly assembled and looked almost real, especially from the air—or everybody hoped they did.

Some had no wings attached, which looked kind of stupid, at least to the men on the ground. The provisional hangars were constructed so that each covered only the wings and engine of the plane, leaving the rump sticking out, and someone had ordered only dummy rumps made to save time and money.

The more complete fakes were positioned in the open as if ready to take off. It looked like real again, although the gun crews felt somewhat funny. "Aren't we here like sitting ducks, protecting heaps of wood?"

The sergeant, as usual, had a ready answer. "This will give you smart asses a chance to really get them for a change."

This remark intensified their determination.

It was a long afternoon with no action for the battery until the sun was setting, when again the alarm sounded. Everybody was tense, ready for action. This time there were six Stukas coming in from the west. Instead of flying inland and then turning, they headed straight for the airfield. This kept the sun behind them, which made sighting more difficult for the machine guns crews. The big guns' crews were not hampered by this, following the leads from the command center. With the little experience they had gained that early morning they laid a barrage of heavy fire with the result that one Stuck was hit, screaming down and exploding on impact in the dunes. The gun crews cheered and yelled, but the sergeant hollered above the melee, "Watch it, you fools, there is one coming right at us."

And indeed, one Stuka dove right at Bob's gun with frightening speed. Bob and his mate swung the gun amazingly fast to the target and they fired staccato, not heeding the details of coordinates, simply because there was no time to do it differently.

It seemed the plane was upon them when the pilot let go two bombs at the gun. Nobody could follow what went on at that moment. Both bombs hit, one over the gun and one directly in front of it, and the entire installation shook violently. Bob's mate slumped in his seat, not moving, and Bob was slung against the firing box with a force that knocked him unconscious. The machine gun crew behind them fired wildly when the plane pulled out of its dive and hit it in the tail, apparently making the Stuka unstable. The machine wiggled and disappeared over the dunes, rapidly losing height, and crashed into the sea.

The remaining four Stukas made a last strafing run over the battery and disappeared, leaving behind a chaos of burning dummies, one battered gun, and several casualties. The latter were quickly taken care of, including Bob and his gunner mate, and ambulances sped to town with flashing lights. In the Red Cross hospital, it was found that Bob suffered from a brain concussion and a broken jaw, but his mate was not so lucky and didn't make it. Ian and Dan used a couple of hours off duty to visit with Bob, and sitting around his bed they were all very different from the boys they were when they first met only five months ago.

Bob couldn't talk very much but the others told him about their experiences in their duties during the war, which by now was in its second day. There had been no further attacks on the airfield; probably the enemy's reconnaissance planes, which had been flying over at high altitude making photographs of the damage, had provided proof that after the first attack there were only dummies left. Dan boosted his own morale by repeated statements on the first priority of food supply under fighting conditions, but to his chagrin, didn't get any applause. Ian had more news from around the country and it mainly referred to the continued battle in the east and bombing of military installations along the coast.

Soon the visiting hour was over and the two friends departed with good wishes as well as a warning to take it easy with the good-looking nurses. They did not tell Bob about his gunner mate and of others whom they all knew; he would find out soon enough.

During the following days the attacks ceased, duty became easier due to a certain routine, and patrolling the dunes around the clock was considered boring.

Far from boring was the general situation in the country. In the east and the south the armies had to steadily withdraw to the west, despite their fierce defense against an overwhelming force, while the bombardment of bridges and harbor installations took a heavy toll. Clearly, the enemy was set to occupy the country as fast as possible in order to form a front against Britain, separated only by the North Sea.

Although they were advancing, the German Supreme Command had not anticipated it would take several days and they still could not strike to the coast. Paratroops were called in. They landed behind the inundated water line, cutting off the troops in the east and south. They also battled against marines who defended important bridges, many of them located in the cities. Even those measures did not succeed within the German time frame and an ultimatum was sent to the Dutch to surrender, stipulating that if they did not, the Germans would bomb open cities.

In late afternoon May 15, 1940, the troops from the fishing village were ordered to come to the nearby town where other battalions gathered to receive the news that the government, under pressure of the German threat to bomb open cities, decided to surrender in order to save lives of the non-combatant population. The royal family had fled to England moments before parachutists reached the palaces and would install a government in exile to continue the war against Germany from there. Most ships of the navy also escaped to England.

Upon hearing the devastating announcement, the soldiers either stared at each other or openly cried. Somebody began singing the national hymn and all joined in. Never before had Ian sung the hymn with so much feeling. For the first time he realized the historical bond with his countrymen.

A loud voice called after the hymn had ended, "We will not give up. We will keep fighting." The cry was taken over by all the soldiers until it became a roar. It took staff officers quite some time to calm the men down and re-establish order. A colonel urged them to follow the command and not jeopardize the arrangement forced upon the country in order to avoid bloodshed.

The country had given up and a long, horrible night-lasting five years-followed.

Chapter Three

After the announcement of the surrender and the outburst of national pride, the troops had no idea what would follow. As they had done before, each section looked to its sergeants for leadership, but found that even these usually well informed petty officers had no idea what to do. All they could do was to keep their groups together with some kind of discipline, fully aware that otherwise, pandemonium would be inevitable and control lost. Sensing the general atmosphere of the soldiers, the colonel, who had spoken before, ordered that each troop had to return to its respective accommodations and stay there until further orders.

Although this was not very enlightening, at least it was something to follow and Ian's artillery battery crew marched back to the two schools on the coast, where they had been training. Other troops did the same and the square was left empty of soldiers, leaving burghers of the town who had gathered around the military wondering what would happen next. The same question was in Ian's mind when heading for the coast, but since there were no answers he and the others kept going in silence.

Upon their return, there was roll call, the food crew was ordered to the kitchen and the rest to their quarters. In the messroom, Ian and his buddies sat around the tables and only after they had finished the improvised meal did the talk start.

"Are we going into POW camps?"

"Why don't we go home; it's all over."

"What do we do with our rifles and other stuff?"

"What will happen to the country?"

And so it went, on and on, until Ian, who usually took the lead of the group, suggested the men ask sarge, who had become their trusted confidant. One went to find him and after a while the sergeant entered the room, faced the men, and sat down. "I know you have many questions like I have, but until things have been clarified, let's keep our cool, okay?"

He looked around and addressed Ian and Dan. "You two come with me right now."

They followed him and he led them to the sergeants' room where others were already gathered.

A master sergeant spoke. "Since we have as yet not received any instructions on further actions, my colleagues and I are of the opinion that under no circumstances is the enemy to capture our guns and use them against our allies. Therefore, we have decided to nail the guns beyond repair. We have not informed our officers of this because we do not want to put them in a position of forbidding us to do so, mainly since as officers they are under oath to follow the Geneva Convention."

"Tonight, we'll set out to the battery and blow up the three remaining guns. This is an order. Tell nobody and return here at ten o'clock sharp. Thank you. Dismissed."

The last words were accompanied by a wink and a smile.

Ian and Dan returned to their quarters and were met with questions about what was going on. The two friends shrugged them off by mumbling something about a duty roster and the others lost interest promptly. Ian had doubts about the legitimacy of the plan but was behind it wholeheartedly, wondering how to nail or spike a gun. That would be something special. And it was.

At nightfall the small group climbed into a truck carrying buckets and a bag with equipment and went to the beach, without having been noticed by the guard, who was detained by one of the sergeants for an errand. This was accomplished easily, since the guard couldn't care less anyway.

The truck stopped on the boulevard. The soldiers took the buckets to the deserted beach, and following the master sergeant's instructions, filled the buckets with wet sand.

After arriving with their load at the perimeter of the battery guns, which had not been moved from previous positions, the small group unloaded the buckets and bag. The sergeants filled the gun barrels with the wet sand, and when the task was finished, the master sergeant went to the command post nerve center, making adjustments and taking out the emergency remote control cabinet. The recruits were kept at a distance, together with the sentries guarding the battery and empty airfield. The sentries obviously knew what was going on.

The next move they observed in the semidarkness was the loading of each of the three guns, and as an afterthought, the fourth and damaged one.

"That's for good measure," Ian said to Dan.

"Now we are going to see fireworks, I bet," Dan replied to nobody specific.

Apparently the work was done. The petty officers returned to the truck where the others were staying and the entire party took off for a safe distance. They settled behind a dune; the leader called, "Now," and shortly thereafter a forceful rumbling sound echoed through the area. The group didn't move for another fifteen minutes and then approached the battery, using flashlights to inspect the damage. The barrels were split open and the firing mechanisms blown. The master sergeant grunted with satisfaction, "Well done. Let's get out of here," and off they went, expecting people to come and investigate, but nobody appeared. The truck was parked near the school. The group dispersed and entered the school in twos and threes without causing alarm or stirring up questions. Ian and Dan felt like conspirators and were mighty proud to have been part of it, little as that was.

The next morning, during inspection, the officer on duty announced that the battery sustained extra damage and left it at that. For good order and understanding, he ordered that every soldier had to take care to maintain his rifle and other weapons. It was clear that the staff had decided to stay aloof from the action and not pursue it further.

Hearing that statement, Ian and Dan looked at each other and both felt the announcement was anticlimactic; not only that the expected "fireworks" in reality were subdued but also that now they wouldn't be considered heroes.

Main activities for the next couple of days consisted of letter writing, visits to the bakery opposite the school, occasional guard duty, card playing, and last, but not least, gossiping about the situation the country found itself in as occupied territory.

Radio broadcasts were of little help since all national stations had quickly been placed under German control and were considered biased. The government in exile had started transmission from Britain under the call name Radio Orange, which gave another picture. But at that time it was not very encouraging since the European theater was not going well for the Allies.

New orders were issued. The entire battery had to move from the village to the nearby town, which, at least, created action. They were trucked to real barracks just outside the town where it all had begun in January. The barracks were occupied already by other units and this latest addition made the quarters very crowded but the artillerists were finally glad to be under a more comfortable military roof. Again they waited for new orders with nothing to do other than stand guard, which, due to the large number of troops, wasn't very often. "We are occupied and haven't seen a single German soldier" was the general observation.

That last remark was soon rectified. One morning the sentry noticed that a small group of men in military uniform on funny-looking bicycles was heading in the direction of the camp. He called the officer on duty, who observed the group through his binoculars, calling out, "The Germans are coming!"

This exclamation went through the camp like wildfire and everybody ran to the perimeter to watch.

The German paratroopers, who were dropped from transport planes with their specially constructed bikes to control the area, noticing a great number of armed soldiers, jumped from their vehicles, and took cover. For a while nothing happened, until a commanding officer in the camp shouted, "Wave a white flag, for heaven's sake." Ingeniously a bed sheet was tied to a pole and displayed. The Germans quickly mounted their bikes, rifles at the ready, and came to a halt at the gate. They were war-hardened, no-nonsense men and their leader called for the camp commander in German. The camp commander soon arrived and was promptly told to rally his men with their weapons for inspection. Later, Ian thought about this episode like it was a scene from a comic opera: ten German soldiers conquering more than a thousand self-imprisoned Dutch ones. But at that time it was not a laughing matter.

The situation became very tense. The Dutch troops could easily have blown the handful of enemy soldiers to smithereens, but using enormous will power and discipline, the staff strictly adhered to the conditions of the surrender, and the dangerous moment passed.

Events from that point on happened so fast that in Ian's observation and participation it became a blur and only much later did he recollect the facts. Their weapons were collected and stored in a warehouse under a German guard. White cloth (again bed sheets) was cut into small two-inch triangles to be sewn on the left upper arm of the tunic as a sign of surrender.

More German troops arrived, taking over the guard system of the camp.

Dutch administrative officers, having received the latest instructions from the government, and no doubt sanctioned by the German command, started categorizing those who, before having been drafted, were employed in work considered essential for the country's economy and services. Others who did not fit in this category were going to be relocated to garrisons closer to home or to their previous place of employment.

Thus the moment had arrived when the three friends would be separated. Bob, who had been recovering in the military hospital, was sent home for recuperation. Dan found refuge as help in his father's bakery, while Ian, as a student, was relocated to a garrison closer to home.

This intermediate period, lasting only a few weeks, was filled with athletic activities under supervision of their own officers and still nobody had thoughts of simply disappearing. One day while doing track and field exercise, Ian met an attractive-looking girl in a nurse's uniform and discovered they came from the same area. They exchanged home addresses and that was that.

After arriving at his final destination close to home, Ian, now a corporal, commanded a unit whose task it was to remove all barbed-wire barriers along the river. There was little enthusiasm for the job. Finally, he got his first furlough pass to visit his family. The reunion was joyful since they all had come through without a scratch, but not without hardships, both physically and mentally.

Ian's father asked him what he was going to do—a question Ian had thought about for a long time without finding a direct answer. His naval aspirations were up for grabs, but deep down he felt a longing for the sea, to be free and away from suffocating clutter. He had little choice: military service was out of the question, money for further study nowhere to be found, and staying in the barracks was a highly uncertain activity that could end at any moment. And being back home, filled up with his family, was no solution either. Life was completely screwed up and something had to be done about it.

Mid-summer had arrived and the war theater looked even more grim for the allies. Belgium was forced to follow in Holland's footsteps and surrendered after heavy fighting. This enabled the German armies to enter France from the lightly protected—north-behind the famous Maginot Line—attacking it from the west side with its heavy guns facing east. The French armies, rushed to the beleaguered northern part of their country, put up heavy resistance that took many months, but were gradually losing ground. Radio Orange kept transmitting upbeat messages to which the listeners in occupied countries hung their hope of a change for the better, although this did not appear likely for some time to come.

Several weeks after Ian visited his folks, the problem for him and many others who were in a more-or-less similar situation was taken off their shoulders. During morning inspection, orders were given that the troops remaining in the garrison were going to be sent to Germany. The German supervising officer, making the statement, ended the announcement, "You men are going to participate in our efforts to create a better world. You will take the places our men left behind when they were called for military duty to protect the freedom of all European countries. Sieg Heil!"

These last words had a chilling effect on the group, even more so than the message itself, and only after they were dismissed did it dawn upon Ian that far-reaching meanings were behind them.

He was sure that members of his unit would come to him with questions for which he had no answer. Since their own officers were all in POW camps, the next in command was a sergeant, to whom he went for an explanation. The latter was already besieged with questions by other corporals and to keep some sanity in the whole affair, a meeting was held in the mess room.

"I am sorry, men, but I don't know any details to help you with," said the sergeant. He was a career petty officer with many years in the army, assigned to the task of keeping order and discipline under the difficult situation.

"I promise I'll do everything I can to clarify what the plans are and let you know."

No work detail went out that morning; everybody stayed, made guesses, went as far as threatening to desert or simply to disappear. It came close to mutiny when all the troops were called to the parade ground. The German officer who had delivered the message earlier was there and declared in a biting tone that as prisoners of war they had, as a special favor, two choices: either to be sent as POWs to a camp in Poland or to choose to go to a German work camp, in a quasi-military status with restricted liberties, performing work as ordered.

The youth in Holland had grown up in a law-abiding atmosphere. They obeyed the law and had great respect for those who represented the law. A constable on a bike in a village was an authority you wouldn't mess with; a parent's word was accepted without rebuke. Of course that didn't mean boys and girls were saints, far from that, and many had invented ways to circumvent situations deemed too strict or not to their liking. But all this had changed abruptly, and the beginning of rebellion against oppression took form.

Ian slipped past the sentry who was, by arrangement, distracted from his duty, which he didn't take very seriously anyway, and went into town to see a friend of his father who might shed some light in a situation like this. The friend held an important position in the local government and listened to what Ian told him. He was clearly upset about what he heard from Ian. "All right, my boy, sit down and I will make some phone calls."

When he returned his face was somber and Ian felt that no good news was forthcoming. He knew he was right when his father's friend told him that the main question was whether Dutch or German law would apply, or even martial law. He said his own acquaintances whom he had called couldn't tell him either. Secondly, was the German officer bluffing when threatening to send them to Poland as POWs in order to get slave labor to Germany? Then he looked at Ian and told him in strict confidence that plans were made to provide men like Ian with cover to avoid imprisonment. Those plans were still in an embryonic stage and it would take considerable time to work them out on a country-wide basis, if at all. The best solution he could suggest to Ian was to go as a sort of civilian to a German work camp for the time being and to keep in contact with him. He would let Ian know when progress was being made, adding that it would be easier to return to Holland from a work camp than from a POW camp father away.

Ian didn't like what he heard but could not come up with a better solution, and returning to the barracks, he told his comrades what the consequences of the choices were, without mentioning the cover-up plans. Once more he told his listeners that the other option was going home and awaiting what would happen. Those who could do so would take the risk of being picked up and pressed into who knew what. Ian had, at that time, no way of knowing that a few years later every man in Holland who was not employed in work considered vital by the Germans, would be sent to Germany as slave labor.

As for himself, Ian decided to go home, run errands, and bide his time. Two days after his return home in the village, he was approached by a local government official whom he knew very well. This man, in careful words, told him that he belonged to a small group that had established secret contacts with England and he had been informed that the contingent of the troop in town to which Ian belonged was destined to do labor work on roads near a plant in Germany where planes were built. The location of the plant was rather obscure since at nightfall the Germans covered the whole area in a blanket of dense fog, which made it a difficult target to bomb. The plant was located in a valley, making it possible to fog even in daytime when necessary, although in the early phase of the war, Allied bombers did not make daytime bombing raids deep into Germany. The man suggested that after Ian had a better knowledge of the exact location of the plant he might be able to escape from the camp, work his way back, and pass the details to him. Thereafter Ian would be provided with necessary papers and be located in the heavily populated west of the country.

"And what shall I do next?" asked Ian.

"Well, we know that you would like to continue your study," the well-informed man said. "You will get funds to do so." He added, "Think about it, but don't take too long. Time is pressing. You take a risk; it is up to you," and he left Ian in a state of turmoil. Working as a spy? How to get out of there and back into the country? Did he risk his life? And the worst part was that he could not even discuss this with his father or friends. Unable to sleep, he tossed the pros and cons around in his mind and finally came to the conclusion to take it. There might be the opportunity to study to be a seagoing officer and be ready to sail when the war was over.

Chapter Four

The following day he told the official his decision to go. Thereafter his life took on a dream-like quality.

Within a week Ian found himself with a group of men dressed as civilians on a train heading into Germany. The trip took two days, during which Ian, mindful that one day he would have to find his way back, made notes of the names of the various stations they passed. Finally, they disembarked and were marched to an isolated camp, guarded by members of a quasi-military organization. As expected, they were put on road repair work, including railroads, and worked in groups under watchful supervision. After the long working hours they were free to leave camp until curfew time. But in the beginning nobody went out to the nearby town. They were exhausted from the heavy labor.

A couple of weeks went by until Ian went to the town with some others. It was a drab settlement without much entertainment other than pubs, which were not easily recognizable in the completely darkened town. Apparently almost the entire population worked at the plant and Ian made it a point to visit the same pub to become better acquainted with the regulars and slowly gain some recognition.

By now he had a pretty good impression of the exact location of the plant and by working on a railroad seven days a week got a good idea of freight train schedules and directions. His Boy Scout experience proved to be quite helpful. Once a month they received their food-ration cards and after two months Ian decided he had gathered sufficient details to produce valuable information. As part of his escape plan, he made friends with Tom, another young man who, like many others, was lured into Germany. Tom bore signs of being homesick and hinted that he was fed up with the work. Ian probed carefully into Tom's background and decided that he was to be trusted.

The two became friends and Ian suddenly told Tom that he, too, would like to return to Holland, watching Tom's reaction.

"How would you do that, with the guards, and what about money?"

Since they were earning some money for their work, that wouldn't be a problem. Ian told him that the time to disappear would be when they got their monthly food rations and suggested they buy as much as they could carry for the trip.

They stacked food away little by little in a hiding place outside the camp. One evening after work they walked away, collected the food, and marched in a westerly direction along a railroad leading that way. At times, the two men had to duck in a ditch when a train passed or when a road crossed the tracks, even if there was no traffic. Ian explained to Tom that for the first two nights they had to walk, hiding during daytime, because, no doubt, they would be missed and the trains and buses checked. Luckily, the weather held, and although they were dog tired, their progress was not too bad. They followed the tracks and when they neared a railroad station in darkness, Ian checked the name of the station with the notes he had made when they traveled to the camp.

On the third day of their escape, both young men looked like bums. They had slept once in a forest and once in a haystack and only washed themselves when they found a little stream. Both decided it was time to take the risk of entering the next train station, changing into other clothes, and buying tickets on a train heading west.

That morning, after three hours of walking in daylight, they came to a station and entered it with pounding hearts. They had no idea whether their escape had alerted the authorities. To their relief, nobody took any notice and after a quick change of clothes they studied the train schedule. They settled on a destination about four hundred miles from where they were, still far enough from the Dutch border to avoid suspicion. They purchased tickets without any questions and after a wait, boarded the train, careful to avoid compartments with soldiers. Ian concluded that it was less complicated to travel within Germany than in occupied countries.

Shortly after the train pulled out of the station, they fell asleep and awoke with a shock when somebody shook them. Startled, they contained themselves, seeing it was the conductor requesting their tickets. By now their German was sufficient not to arouse questions and the conductor punched a hole in the tickets, looked at the two, and told them to attach their tickets to their coats so that he could see them and not awaken them again.

Ian, who had a good tongue for foreign languages, thanked him for his kindness and thought that there were some good Germans after all. The rest of the trip passed without further incident. Tom and Ian avoided sitting with each other to avoid detection. It was getting dark when they arrived at their chosen destination and they went to the coffee shop to buy refreshments. When they looked around they noticed MPs, which gave them a shock, but soon they saw that only military personnel were being checked.

The question was what to do next. Should they continue walking in the dark along the railroad tracks, or travel by train?

Encouraged by their previous experience, they decided to take a train again, this time to a station close to the border. Crossing the border would be quite another matter. No doubt there would be document checks, which would show that they were Dutch and without a furlough pass. Ian didn't want to think about the consequences if they were caught.

Germany at that time was a typical train-traveling country. Private cars were out of bounds; the military and government officials were practically the only ones allowed on the road. Commercial trucks were strictly used for hauling foodstuff and other essentials necessary to keep the home front operational.

Such was the reason that railroad stations were always crowded at any given time, day and night. Therefore it was not difficult for Ian and Tom to mingle with the crowd and this time purchasing tickets seemed almost routine. They had several hours until their train departed that they spent dozing in the waiting room with many others doing the same. In the wee hours of the next day they boarded the train that brought them to a station close to the border. Ian estimated it was about fifteen miles away.

They packed their luggage with some clothes and their diminished food supply and started walking on the main road heading west. It was mid-afternoon when the sun disappeared and a light drizzle set in.

"We can't keep going on the main road," Ian observed. "This way we will be heading right into the checkpoint at the border."

Tom agreed. "We better take a side road. I don't think there will be border patrols because, in reality, there is no border now."

Ian had, without saying anything to his buddy, been worrying about possible patrols and was relieved when Tom made his statement.

"You are correct. Let's make a little detour and then go in a westerly direction. We still have some daylight hours left to see where we are going."

Soon they reached a smaller road going in a southwesterly direction and marched faster with the feeling they were nearing their homeland.

"We are like horses smelling the stable," Tom smiled, and both were thinking how nice it would be to hear their own language again and to be amongst their own people. With these upbeat thoughts in mind they didn't pay attention to the surroundings until Tom suddenly grasped Ian's arm, whispering with urgency, "Duck, quick."

They promptly went over the berm into bushes along the road.

"What was that for?" asked Ian, annoyed.

"Look carefully to the right and you'll see."

They crept cautiously through a thin line of trees and held their breath in shock. Straight ahead was undoubtedly a POW camp with heavy barbed-wire fencing and watch towers.

"Wow. We almost went right into it. Thank heaven you saw it just in time," Ian said, and patted Tom on his back.

Apparently they had taken a less desirable road and went through the little forest and plowed fields back to the main road. They had wasted time and it was getting dark. The light drizzle changed to rain. Noticing a small building off the road, they jumped over a ditch and as they neared the building, saw it appeared to be a shelter for cattle. There was loose straw on the dirt floor and the two bedded down in luxury they had not encountered for several nights. Just before falling asleep, Tom asked what the name of the last station was. "Leer," answered Ian, half asleep, and then wanted to know why Tom was asking.

"Well, there is something wrong with that name," mumbled Tom, and apparently tried in his half-conscious mind to figure out what that something was. Suddenly he sat upright. "I smell cow dung."

Ian, now also awake because of this outburst, said, "I don't give a damn what you smell; what do you expect to smell, roses? We cleaned our spot as good as possible and if you don't like it that's just too bad." As an afterthought, he added, "And what about Leer. I don't see any connection."

Smell or no smell he did not get an answer from Tom, who had fallen asleep. Ian muttered some words connected with empty brains since the German word for empty is "leer," and slept.

The next morning they rose early and didn't talk about last night's embarrassing discussion, excited as they were about the possibility of being home soon. With the previous day's experience in mind they carefully took a dirt road to get off the main road and scanned the area ahead at each curve.

Traveling in daytime meant a certain risk, but they took that at face value. Not knowing whether there would be any kind of fencing left at the border after the surrender, they preferred to reach it in daylight. After some hours marching, during which they did not meet a living soul, they suddenly came to a canal. The dirt road made a T. They could not cross since there was no bridge in sight. Unfortunately the canal ran in a north-south direction, which did the wanderers no good.

"Maybe if we follow the dirt road along the canal, either to the left or right, we may find a foot bridge to cross," suggested Ian, hopefully.

"All right, let's try and turn south."

Ian agreed. "Who knows, maybe the canal is the border."

Although the weather had improved during the night, their clothes were still damp and their feet, encased in wet socks, were hurting. Both became aware that they carried a pungent odor with them, looked at each other, and began laughing.

"You look like a real bum," said Tom.

"And you smell like a sewer," said Ian.

At the declaration of this reality both, without a word, left the dirt road, crossed the levee, and slid down to the water's edge.

"Can you swim?" asked Ian.

"A little bit," confessed Tom.

They undressed, stowed their clothes in their backpacks, and shivered.

Ian didn't have much faith in Tom's swimming capacity.

"You and I will swim together to the other side, which is not far. Then I will come back and take one backpack at a time, which I must hold above water."

He was right. When Tom hit the water he started splashing and pedaling like a dog, without making any headway, so Ian quickly took him in tow. The two landed safely, after which Ian crossed the water twice with their meager belongings. They quickly dressed, and feeling better, went over the levee on the west side.

There was no road on that side of the canal so they had to plow through farm fields until they reached a foot path, which they followed. Half an hour later they halted, hearing the sound of a motor and voices.

They took cover. After a while they saw two men and a farm tractor. Ian and Tom were looking at the two men working in the field and could not decide what to do. Were they in Holland or not? Could they trust these farmers? It was noon and the tractor motor was shut off. Both farmers went to the side of the field, sat down, and took their lunch boxes. They were seated pretty close to the spot where the two friends were hiding, but now Ian and Tom could hear what they said.

It didn't help them figure out what side of the border they were on since both men spoke in a dialect used on both sides. A language doesn't change with a border line, especially not in farming areas. None the wiser, they continued to listen in the hope of picking up a word or meaning that would help determine where they were.

This went on for some tantalizing time. The farmers had a healthy appetite and it was mouth watering for the two to see the thick sandwiches and smell the real coffee. Their own food supply was about exhausted.

Suddenly, Ian grasped Tom's arm, pointing to the tractor in the field. Tom looked at him with questioning eyes, not understanding what he meant.

"What is it? Do you have a crazy idea to steal the tractor and run away with it?" he whispered.

"Of course not, stupid," hissed Ian, losing his temper. "Look at the license plate on the tractor. It is a Dutch license plate."

And throwing all caution to the wind, he jumped up and ran to the two men, who were too astonished to move.

Tom followed and the four sat together, the farmer and his farmhand listening to their story of being pressed into a kind of slave labor, their escape from the camp and travel to Holland— because that is where we are, aren't we?

The farmer looked at them and nodded with a faint smile on his weather-beaten face.

"Yes, you are in Holland," he confirmed to their delight, and went on. "You two better come with me to the house. You look like you are starved and a wash-up under the pump won't do any harm. Then we can talk."

He left instructions with his helper to continue their work and took the two vagabonds with him to his farm, which was not far away. On arrival he called his wife and told her about the pair. She disappeared into the house and returned with towels and soap, telling them where the pump was.

"When you have cleaned up, come into the kitchen. I'll make you something to eat."

They thanked her for her kindness and washed themselves.

"I think we really smell," remarked Tom. Ian grinned.

"That's why we have to make toilet in the beautiful fresh Dutch air with darned cold water. I think the canal water wasn't enough."

When they were finished they entered the kitchen and almost keeled over, smelling the food the farmer's wife had prepared on short notice—thick slices of bread covered with a heavy layer of butter, and on a side dish, slices of bacon, as well as homemade sausage. Tom reached out for the food, but, just in time, caught a warning glance from Ian. He got the message and both were silent for a moment, then said, "Amen," and could no longer restrain themselves.

After the meal they sat together and the farmer told them about what had happened in the world. His information was rather different from what they had been told during their stay in Germany and Ian suspected that, although it was forbidden, the farmer was listening to Radio Orange from London. But whatever sources were available, the news was not good at all. After Holland and Belgium fell, the German armies and air force fought hard and occupied the northern and central parts of France, while the southern part remained "neutral" under a German-controlled puppet regime. Denmark was overrun and Norway, after prolonged and heroic resistance, had to capitulate. The entire North Sea coast, including the channel, all opposite Britain, was under German control. There was no "hanging of laundry on the Siegfried Line," and the "We are sailing to England" song was blared on all German stations and sounded threatening.

All this news made Ian and Tom feel a stronger urge to get to their home towns as quickly as possible. The farmer agreed to change their D-marks for guilders so that they needn't go to a bank. They also got information about transportation to their respective destinations.

"Tonight you better stay here. I will show you a good place to sleep in the hay," the farmer said.

That night when they nestled in the hay, Ian warned Tom, "And no nonsense about cow dung, you hear." Early the next morning, after a man-sized breakfast and getting extra sandwiches "for the road" they took leave from the hospitable couple with many thanks. On their way to the bus station both fell silent, knowing they were about to part company. Ian was closest to his home town, while Tom had to travel further south. At the station they shook hands like the old friends they had become and promised to keep in contact. Tom's bus had already left when Ian boarded his. Ian felt strange being alone.

The landscape was rather monotone and flat with only occasional forests in fall colors, but to Ian it was beautiful. From the bus he took a train to the town near his village. Not knowing whether his folks were alerted about his escape and not wishing to be recognized, he got off the train and walked toward the village, which was one hour away.

He decided to go first to the home of the official who had asked him to go to Germany on his special errand before showing himself in the village and his parents' home. The official lived in a secluded area, so the risk of meeting somebody was small.

While walking, Ian realized how much his life had changed in such a short time, that he couldn't even arrive openly in his own neighborhood. He felt like a thief in the night.

Arriving at the official's house, he rang the bell and was greeted by the lady of the house. She obviously knew about where Ian had been because she looked around to see if anyone had seen him and rushed him inside.

"Welcome back, Ian. I'm glad you made it. My husband will be home in a couple of hours. I'll make tea."

Sitting in the living room sipping tea, they exchanged news. She told him about life in the village and that his family was okay, and he told her about his German adventure. "While you wait for my husband, why don't you write a report for him. That way we won't lose time," she said. Ian detected some urgency in her words, and did as he was asked.

After a while the back door opened and the official came in. He was pleasantly surprised to see Ian.

"By golly, I am pleased to see you, my boy. Tell me everything."

His wife told him that Ian had written his report, adding that he had not seen his family yet but had come straight to their house.

"Very good, very good," the man agreed to the precaution. "Nowadays you have to be careful even here, and you really have learned fast." It was suggested that Ian should stay with them for the night and visit his folks after dark.

That evening Ian was reunited with his family, talking a mile a second, and felt at home, albeit for a few hours only.

Chapter Five

It was well after curfew time when Ian returned to his host's home. Sure as he was that there was little German control over the village, he entered via the back door this time and slipped into the dark utility room. Since the occupation, the entire country was darkened, and even the lamps on bikes were covered with black material with only a small slit cut out for recognition.

He found his host still up. "Hi, Ian. Did you have a good time with your family?"

Ian said he did.

"You haven't told them anything about our arrangement?"

"No, sir, I just told them I was fed up with the whole affair, and that you would help me get a job somewhere."

"Very good. I have read your report; it is quite detailed and I have only a few questions, to be dealt with later. Now, about helping you. What are your plans, in general?"

Ian had thought about this moment for a long time, the moment when hopefully he would be asked such a question.

"What I really want is to study to be a Merchant Marine officer. That is still possible, but then I have to go to the west of the country where the schools are," Ian said, and looking his host straight in the eye, continued:

"To do so I need money. During the short period in Germany I earned some, but had to spend funds for train and bus travel, so there is not much left. I can't ask my dad because he has to take care of his family."

Ian had prepared himself for this moment and felt that the time for vague but well-intentioned propositions had passed. It was now or never.

His host looked pensive and the silence between the two continued for minutes. Ian had laid it upon him with the clear and simple facts and waited.

"All right, young man. I think your mind is made up and I am sure you made a good choice under the circumstances. What I can do is to provide you with necessary documents such as identification pass and rationing coupons, which you'll need wherever you go, plus some travel funds. As for a job, you must let me know what city you will be in for your study and maybe I can be of some help there also."

Ian had a feeling of relief when he heard those words and thanked his benefactor, who added, "It is getting late. Let's sleep on it and I'll see you in the morning."

The next morning Ian was told that it would take a couple of days to have his papers prepared. He thought it would be a good idea to see some of his friends in town. His host agreed and Ian took off on his bike, which he had picked up the night before at his parents' home. He rode toward town, cautiously avoiding the main road. He was apprehensive and realized that in such a short time it had become routine to avoid others, even in his own neighborhood.

He was following a dirt road through a forest when he saw a man in a blue uniform coming from the other direction. His first reaction was to turn around and race off, but then he heard his name called. He stopped and saw that it was the village constable, pedaling toward him.

"Hi, Ian, good to see you back, safe and sound." The greeting words had a hidden meaning, Ian felt, and not sure what else to say, he told the man that he was glad to be back. He anxiously awaited what would follow.

Nothing happened. The constable climbed on his bike and said, "Young fellow, good luck and be careful. Today there is no control going into town."

Wow, that was close, Ian thought, and pedaling quickly he reached town, realizing that apparently there were not many secrets in the village and the earlier he disappeared the better.

He found only one of his friends in town, who told him he was planning to go to textile school in the east. Ian mentioned his plan to study in the west. Neither of them talked about what they had been doing during months past, as if by unspoken agreement. Then his friend said, "Do you remember Henry? He used to be with us until he left town. Now he is back home and I heard that he found work out west and is leaving soon."

Ian asked his address, thinking it would do no harm to talk with Henry. Perhaps they could go together. He found him home and after reminiscing about the good old days, Ian informed him of his plans. Henry was enthusiastic.

"Why don't we go together; I have rented a room and board in Scheveningen and maybe they have room for you also."

That was it, Ian thought, and they made it a point to agree to meet each other in two days at the railroad station, the same one where several of Ian's travels had begun. On his way back, Ian realized they had not told each other what kinds of jobs were waiting for them. This was convenient since Ian actually had no job there yet. He shrugged the thought off. He was elated about going to the town of Scheveningen, which was just right for his purpose.

Ian's host was also pleased when he heard the news. "Great, and as soon as you have an address, let me know. I have some contacts there and possibly can line something up for you."

Hearing the news, his family understood his desire to leave the village. Two days later he found Henry waiting for him at the station. This time the trip was entirely different from when he traveled as a greenhorn recruit excited to join the army. Now there was no singing, no jokes, and no hilarity at all. Instead, the passengers looked out of the window or had their eyes closed.

It was late fall and the scenery was bright with colors in the afternoon sun. The inundated fields had been drained and German soldiers were everywhere. Air strikes on moving targets by RAF fighters were not yet common in the early phase of the war in Holland, but nevertheless people kept a wary eye on the skies.

Henry and Ian reached The Hague rail terminal and took a streetcar to Scheveningen, a nice short trip through the dunes to that town. Before the war it was a glorious beach resort with rows of hotels overlooking the North Sea and plenty of night life. They went directly to Henry's address, a row house on a canal, and were welcomed by Mr. and Mrs. Lipman. Henry explained why Ian was with him and asked whether they might have another room available. The couple looked at each other and Mrs. Lipman explained that their home was not a boarding house but that they had taken Henry to have an empty room occupied, which otherwise could be requisitioned by the Germans.

Well, they would talk about it and meanwhile Ian could sleep on a couch in the living room. Mrs. Lipman, a very charming lady, prepared an excellent meal and Mr. Lipman, a music teacher, told them about the history of the town, which long ago had started as a fishing village safely tucked behind the dunes. Now the place was crowded with German troops who occupied all the hotels. Barriers had been erected along the beach and the previously Dutch bunkers were manned again. Much of the area was out of bounds for civilians. The dunes were, for the most part, still open for the public but only from sunup to sundown.

The next morning during breakfast Mr. Lipman told Ian that they had discussed the matter of his staying with the family, which included their daughter who was in high school, and by rearranging some rooms, he could stay with them.

That settled, Ian asked Mr. Lipman where the nautical academy was located, and when told, he didn't lose any time getting there. He went to the administration office and inquired about enrollment, declaring his goal of becoming a Merchant Marine deck officer.

The clerk looked at him and explained that lately the school had changed its program, under pressure from the occupation force, and was now educating students to become mates and skippers on the fishing fleet. Part of the program would apply to the Merchant Marine also, but not all of it.

Ian absorbed the blow to his plans. "Is the fishing fleet still going to sea?" he asked.

"Yes, but only during daytime and under protection of German patrol vessels" came the reply. Clearly Ian was caught unaware by the complication of the situation, and noticing it, the clerk mellowed somewhat.

"Do you have any practice at sea on a fishing boat, or do you have experience with fishing methods?" he asked, trying to be helpful.

Ian thought about his fishing experience as a youngster, consisting of fishing with a tree branch equipped with his mother's yarn, a bent pin, a piece of cork as float, and a ball of wet dough as bait. Surely that was not going to impress the clerk, who watched him closely; Ian put up his hands in a gesture of helplessness, ready to leave the office.

Just before crossing the threshold, he heard the clerk say, "Wait a minute. I just thought of something." Ian turned around not knowing what to expect.

"I know a teacher living in town who gives private lessons to Merchant Marine officers who were on shore leave when the war broke out. Maybe he can help you," the clerk said, and scribbled a name and address on a piece of paper, adding,

"Good luck." Without looking further at Ian, he went on with his paper work.

By asking a passerby for directions, Ian reached the address, located in an affluent neighborhood, and rang the doorbell. A lady opened the door and asked what he wanted. Ian explained his purpose and was told that Mr. Wide would be home in two hours. Ian thanked her and said he would be back at that time. He strolled through the area, went into a lunchroom for a cup of coffee, and tried to satisfy his appetite with a portion of coupon-free pastry, which looked delicious, but after the first bite, Ian found that the crust was the only substantial portion of the pastry. The rest was a fluffy nothing. He asked for the name of the concoction. "Hague bluff," the waiter told him and handed him the check, which was not fluffy at all.

At the appropriate time, Ian was back at the address and this time the door was opened by a heavyset man with a deep voice. "Yes, were you here before?" he asked. When this was confirmed, he invited Ian to come in and led him to his study. Mr. Wide looked like a man used to giving commands and getting to-the-point answers. Ian wisely decided to give him his story straight, omitting only the spying part.

Based on the questions and answers it looked like Mr. Wide would tutor him under two provisions: that he had to do all the homework he could handle and that Ian could not get more than a simple written statement from him, declaring that Ian was a private student. As to the first item, Ian told him that for the time being he had all the time in the world, and to the second that, also for the time being, he would take his chances. Thus satisfied, Mr. Wide gave him a list of books he needed, told him the financial arrangements, and set the day of the first lecture. It was all done in a very efficient way and when Ian returned to his room, he told Henry what happened.

"I really struck pay dirt today and I am sure that this teacher can prepare me for exam in the shortest time possible, maybe in two years."

"Two years!" exclaimed Henry. "How are you going to pay for all this? Did you find gold somewhere?"

"Well, I figured two years based on working and studying in free time."

"Working what and where?" Henry stubbornly wanted to know, not having been informed about Ian's deal with the official in his village.

"I'll find something. I don't care what. The main thing is that I can study here, partly thanks to you, my friend" and Ian slapped Henry on the shoulder.

"You better find a job considered important enough to carry an "Ausweis" because it swarms with Germans here and if you are only a student they will kick your ass right over the border into a labor camp, or worse." Henry was really trying to act as the devil's advocate.

"Shh, not so loud," warned Ian. "The Lipmans are good people and there is no reason why they should worry over me, so pipe down, fellow."

He sat down and wrote a letter to his benefactor in the village, giving his address and informing him about the teacher giving him private lessons, and at the end of the letter mentioned the need for a job, not only for financial reasons, but also for his safety.

The days went by and the new lifestyle was entirely different from what he had experienced so far. He participated in a close and happy family life and most of the time it was as if the world outside could not penetrate within.

He had purchased the study books at a second hand book store, prepared for his first lecture with Mr. Wide, and was looking forward to receiving a reaction from the gentleman back east.

Finally word came that a job was arranged for him. He would be a parking garage attendant in the city of The Hague. The job was "honored" with a document, signed by a city official, with the declaration that Mr. Ian Halls was employed by the city with the duty to protect and safeguard government property, including vehicles of the Third Reich forces. The document was beautified by several official-looking seals, stamps, and signatures, things the Germans adored.

Ian showed the piece of art to the Lipmans and Henry. The former congratulated him, glad as they were that both boarders had good papers which would not put them in jeopardy when there was a check. They knew that Henry was working in a furniture factory and that his position was also backed by documents.

The first winter in occupied Holland brought hardships to the population, but the people made adjustments to life; there was not yet starvation and national pride remained unbroken, despite the increasingly brutal behavior of the Germans.

Ian's work, parking vehicles and issuing parking tickets for bicycles which were left with him and his colleagues by civilians when shopping downtown, was not very demanding, but served him well. His study required much spare time, which he gave, full of enthusiasm and energy. He envisioned the day when he would be on the bridge of a vessel as an officer, navigating the oceans to faraway lands. In addition, he enjoyed his friendship with Henry and the warm contact with the Lipmans.

It wasn't that nobody cared what was going on in the world, a great part of which was torn by battle, but they could only follow what was announced by radio and newspapers, biased as they were. It was not that they had a selfish approach to the development at large, but the fact that they were occupied with the day-to-day necessities of their lives. Churches were full at Sunday sermons, since people sought leadership and support from clergy who often dared to challenge the conquerors. The same was true of theaters where artists courageously performed biting critiques and German songs laced with humor, which everyone needed to survive psychologically. Cinemas, where only heroic German propaganda films were allowed to be shown, were mainly used by the public as a warm shelter or for cozying by lovers.

Although busy with his work and study, Ian felt lonely in a town where he was a stranger and he remembered the girl he had met when he was in the transition camp. He wrote a letter to her home address, telling her what he was doing and asking her for a reply. Not long thereafter he received word from her, informing him that she was considering coming to The Hague to visit with her sister and family who lived there. Giving the day and time of her arrival by train, the letter ended with the question, could he be at the station to meet her, and they could go together to her family? The letter was signed, "Best regards, Jenny."

Ian found where her sister lived on a street map of The Hague, checked the streetcar connection from the station, and managed to arrange time off to be there. The train arrived. He had taken a strategic position to watch the stream of arriving passengers and was confident that he would recognize her. That confidence faded when the flow of arrivals was thinning considerably and still there was no sight of her.

He pulled the letter from his pocket. Did he have the right date and time? Was he at the right gate? Scanning through the letter and getting more nervous, he heard a female voice behind him. "Are you staying here for the next train?"

He turned around and looked into the laughing face of the girl he was waiting for.

"How could I have missed you?" he stammered, looking at her with admiration. Boy, this girl looks great, even better than I remember, flashed through his mind.

"Well, very simple. This station has two exits," she said, and both young people started laughing.

They shook hands, Ian took her suitcase, and they left the station. The two had much to talk about and Ian ignored streetcars passing by as they kept walking. He wanted to stretch their being together as much as possible, a selfish approach with which he had no qualms. After almost an hour, Jenny, who had already asked a few times when they could get a streetcar, now became anxious to meet with her family whom she hadn't seen for many years and asked him if they were going to walk all the way.

Ian got the message and excused himself lamely, not having been in the city proper many times before. Jenny, who had also enjoyed talking with him, felt with typical female intuition what Ian was doing and told him that she would stay with her sister's family for several days.

"Maybe we can see each other again before I leave," she said, and added, with an understanding smile, "Then you may find the right streetcar."

Ian felt like he'd been caught with his hand in the cookie jar; shortly thereafter he miraculously found transportation and delivered Jenny to her destination. She was greeted by her family with cries of joy. He excused himself to give them time together, but not before arranging to see Jenny again before she left.

The days until that moment couldn't go fast enough for Ian and their time together was one of mutual understanding and liking. They made it a point to write each other and said good-bye. This time Jenny's family saw her off to the station. Ian suspected that they would make sure she was on time.

Chapter Six

Life, with all its ups and downs, went on. Spring and summer brought more rationing measures, stricter curfew, and many empty stores. Thousands of men whose employment was not considered vital by German standards were shipped to Germany to work in factories or as farm hands.

Ian's luck was holding and his occupation was still recognized necessary for the well-being of the country, something he had doubts about but surely wasn't going to question. Every week was a benchmark and nobody looked farther ahead since the horizon was blocked from view.

The correspondence between Ian and Jenny warmed and when Jenny visited The Hague again she had some news. She was moving to The Hague to work as an assistant for a dentist who had his practice in his home on the outskirts of the city. She would get a room in the house and live there with the family.

They both fell silent and Ian took her in his arms and kissed her. They stood there in full daylight on the sidewalk of a busy street, completely engrossed in each other. Passersby smiled understandingly and one old lady took her time observing them. "Bless you, children. Use every minute of your luck in this crazy world," she said, and then shuffled on.

"Will you be my girl?" asked Ian.

"Oh, yes," Jenny answered, and with these simple words both knew their lives had changed.

"Let's go quickly to my family so I can tell them that I will stay here. My sister and brother-in-law will be excited."

"And what about us, don't forget to tell them that," Ian felt it necessary to remind her.

"Of course, my love. That is the first thing I will tell them."

This time he immediately found the right streetcar and when they told their news at her sister's, there was great joy. Her brother-in-law pulled out a bottle and they drank to their health and luck.

From then on Ian's life was fully occupied by Jenny, his study, and his work. His study especially was given every priority and every minute of his time since he felt there was no guarantee of how long he would escape deportation. Whenever the two lovers could be together, Jenny understood Ian's drive and did not disturb him other than with an occasional kiss or embrace. Stolen hours were used to lay in the sun in the dunes.

The homes of Jenny's family and the Lipmans became the centerpoints where they could be with the friends they made from membership in the local rowing and sailing club. The club gave them the opportunity to go rowing and sailing on the canals and lake not far from the city. When organizing a party, the hours had to be adjusted to the curfew, so all guests had to arrive before 8 P.M. and could not leave until after 6 A.M. Such gatherings, therefore, had to be with very good friends—others were rigorously excluded.

Everyone had to bring whatever food and drinks they could spare or had squirreled away, and this approach resulted in some surprising combinations which were a far cry from a balanced meal or drink. But nobody cared, since the main thing was to be among friends and have a good time for a change.

The winter of 1941 brought more restricted rationing; German troops had priority on all necessities to fight the war. Food was taken from the suppliers and sent to the German population. Leftovers were for the people of the occupied countries.

Medieval barter systems sprang up. Money quickly lost its value since there was little to buy. Secondhand stores began acting as a go-between for parties who had something to offer in exchange for something they wanted. Neither Jenny nor Ian had accumulated valuables to barter with and consequently they stayed out of that activity. They both had to rely on what their coupons allowed them to buy. It was a time-consuming ordeal going through so many shops on their occasional trips downtown to The Hague to purchase clothing.

Not many people expected the war to go on for so long, but another year went by. The United States joined the Allies, as did Russia, while Japan was on the side of the Axis. The result was that Germany, Italy and the other European Axis members had to fight on two fronts, while the U.S. had to focus heavily on actions against Japan.

Hope was growing in the occupied countries that the tide would turn, but it was slow in coming, although the output of the gigantic weapon and war material production from the United States began to take shape. In 1942 Holland received another shock: The Netherlands East Indies, a Dutch colony for 300 years, fell to Japanese invasion forces that steamrolled through Southeast Asia.

The pressure on Germany, fighting on two fronts in Europe and North Africa, grew, resulting in Germany taking more severe actions against the Jews and Gypsies, as well as pressing more labor from occupied countries into their industries. In addition, the so-called "protection" troops were replaced by contingents of other German divisions, amongst them the hated Gestapo, who brought terror to the Dutch and other countries under their heel.

Resistance movements began gaining momentum, but for Jenny and Ian, who both came from another part of the country, it was not possible to enter into those circles. They were organized on the basis of personal acquaintance and known background. That principle was the only security for survival in the often risky and dangerous activity.

Under the circumstances, Ian devoted more long hours to his study in order to be ready for the exam for third officer Merchant Marine. He could only apply for the theoretical part of the certificate because he did not have the required twelve months at sea. But that would come later, he figured. First get the attainable part completed.

He did not want to talk about it, but a disturbing thought kept gnawing at his mind. There was a good possibility that, as soon as he had passed the exam, his excuse of studying and his job as parking attendant would vanish.

He cautiously talked with Henry about the general conditions of the time and then touched on the subject of how Henry felt about being safe from press gangs.

"Well, I am not sure whether I can escape being sent to Germany much longer," Henry told him, adding, "several others doing the same type of work have been forced to work in German factories already." Ian felt that this was the right moment to come out in the open and he told Henry that he, too, was having second thoughts about being able to remain in Holland.

And then he disclosed to his friend, under promise of confidentiality, his plan to escape to England right after he passed his exam, which, according to his teacher, could be only some months away.

"I'm going to buy a foldable canoe and equipment, provisions, and a compass and cross the North Sea."

Henry, a real landlubber, looked at him with great surprise.

"Simple as that? Why haven't we done that some time ago? And, and . . ." The questions were fired at Ian rapidly.

He was prepared to answer since he had toyed with the plan for quite some time, without even discussing it with Jenny.

"As far as I know, foldable canoes were very popular in southern Germany. I read some articles about them. You fold the body in one bag and the frame in another. Some have a small sail on a collapsible, sectioned mast and most are for two people. Like a kayak, you have a watertight cover around your middle and over the sides. I know one such canoe is for sale in the sports shop downtown. Think about it, and if you want to be in, let me know and we'll go through the details. I'll give you two days because the most important step is to buy the canoe before it's gone."

After this long tirade Ian took a deep breath and looked at Henry to see his reaction. He noticed first bewilderment, followed by a bright expression in his friend's eyes.

"I am flabbergasted about all this. It is clear you have it all figured out. But I'll take the two days to think it over, not to say yes or no but more to get all the consequences in my mind" was Henry's answer.

Ian, knowing his friend and understanding his reaction, felt sure that he could count on him. He appreciated the fact that Henry would approach the plan with his mathematical mind, going over details Ian might not have thought of.

Two days later the two young men sat together in Ian's room. Henry's first words were, "I will go with you," and that said, both stood and toasted to their luck with a glass of beer, procured for the occasion by Ian. They both bent their heads over a sea chart, which Ian had received from his teacher learn to reading it. They studied the nautical almanac, which gave tidal currents, high and low water times, and a host of maritime information. There was also a chart of the southern section of the North Sea. Ian recalled the look on Mr. Wide's face when he had asked for that particular chart. Henry had never seen such a sea chart in his life and was astonished by all the details.

"I never realized that there is so much to it," he confessed.

"Why do you think it takes years of study to know navigation and a multitude of related topics?" responded Ian with just a little bit of annoyance in his voice. But he quickly realized it wasn't fair to put Henry on the spot. "I am sorry. I shouldn't have said that. You know things about woodworking I haven't the slightest idea of."

Henry smiled. "It's okay, I have never been at sea, so be prepared for more stupid questions."

Both grinned and their camaraderie was re-established.

Since the most important item was the canoe, the first Saturday morning both were free they set out for the shop. With pounding hearts they entered, looking around to see whether there were any German customers. At that early hour the shop was quiet and they approached a man behind the counter who was shuffling papers.

Ian told him that he and his friend liked water sports and were considering buying a canoe to go out on the canals and nearby lake. The shopkeeper led them to the back of the store where a number of canoes were stacked on shelves. They had seen the foldable canoe already, but went through the motions of looking at the others first. Ian looked questioningly at Henry and said loudly to him, "I had not thought about where to store a canoe; we are not located at any water access. How do we do that?"

The shopkeeper eyed him with raised eyebrows. It was clear he thought the two were not very smart.

"What a shame, and I was so much looking forward to paddling on the canals," Henry put in his five cents' worth. The shopkeeper was called away to attend to supposedly real customers. Ian and Henry told the assistant their predicament without dramatizing it too much, hoping to get a more willing ear. Ian decided to take the bull by the horns, "I read an article in a boating journal about a kayak-type of canoe, which can be folded into two bags. That way you can take the whole thing with you to wherever there is a river or lake." Ian paused awaiting reaction.

The assistant's face lit up, as if suddenly remembering something.

"Now that you mention it, we might have what you are looking for. Come with me." They followed him to the front of the store, pointing to the foldable canoe, which was in two bags with a small sign indicating the contents. It was in the same spot where Ian had noticed it on a prior excursion when his plan began to take shape.

He explained to the two friends how to put it together and that it included a lightweight, short mast and a sail, plus two paddles. They asked the price, which was rather stiff, but without even glancing at Ian, Henry resolutely said, "It looks great. We'll take it." The shopkeeper, finishing with his other client, came to them from behind the counter.

"Wait a minute, gentlemen. This is the only model we have in stock and heaven knows when we will be able to get more. They are manufactured by a company called 'Wassersport' in Munich."

His assistant, eager to make a sale, said something to the effect that the longer they kept it in the bags, the more risk that the pliable canvas, covered with elastic rubber paint, would start cracking.

The remark was not to his boss' liking, but since the canoe was for sale and the price agreed upon, he shrugged. "All right, but you take it with you today," and with these words went back to his station.

Ian and Henry were elated about accomplishing the first phase of their plan and had a problem not showing it. Prepared for the purchase, they paid cash, thereby avoiding questions like their names and address. They lost no time in each taking a bag and leaving the shop, not sure about the shopkeeper's attitude and his reluctance to sell that particular canoe.

The two bags were tied to the carriers on their bikes and without any problems they arrived at the Lipmans' home, where they were met with questions.

"Henry and I have bought a canoe and we plan to go to the canal and lake to do some water sport on the weekends," Ian told them.

Mr. Lipman looked at his two boarders quizzically, but did not ask any questions, although both had the impression that he did not accept their explanation at face value.

The next two months were very hectic for Ian. His study, his work, Jenny, and the escape plan all required attention, devotion, and, most of all, time. Having accumulated sufficient funds from his work, he asked for a leave of absence to study for his upcoming exam. This was granted with the warning that most probably his job would be taken by somebody else, since there were many who would do anything just to stay in Holland. "Well, that is the risk I'll have to take," Ian said, with the feeling that he was already burning his bridges behind him.

Jenny was very concerned when he told her about his job, especially since she knew nothing about Ian's idea to escape to England and wondered why he and Henry had bought the canoe, spending money on something he hardly had time to enjoy. But she loved being on the water whenever she was invited to come.

The two buddies trained very hard, not only in paddling, but also in putting the canoe together blindfolded, since they would have to do that in the dark when the time came.

Henry, having more spare time, scrounged through the town to purchase a compass, canvas bags for food, flashlight, sea biscuits, water jugs, and other essentials. He spread out the purchases among different stores as much as possible to avoid suspicion. It became more difficult to hide all that stuff in their rooms and one night Ian and Henry decided that it was only fair to inform Mr. and Mrs. Lipman about their plans.

"I knew it, I knew it," exclaimed Mr. Lipman, asking Henry what he would arrange about his job. "I simply don't come to work and when they come here and ask where I am, just tell them that I left for home to look after my parents," Henry answered.

Mr. Lipman assured them that, when the time came, he would think of something and not jeopardize the safety of his family and himself.

Another hurdle was crossed when Ian told Jenny about his plan, to take effect after he passed his exam. She did understand his reasoning, of course, but would not accept that Henry was going with him. "You say you love me. Then why can't I go with you instead of Henry? I can paddle as well as he can," she exploded, adding, "I thought we would do everything together."

Ian had a difficult time explaining that both he and Henry were at greater risk to be picked up than she, and he made her a solemn promise to marry her when the war was over.

"You haven't even proposed to me, you dumb and stubborn man. But my answer is yes," and she smiled at him.

They embraced for a long time, envisioning what it would be like when they could be together always, with no sneaking around stealing every minute available.

Jenny made one condition. Right after he passed his exam they would organize a hell of a party with all their friends and her family. Ian wholeheartedly agreed, as he would have agreed to almost anything.

Chapter Seven

The dunes farther inland were still open to the public during daylight hours. A couple of weeks before Ian's exam, Ian and Henry found a hiding place for their canoe and equipment, which they would have to bring in small parcels.

They went to a section closest to the beach and as far away as possible from watch towers. Near that section, on a high dunetop, they could look over the water and noticed strings of barbed wire at the foot of the dunes, closing off entry to the beach.

Henry remained undaunted; as a true purchasing agent he made a mental note to buy a wire clipper as part of their outfit. Having obtained a good impression of the situation, they started to bring in the equipment for their planned voyage in piecemeal fashion and hid it in a shallow hole near some trees. Each time they covered the deposit with a thin layer of sand and laid branches on top.

Everything except perishable food was delivered without detection, which the friends considered a good omen.

The examination dates arrived and when the certificates were issued to the successful candidates, Ian received one of them. Jenny had been waiting in the lobby of the building in which the exam commission was located and when she saw Ian appear with the document in his hand, she ran into his open arms. There were more scenes like that and everybody was laughing and chattering during the happy moment. Then they all dispersed, going different ways to an unknown future.

Relieved that there was nobody to press them into any kind of marine service, Ian began to think that maybe the situation was not so bad after all. Having arrived home with that thought in mind, he discussed it with Henry as soon as the congratulations were passed.

"Forget it, buddy. Even during the last two days several men working in the same department as I were absent and it is obvious what happened to them," Henry assured him.

Since the first danger period for Ian had passed and nobody knocked at his door, there were two important items on his agenda: first, to arrange a party, and second, to obtain a weather forecast. The former was in good hands with Jenny, but the latter was not so easy since the national radio stations did not give information on expected winds, precipitation, and sailing conditions. Only the forbidden Radio Orange was the source of details Ian needed.

They had discovered that Mr. Lipman had many times told them facts about the war theater which he could only have heard by listening to that free station in England. Having taken Mr. Lipman into their confidence about their plans, Ian told him what he needed to know about the anticipated weather pattern. Most important was that there be no stormy fields on the North Sea, and an easterly wind, which would offer a less heavy surf to get through as well as use of the small sail once out of sight of the coast.

"I'll see what I can do," answered Mr. Lipman, without giving himself away.

The party was a great success, lasting through the night, and as had become almost natural, nobody asked Ian about his future plans; that was something people kept to themselves and left it always to the person to talk about or not.

For Jenny the party was not only to celebrate Ian's accomplishment, but also made her aware that soon her fiancé and his friend would be in a tiny canvas hulk on the often treacherous North Sea, which even in peacetime was considered a daring adventure. However, there was not much choice and she didn't want to think about the alternative.

In the midst of spring, almost two weeks after Ian had passed the exam, Mr. Lipman told him that the weather forecast sounded like a period of not-too-strong easterly wind and sunny skies, which would hold for several days. It was on a Friday when they heard the good news, and the decision was made to enter the dunes Saturday afternoon, taking food with them. They would hide near the spot where they had hidden the canoe and other materials and wait until nightfall.

Both men had decided not to inform anyone, not even Jenny or family, about the day of escape, for reasons of security for those staying behind and to give especially Jenny and the Lipmans at least one night without worry.

They set out to the dunes as if taking a walk and had no problem finding the chosen spot. They did not head for that spot directly, but as had been done on previous visits, walked around. Not noticing anything alarming, they settled and waited until dark. Both were filled with their own thoughts while waiting and the enormity of the undertaking became so overwhelming that talking was a better diversion than silence. So they talked about various subjects, anything except the coming adventure.

The expected east wind slacked off and feather clouds began to form, which Ian didn't like. He knew, based on the meteorology he had learned, that it could mean more wind and even a change of weather. He did not want to alert Henry by announcing the probability of the latter.

Que sera, sera, he thought; they were on their way and better not scramble back.

Finally, the sun disappeared below the horizon and the gully in which they were waiting was getting dark. Eager as they were to get going, it became a strain not to start, but better judgment told them to wait another hour. Then the time came to pack, and under heavy burden, they headed through the dunes toward the beach. Using the wire cutter, they made an opening in the barbed-wire barricade and now they noticed, to their relief, that it was not electrified. Everything remained quiet and they could detect no patrol. In that phase of the war an Allied invasion was not anticipated.

They were through the barricade and on the beach, hoping there would be no land mines. The surf was heavier than expected by the sound of it and the wind had shifted to the west, contrary to expectations, something that happened often during spring.

Their previous training putting the canoe together blindfolded paid off and it did not take long to load all the gear on board, although under the tension, they felt it had taken many hours.

"Do we have everything?" whispered Ian.

"Yes, I checked. You have your papers?" asked Henry. Ian felt, under his duffel, the small package with his ID and some other identification documents wrapped in oil cloth.

"Yes, now let's shove the canoe into the water. You set in first and I'll hold the canoe steady into the waves. Close the cover around you quickly," commanded Ian. The canoe rocked in the surf. Ian pushed it completely afloat and swung into his rear seat. Henry passed a paddle to Ian and both strained their muscles to get through the surf. The canoe pitched heavily, throwing water over the decking, and despite their sea clothing the two started shivering. They made little progress but finally got through the surf breakers, coming into an area of long swells. The wind was now against them, strengthening in force. Ian gritted his teeth and cursed under his breath. "Rotten luck. Why does it happen to us after all the work?"

The canoe's length was badly synchronized with the waves, plunging at times with a loud smack into a valley between two waves and thereafter, shuddering in its frame, diving into the next wave. Every minute it became more difficult to keep heading at an angle into the rollers and suddenly they lost steering altogether and Ian shouted, "Paddle, for Christ sake." No response came. Henry was leaning over the side, violently seasick, and had lost his paddle in his agony. With Henry hanging over the side, Ian by himself could not keep the canoe on course and the waves were coming broadside. The craft rolled over. Miraculously, Ian freed himself from the canoe, which was floating upside down, felt the cold water already numbing his senses, and while gripping the end of the canoe, tried to see in the semidarkness what happened to his friend.

By sheer will power he worked his way along the wildly plunging craft to where Henry had been seated, and not seeing any sign of him, grabbed under the canoe and felt Henry under water, struggling to get out of the canoe. The two jugs with drinking water were squeezing his legs to the side and with a terrific effort they both pulled the jugs away and Henry, miserable as he was, came up, gasping for air.

They both hung onto the canoe, which had sufficient buoyancy to keep them afloat. With clothes and shoes on, swimming was out of the question and the cold water began penetrating their bodies. Once when they were on top of a wave, Ian thought that above the sound of the by-now-stormy wind he heard the growling of the surf. Could it be that in reality they were so close to the beach? He shouted his findings to Henry who only shook his head. Nevertheless, they both listened when another wave top carried them over, and unmistakably, they heard the surf.

The nightmare continued. It was still dark and it became more difficult to hold on to the canoe. Then, at almost the last moment, they felt the undertow of the surf, which took them cascading, loosening their grip on the canoe and whirling both on the beach gasping for air. They laid there for quite a while too exhausted to move and cold to the bone. Ian stirred and then realized the dangerous situation they were in, laying on the bare beach with daylight only a few hours away. When found, they were sure to meet execution. He crept to Henry, shook him roughly out of his lethargy, and said, with despair in his voice, "We better move out of here fast. We must find the hole in the fence and get off the beach." Henry nodded and both stumbled up, crossing the beach to where the dunes began.

Finding the line of the fencing and reckoning which direction along the wires to follow, they crept along slowly and cautiously, feeling for the hole. It was hard work because they had clipped the barbed wires as low as possible above the ground to avoid detection, a measure which now worked against them. It had started to rain, adding to their misery, but both were now in such a state of exhaustion they could not care. They doggedly plowed on, not feeling anything but obsessed to find that hole for their escape. That obsession was so strong they almost missed it. They had taken turns moving along the wire, touching the lower lines hand over hand, and were wounded several times by the sharp barbs. It was now during Henry's turn that he suddenly came to a halt, shaking his head as if coming out of a trance, and called out to Ian, who was ahead of him, "I found it!"

Ian turned around. "Where?"

"I passed it," Henry said sheepishly.

"You passed it?" Ian couldn't believe his ears.

"Yes, I passed it not long ago and only just now realized it was what we are looking for." Henry's tone was defensive. "Well, we must move slowly back to find the passage. It will soon be daylight."

With renewed energy they trod back along the line and found the open spot, crept through it, and worked their way uphill into the dunes until they found protection from the wind—but not from the rain—in a shallow gully, where they fell down, out of breath, with no strength to move on. Laying close together in search of body warmth, having lost everything and realizing the complete failure of their plan, both didn't care what happened to them any more.

But their youth gave them a reserve will power never tried before and with the first daylight they stirred back to reality.

"It is getting light, and soon the dunes will be open. We better begin walking, otherwise we invite pneumonia." Ian urged Henry and himself into action. They had no idea whether the canoe with their belongings had sunk or would have washed ashore; if so, Ian hoped it would be away from the spot where they had gone through the wiring.

The westerly wind was still blowing, breaking up the clouds, and the rain lessened.

"We can't be wetter than wet," observed Ian, trying to get away from somber thoughts.

They plowed on, following the shallows and avoiding the tops of the dunes. When they neared the town and got out of the dunes, they heard churchbells and realized it was Sunday morning. Meeting the stares of churchgoing people, they began to feel uncomfortable and wished they could run to their rooms. They were worried somebody would notice their condition and warn authorities.

"We sure must look like a pair of bedraggled gypsies," chuckled Henry, with a freshly returned sense of humor, and looking at the appearance of his buddy, couldn't hold his laugh.

Ian was glad that Henry's spirits had lifted and shifted their walk into high gear, causing a sloshing sound in their shoes. They felt better already when they turned the last corner to the Lipmans' house, and ringing the doorbell, prayed somebody would be home. The door opened and Mrs. Lipman stared at them with unbelieving eyes. "Oh my god, what happened to you two," she exclaimed and just stood there without making a move. Then Mr. Lipman arrived at the door, realized with one glance that something had gone amiss, and pulled the two inside. Before closing the door, he cast a quick look into the street to see whether somebody had noticed the wet procession, but all was quiet at that hour. When Mrs. Lipman was informed with a few words that last night would have been their day of escape to Britain she ordered the two to the bathroom to get out of their soaked gear and told her husband to get dry clothing for them.

After a hot shower both conspirators went to bed under extra blankets, thankfully gulping hot tea, which the motherly hostess had made. Nobody asked any questions—that would come later—and they fell asleep almost immediately.

Late in the afternoon Ian and Henry came into the living room, looking and feeling much better, without a trace of cold or fever. They told what happened and Mr. Lipman asked if they had lost any identification papers. Both young men looked at each other, automatically feeling in their jacket and beginning to be alarmed. "Don't worry," smiled Mrs. Lipman. "I found two packages in your coats before I put all your clothes in the laundry and I think the contents remained pretty dry."

With a sigh of relief they took their papers from her. "Fine, so far so good," Mr. Lipman said. "So we can assume that whatever is found on the beach, there is no trace left for identification. Therefore a search party would not know in what direction to start, and if they are going to use dogs, your scent will not be detectable because of the rain."

Acting as the devil's advocate, he continued. "In the highly improbable case that somebody might come to the door to ask for you, I think it would be better for us if Henry goes to his parents as planned and returns here after a few days. For you, Ian, it is a different matter, since you got a leave of absence to prepare for your exam and now that you have passed it two weeks ago, they might wonder why you haven't returned and applied for your job again."

They discussed the situation and came to the conclusion that Henry would call in the next morning and ask for a couple of days vacation to visit his family for some urgent reason, while Ian, stating that at all cost he would avoid bringing the Lipmans any kind of difficulty, would also go the next morning to his employer and ask for his job back.

After a long night's sleep both friends set out for their tasks; Henry had no problem getting a couple of days off, but Ian learned that, although they had tried to keep the function open, another person had taken his place. They apologized but said they could not offer him work.

The same afternoon he went to see Jenny and during their long walk in the rainy weather he told her their escapade of bad luck and the fact that he was without work. Jenny's reaction on the first part was twofold. She was sorry that it went wrong, but very glad he was back. She was worried about his being jobless and officially having to report to the proper authorities. They, no doubt, would have to send him to Germany.

"What are you going to do now?" she asked.

"I don't know yet. I think it is a good idea to go and see my teacher and explain the situation to him. "

"Can't you continue your study? When you run out of money maybe I can help you. I can't buy very much on my coupons anyhow in this rotten time." Jenny was almost in tears.

"No, I cannot study further. I first will have to sail in the Merchant Marine for twelve months. Then I get my full third mate certificate." Ian held her close to him, proud to have such a girl.

Not wanting to lose more precious time, Ian walked the next day to the tutor's house. He found him at home and the two men sat together talking about the war. This gave Ian the opportunity to tell him about his and his friend's attempt at escape to England and the consequences he was now facing.

Mr. Wide listened without interrupting and when Ian was finished he was silent for a moment, as if deep in thought.

Then he looked at Ian with sympathy. "Ian, I admire your guts to do what you did. But you should have known better than to take off in such a type of canoe, which is by no means seaworthy. You are lucky to be alive, my boy. Now what are you going to do?" The same question Jenny had asked him, thought Ian.

"Well, sir, I really don't know," he replied.

"You need a year practice on a merchant vessel and if you want to further pursue your choice, the best way to go about it is to sign on a Dutch vessel, still allowed by the Germans to sail into the Baltic. It is, however, risky, because the ships creep along the Dutch and German coast in convoy with German men of war as a shield. These convoys are occasionally attacked by the RAF, and although the Dutch vessels are clearly marked, there is no certainty that they wouldn't be hit. Your other two alternatives are either to go into hiding or be shipped out to Germany. Think about it, Ian, and if you decide to go to sea, I have connections with the few Dutch shipping companies plying the Baltic waters."

They deliberated on the topic some more, and then Ian thanked him for his help and walked home, not seeing the area he passed through, his thoughts on what Mr. Wide had told him.

Apparently he had only three choices and he was not very enthusiastic about any of them. I am now twenty-two years old, he thought bitterly, and have met nothing but misery. Depression, military service, surrender, escape from labor camp, stupid work in The Hague, and a loused-up escape. What now?

Feeling very sorry for himself, he looked around, and for the first time on the walk, scolded himself for being such a pessimist. One day the war would be over, he had a beautiful, loving girl, and had made a start with his career, despite all the handicaps. And with head up he stepped on.

Chapter Eight

It was early spring 1944, more than a year since Ian had the discussion about the future with his tutor in Scheveningen. Much had happened during that year.

Ian looked out of the window into a quiet street in The Hague and was in a pensive mood, thinking about his recent past.

Not having much choice, he had, with the help of Mr. Wide, signed on as apprentice mate on a Dutch vessel sailing from a northern Dutch port into the Baltic Sea carrying coal to Finland and bringing lumber back. As soon as he had completed his one year at sea, he signed off and got the desired certificate of third mate Merchant Marine.

One period during his year at sea he recalled very vividly. It happened that after loading lumber in a Finnish port in the Baltic, the ship had to call at a Swedish port to top off to full cargo-carrying capacity.

It was quite a revelation to be in neutral Sweden, where shops were well stocked with merchandise unavailable in war-torn Western Europe. The town was brightly lit in contrast to the darkened cities elsewhere.

During the loading Ian got acquainted with the manager of the local stevedoring company and he was invited to his home for dinner. There he met the rest of the family, consisting of the manager's wife and their two daughters. The main course was succulent gravlaxs, salmon buried in the ground for a specific time, which melted on the tongue, and small potatoes with parsley.

After dinner, the two men sat by the open fire and the host opened the discussion by cautiously touching on the subject of escaping to England via the Dutch Consulate in Stockholm. Without directly asking whether Ian had considered such a move, he told him that it had been tried before with often disastrous results. Escapees who had not mastered the Swedish language had asked in Stockholm in English where the Dutch Consulate was located, and any passerby not fluent in English assumed the foreigner was asking for the "Deutsch Consulate." Hence the escapee was directed to the German Consulate and never heard of again.

Ian understood what his host was driving at. "I have heard about people jumping ship when in a Swedish port. Personally I do not intend to do so, since I am concerned with German repercussions against my family."

Then a thought had struck him. "But if I know somebody who, for urgent reasons, is trying to escape from the Germans, could I refer him to you for help?"

"In principle, yes. But you and I must be careful that such a person is not a traitor, acting as a whistle blower for the Germans."

He gave Ian some useful information, which could be passed on to would-be escapees, such as the exact address of the free Dutch Consulate and not to ask or talk to anybody in German. Also, he handed to Ian an English-Swedish pocket dictionary. Shortly thereafter, the ship was ready to sail and Ian felt like he was leaving good friends behind. During subsequent trips when the ship happened to call at a Swedish port, Ian twice had the opportunity to help Merchant Marine students, who had signed on as apprentice sailors, take their chances reaching England.

Each time he was in port in Holland for a few days he went to The Hague to see Jenny, to whom he now was engaged.

The Lipmans, like practically the entire population of Scheveningen and other coastal towns, had been evacuated and Ian had no forwarding address. The dunes were completely closed and the west coast looked like a huge fortified area. It was apparent that an Allied invasion was expected.

His friend Henry was also "relocated" to a labor camp east of Berlin. Once, when his ship was in a Baltic harbor, Ian had traveled to see him on a Sunday; the reunion was great. Henry lived in barracks with other detainees from Holland, and their lives were very monotonous. They worked long hours in factories, walking back and forth; ate tasteless food; and slept. The only excitement occurred during alarms when Allied bombers appeared. After that visit, Ian was glad that he had chosen the sea.

Now he was staying with Jenny's family and enjoyed their togetherness. During his time at sea he had squirreled away extra foodstuff, and this together with his rationing coupons and the help of her husband's job with the city parks department enabled Jenny's sister Sue to keep food on the table. Sue's husband's job included the opportunity to grow potatoes on small plots reserved in the parks, and part of that staple was used to barter for other essentials.

The whole situation was dismal and the people in the big cities were facing hunger. The conquerors were less tolerant and the collaborators were more vicious. No wonder Ian was not in the mood to study. Jenny was also under stress because of her work condition: the dentist's family had its own problems.

A friend of Ian's from his Boy Scout years back in the east had married and was living in a suburb of The Hague. Ian and Jenny visited the couple a few times and a warm relationship developed. His old friend, Wim, who held a government job, had hinted that he knew people in the partisan underground world through which one could obtain addresses of safe houses in case of prosecution by the Germans. They had not discussed the topic further at that time, but now, while Ian was staring into the street, the thought came back to him to disappear from here and go to a rural area, work on a farm if possible and avoid deportation, hunger, and related threats. Moreover, he was sure that Jenny was feeling more and more the same way.

So when Jenny came on a Sunday, he suggested going to see Wim and his wife Cora, which they did. There was little chance that they would not be home, because there was no public transportation, the shops were closed, and there was no outdoor entertainment. After greetings, Ian didn't lose time bringing up the subject of packing and going to the rural north to work on a farm and await the end of the war. The young couple looked at him. "Did you have a feeling that we have been planning to do just that?" Cora wondered.

"I got some disturbing news at the office and it looks like my chances of remaining are in jeopardy," Wim added.

Jenny looked at their friends, and then at Ian. "Are you planning to go underground?"

"For the past days the thought has crossed my mind, also I figured that for you, too, it would be necessary because your situation and condition are rapidly getting worse," Ian said defensively.

"Well, if we can stay together, I am all for it," Jenny replied. They went into more details and the feasibility of the plan. When it was time for Jenny and Ian to leave, Wim said that he would talk with his contact person and let them know, adding, "No word to anybody. When we do it, we want there to be four of us to help each other."

Two days later, Wim came to see Ian and told him that he had obtained safe addresses for when they decided to go underground.

"Where would we go?" Ian asked.

"To the north part of the country, a province called Friesland. It's a very rural area with lots of farms and not crowded with soldiers, but, of course, you find Germans everywhere," said Wim, and continued, "How about it. Are you and Jenny with us?"

Ian did not need any time to answer that they would go, and the two men made the arrangement that all four would meet at Wim's home the next afternoon to discuss all the details.

"If it is getting too late for you to be back home before curfew, you and Jenny can stay overnight with us," Wim offered.

"All right. Let's see how it works out. I will go over to Jenny and let her know," Ian agreed.

Jenny was a very courageous young woman and when Ian gave her Wim's message, she was all for it.

"Are you saying that you and I will stay overnight at Cora and Wim's together?" she asked, with a naughty light in her blue eyes.

"If it gets too late, yes!" Ian caught on quickly and in a vision saw them making love. He looked at her and their eyes met, both understanding each other's thoughts.

Reluctantly breaking the spell he dashed off to be inside at curfew time.

The next day the four went through their plan in detail. Together they had two functional bicycles on which they could load their luggage, using them as pack mules. They had to walk, but if someone became tired she or he could sit on a bike for awhile and be pushed for the ride. To reach the first address in Friesland, the routing had to be laid out. Cora's parents lived in Amsterdam and she suggested going there first, staying overnight and trying to arrange passage on a boat to Lemmer, Friesland, if that could be done without risk of control.

Considering the urgency of the matter and seeing no reason to wait much longer, they decided to start the next Saturday, leaving it to Wim what to say at the office. They would start out as early as they were allowed on the street from Wim's home, which was already in the direction of Amsterdam.

For Jenny and Ian it was too late to go home, and without fuss, Cora made a bed in their spare room. Ian, playing the gentleman, waited until Jenny was in bed before he entered. Then they found each other and the world around them ceased to exist.

There was a difficult moment when Sue and her husband were told of their plan, since Sue didn't want to let go of her baby sister, but Jenny and Ian were determined to go. At dawn they converged at Wim and Cora's and soon they were under way with the two loaded bikes.

If they could make good time, the forty miles would take them two days, depending on which route they took and unpredictable events on the way. It was a chilly and dreary day and the brisk tempo with which they began had to be slowed in the afternoon when they stopped on the side of the road to have some sandwiches. That night they found shelter in a hay stack near a farm and continued the trek the next morning. On the way they tried to buy food at several farms but were unsuccessful since the farmers would only accept bedsheets or blankets or other items as payment, but no money. Finally they found a farmer willing to accept money so they could replenish their meager supplies and would be able to share it with Cora's parents.

They welcomed the sign of the city with a subdued cheer when they came upon it, and after walking through seemingly endless streets, the four arrived exhausted at their first stop with Cora's family. Her father said he would check the following morning whether there would be any control of passengers crossing the Ysselmeer to Friesland. Cora and Jenny would sleep in Cora's bed, while for Wim and Ian, a makeshift bed was made on the floor of the living room. Thus ended the first leg of their journey, which so far had been without any incident.

The next morning Cora's father went to the pier from which the Lemmer boat was sailing and talked to one of the deckhands who, as an Amsterdammer, understood the reason for the question. No, there was no military control, only a check of ID papers of the passengers, and mainly males were checked. When they heard the good news, they decided to take the boat that evening; sailing time was 6 P.M. and arrival at Lemmer 6 A.M. the following day. Crossings were made only at night because of the danger of air attacks.

So they "saddled their horses" again, thanked the family, and marched to the pier. Both men felt confident that they would not have any problem with control when boarding the boat. Nevertheless, they were uneasy when a uniformed guard asked for their papers, looking at the two women. At the question about the purpose of the trip and where they were going, both men answered that they were bringing their wives to relatives in Friesland. Then, after looking at Wim's and Ian's papers, he said to Wim, "You are in government service?"

"Yes, and I took a few days leave to bring my wife to her family." Wim had no trouble with that since Cora, indeed, had family in Friesland.

"And you were in the Merchant Marine? What are you doing now?"

"I got a shore leave and am using it for the same purpose," answered Ian, trying to avoid having to prove that Jenny was his wife, which he couldn't. Other passengers had meanwhile formed a long line, and seeing this, the officer let them pass with their luggage.

There was no place to sleep on the packed boat. The night was long but the four wanderers didn't mind. Their undertaking had gone smoothly so far and they spent the time on board dozing.

On arrival, there was the usual trampling of passengers to get ashore as quickly as possible and soon the foursome was out of the town in the direction of their first address for a night's shelter.

It happened to be a farm and the farmer's wife took them in the kitchen to warm and dry since the weather continued to be wet and cold. The evening meal was so abundant and rich that all four, not having had such food for a long time, were miserably sick that night.

The farmer and his wife had not asked them any questions other than who had referred them, and Wim had told them. Apparently that was sufficient, but the farmer told them that because his farm was close to town he could not keep them. Wim told him that they knew the situation and that they would continue the trip, not disclosing any destination, but asking for general direction.

This experience was repeated two times, each time at a farm, until they arrived at the house of a notary whose address was given to them as an end station.

The nameplate at the entrance to the big house in a small town read "Notary De Jong," which verified Wim's information, so they entered the path to the front door and knocked. After a while the door was opened and a lady looked at them and at their two loaded bikes. "I am Mrs. DeJong. What can I do for you?" she asked. The four introduced themselves and Wim told her the names of his reference. After hearing their story, she told Cora and Jenny to come in, and asked the two men to put the bikes behind the house, adding, "We don't want to advertise your arrival."

When they were all seated, Mrs. DeJong, who obviously had dealt with situations like this before, called her two daughters in and told them to go by bike to a farm at the south side of town and tell the farmer that four guests would be coming this afternoon to stay for a few days until other arrangements could be made. The daughters apparently knew which farm their mother meant and disappeared. Some kind of tea was offered and Mrs. DeJong told them the notary was unavailable, that she could not accommodate them for safety reasons, and to mention only their given names to anybody. They would hear from her when a more permanent solution was found. "You are married?" she asked. Wim affirmed, while Ian could only say that he and Jenny were engaged.

"Well, the farmers around here are religious, and I'll have to find separate accommodations for you two," she said, with a twinkle in her eyes, looking at Jenny, who to her own surprise, felt that she was blushing. In half an hour the daughters returned and all they said to their mother was, "It is arranged. They are expected before dinner."

Later that afternoon they thanked their charming hostess and followed her directions to a beautiful, big farm. Again they were given a warm welcome by the family, consisting of a farmer, his wife, three sons and a daughter, plus a maid. The discussion started haltingly in Dutch until Jenny, whose parents were Frisian, understood why, and to their delight the family changed right away to that language. Frisian is not a Dutch dialect but a language with its own grammar, closely related to Swedish and Norwegian, a remnant of 400 years of invasions by the Vikings. Hollanders, as they are called by the Frisians, do not understand Frisian and have to study it.

So, with translations back and forth, the ice was broken and a lively discussion took place until bedtime. Wim and Ian were given berth on a hayloft, while Cora and Jenny shared beds with the daughter and the maid.

While they stayed at the farm, awaiting word from Mrs. DeJong about their final destination, the two girls helped the farmer's wife and the men made themselves productive in the huge stables. On the third day, Mrs. DeJong came and the farmer, his wife, and the four friends sat around the table in the kitchen to hear what message she brought.

For Cora and Wim there was a place on another farm not far away. Cora was to help in the household and Wim as farmhand, and both were to help milking the cows. There were some grins when milking was mentioned, but the young couple looked around and said in good humor that they would show how the Hollanders milked a cow.

The solution for Jenny and Ian was a bit more difficult; Mrs. DeJong had contacted a doctor's wife in a nearby village who found a farm, but with place for only one and preferably the young woman. That left Ian nowhere and he didn't look happy. At that impasse, the farmer's wife spoke. "We have thought about it and I would like to have Jenny stay with us. She can help with the cooking, and there is lots of knitting and clothes mending to do in our household." Jenny looked at her and said simply, "I would like that very much."

That, to his dismay, left Ian in a position to go to the other place as a sort of second choice. Then he smiled and said to Jenny, "We'll get married right away and then it will be easier to find a place to hide." "Oh no you won't" was the immediate reply from all four women. "No way; when you go underground, there will be no wedding here," Mrs. DeJong was adamant, and Ian looked helplessly to Jenny for support. "You promised to marry me when the war was over," she reminded him tactfully, afraid that he would screw up the whole deal.

"How far is it from here to the other place?" Ian wanted to know. He was told about eight miles, so he had no excuse. He hoped that he and Jenny could see each other occasionally and when he said so, Mrs. DeJong and the farmer's wife both agreed that it would be workable. Jenny would come to him to visit since that was less risky than Ian going through town.

The next day the four friends parted; Cora and Wim together to their shelter, Jenny staying at the farm which was called "The South," and Ian on his way to the place of his immediate future.

Chapter Nine

In the morning, Ian said his good-byes to his hosts, his friends, and more intimately, Jenny. He climbed on his bike, which was less loaded without Jenny's belongings, and rode to the house of Mrs. DeJong in town. One of her daughters was waiting for him and together they took off.

She informed him that they were taking some back roads to avoid the police station as well as eventual military traffic. It was a nice morning and Ian, despite his earlier misgivings, began to enjoy the ride through pastures with widely spread farms, going over a narrow canal via an old stone bridge. His "ride" was a pretty girl who told him much about the surroundings and the people he was going to meet.

Soon they arrived at the doctor's house outside the village. The doctor's wife, Mrs. Goes, asked them in, and after a short introductory talk, his guide returned to town. Mrs. Goes, a friendly lady, quickly put him at ease. "Ian, you'll find the Brand family very accommodating. They are good people, well established in the area for many generations. They have no children and the wife is past the age of having them. They farm more because it is in their blood than out of financial necessity. They have a maid and a farmhand, and both are trustworthy. They speak Dutch fluently (and here Mrs. Goes smiled), have done some traveling, and you will find them interesting and I am sure that will work both ways." Ian thanked her for the introduction, which did not sound so bad after all, and together they walked to the Brand's farm, half a mile away.

It was an old-style farm, less pretentious than "The South" but well kept and clean. Mrs. Brand let them in through the front door into a showroom-like living room and excused herself to call her husband. Mrs. Goes made a mocking face to Ian and whispered: "You are getting the royal treatment, my boy. The front door is only used for weddings, births, and funerals and I bet you'll never sit in this room again."

Ian was amused, and then the Brands entered the room, shaking hands and inspecting Ian openly, apparently not disliking what they saw. In brief terms, Mrs. Goes told them Ian's background and added that she personally would vouch for him, something Ian was surprised to hear not ever having met her until half an hour ago. Anyway, her assurance about Ian met with satisfaction as Ian observed, and he looked at the two more closely. The farmer was short and heavyset, with red cheeks and very lively gestures. His wife was tall with an appearance of "old farmer nobility" and when their eyes met Ian was aware of her quiet authority. Mr. Brand said to Ian, "You can call me 'Boer' and my wife, 'Vrouw,' both being Dutch for 'farmer' and 'wife.' Thus they created an easier atmosphere to address than the perfunctory "Mr. and Mrs." Calling each other by first names is not at all as usual in Europe as in the United States.

"Well, that is arranged then," Mrs. Goes said with a tone of relief in her voice. "We only have one condition," Boer Brand interrupted. Mrs. Goes was concerned that the deal would fall through, and quickly remarked, "It is understood that you will give him board and lodging, and that he will do any work on the farm without payment." Mrs. Goes felt it necessary to say, but that was not it, because Boer Brand shook his head.

"I don't mean that. Our condition to take Ian into our house is that he will not engage in any armed underground action. We see the Germans as our enemy, but do not want Ian, and thereby ourselves, to take more risks than we do by having and holding him under our roof."

Ian could appreciate this viewpoint of the two elderly people, and he simply made the requested promise. Mrs. Goes was leaving, after thanking the Brands for their cooperation. Vrouw Brand let her out, again through the front door, and the two women talked for a short while.

Boer Brand stood up and said to Ian, "Well, that is that. Come with me and I will show you our farm." Ian followed him to the stable which housed cows and two horses. The milking cows were each in their own stall looking at the wall, which had small windows. "Now they can look outside and are not so bored," the Boer said with a loud laugh. They walked along the narrow path behind the cows, only separated from the bovines by a foot-wide gutter, and suddenly the Boer took Ian by the arm. "Quick pass that one," he urged and they both hurried, Ian not knowing why.

Then he got his first lesson. "This cow has a light cold, coughing occasionally, and when she does that and her tail goes up, you run a risk of getting sprayed," the Boer said, and again laughed heartily, adding: "Whenever you see a tail rising, get out of the way."

Ian began to like Boer Brand, especially for his sense of humor, and felt they would get along just fine. His host told him that he had another, more modern farm, but that he preferred to stay here, his family farm for generations.

After the tour they returned to the living section of the entire building. In Holland the farms are one main building, housing the family, the cattle, horses, and hay, the latter in the loft above the cattle. This time the introductory show was over, and they sat down in a roomy kitchen where Vrouw Brand had made real tea and thick sandwiches from home-baked bread. Ian was introduced to Wyntje, the maid, who eyed him with some suspicion. The Vrouw noticed it, saying to Ian, "Wyntje has trouble with talking Dutch, which she thinks is pedantry since even the minister and the doctor speak Frisian." Ian smiled at her and promised that he would pick up Frisian as quickly as possible, something he should not have said because it is not an easy language.

After the "snack," which was more like a meal, Vrouw Brand showed him his quarters, a partitioned-off part of the loft above the living area, with a comfortable-looking bed, a cabinet, and a chair.

"Make yourself at home, Ian. At six o'clock we have dinner," and with these friendly words she went downstairs. Ian looked at his watch: it was four-thirty. He went down to his bike, unloaded his luggage, and brought it to his area, where he stowed it in the cabinet. He sat on the bed, wondering what Jenny would be doing at this very hour. Going to the kitchen he found Wyntje and asked her where everybody was. After heavy thinking she said, "In the stables, of course. It is milking time." That was lesson number two; you have to eat before milking and thereafter you eat again.

"All right, I'll go there and see if I can help." Wyntje looked at his shoes. "Not with shoes on. Try some klompen [wooden shoes], over there," she said, pointing to a wooden box near the door to the stables. And so Ian made his first, rather painful steps into a farmer's life.

Ian was kept busy every day—milking and cattle-feeding time twice a day, at 5 A.M. and at 4 P.M.; cleaning the stables; cutting and splitting firewood; and moving hay from the loft to the feeding hatches.

He worked with the Brand's farmhand, Sietse, a nice and friendly man. And Boer Brand calls this their easy time, Ian thought, wondering what busy time meant. He soon found out. At the end of May it was time for haying, which was done manually. Since the country was flat and open, it was agreed that it was safe for Ian to be outside; a patrol would be signaled early enough for Ian to hide.

Boer Brand explained that after a farm had been burned to the ground when a patrol was looking for young men they knew were there and didn't come out, the neighborhood established an effective warning system by using young boys and girls who were not under suspicion by the invaders. They passed the word from farm to farm. Most farms had no telephone, so communication was only by word of mouth. This "jungle drum" system worked fine, and when on 6 June 1944, the long-awaited invasion from England into northern France started, this great news was relayed to even the most rural areas.

As soon as Jenny heard the news she was elated, and not knowing whether Ian knew about it, she asked for permission to go and tell him. She borrowed a bike from her hosts, the Bots, rode to the Brand place, introduced herself to Vrouw Brand, and asked where Ian was. Wyntje was asked to bring her to the field where Ian was at work, and when he saw her coming, he threw away the hay fork and ran to her. The two embraced and kissed, completely ignoring Wyntje and Sietse, who looked amused at the two. Out of breath, Jenny told him the news and Ian, who could not believe his ears, jumped with joy. Standing in the hay field, the four were elated and mutually agreed that the war would be over soon.

This hope vanished when, thereafter, the Allied divisions rolling through northern France and Belgium toward Germany reached southern Holland. In an effort to prevent the strategic bridges over the Rhine from being blown up, which would delay the advancing troops, a massive airborne assault around the city of Arnhem was launched. The Battle of Arnhem, as it was called, became a disaster as heavy armored German divisions arrived unexpectedly on the scene, forcing the Allied paratroops to withdraw with heavy casualties. It delayed the liberation of the rest of Holland for almost a year.

During that year, the situation for the Dutch population under the occupation went from bad to worse, especially in the cities. Rationing was severely cut again and again, and many in the cities perished. Power was cut off, all public transportation ceased, the national railways went on strike, and the entire railroad work force went underground in one night. The underground "Home Force" got more weapons, dropped by air from England, which were used for attacks on enemy targets. The response by the Germans was to take hostages who were executed when the partisans did not surrender. Jews were deported in even greater numbers and more slave labor was shipped to Germany.

Jenny was very much concerned about her family in The Hague and one day decided to try to bring food to them. The Bots' family gave her bacon and dried milk, while the Brands, hearing her plan when she visited Ian, donated other non-perishables. First Ian protested vehemently against the plan, threatening to go himself instead. "And get caught right away? No way. I'll go before it is too late and the Ysselmeer crossing is stopped," Jenny insisted. So she went, on a heavily loaded bike, leaving Ian in anguish. One week later she returned safe, looking pale and very tired but triumphant that she had delivered her treasure, which had been received like manna from heaven. She did not tell how she had managed the trip, and Ian wisely did not press her.

Human nature has qualities that surface under stress, and even in the darkest hours there are moments of repose. The churches were packed on Sundays. Courageous clergymen keeping hope and faith in the flock were often imprisoned after speaking out against the invaders. Another most important resource was a sense of humor.

All farmers had to deliver milk to the occupation forces; none was going to the population. People from the nearby town had their own clandestine supplier. The Brands, like the Bots, were dealing out some milk to a small number of trusted people twice a week. The customers arrived at dark and the first time Ian was asked to make the distribution, he saw six people huddled outside the barn door. He asked them into the barn and in lamplight started to deal out two quarts of milk. For some he had to funnel it into a number of small bottles which were stowed in various pockets, others had concocted other devices to avoid detection by controlling officials. One person had ingeniously sealed off the hollow frame of his bicycle, into which the milk was poured. But his real surprise came when one of the notary's daughters came forward, opened her coat and shirt, and pointed to between her breasts.

"In here," she said.

"Huh?" was all Ian could muster.

"Don't worry, I am not going to seduce you," she laughed. "A tinkerer has made me a hollow tin harness around you know what, and nobody will notice."

Ian quickly regained his composure. "It is a pleasure to serve you miss."

When Jenny heard about the gimmick she was not amused and told him to behave, to which Ian remarked that you have to treat customers nicely.

The winter evenings after dinner were long, especially without electricity, and candles were scarce. Boer Brand loved to play checkers and one day Ian didn't say anything when he mounted the small dynamo of his bike on the rear wheel. These dynamos, very common in Holland, are spring loaded and mounted on the fork frame of the bike and their grooved, rotating heads can be snapped on to touch the tire. When the bike travels, the rotating head turns and delivers current to the reflector so that the rider can see where he or she is going. One evening, he asked the Boer, "Shall we have a game of checkers?" "Sure, you switch the light on," answered Boer Brand sarcastically.

"All right, just a minute," Ian responded, and the Brands and Wyntje looked at him as if he had lost his marbles. Ian returned with an old bed sheet which he had obtained, with some prodding, from Wyntje and spread it on the floor near the table. Then he brought his bike into the room. Vrouw Brand, very neat as always, began to protest, but the Boer said to her, "Shh, let's see what he has in mind."

Ian turned the vehicle upside down, resting on the saddle and handle bars, and began with one hand turning a pedal. The rear wheel spun, he flipped the spring, the head engaged onto the tire, and a relatively bright light illuminated the area over the table, obscuring the soft candle light. Everybody cheered. Boer Brand quickly got the checkerboard and the two women their knitting stuff.

From then on their world became somewhat brighter. When Ian became tired of turning the pedal and slowed down, the others started yelling, "More light." By mutual agreement, it was decided to enjoy the phenomena only one hour per night, and it became a ritual.

Winter arrived and the battle lines came to a standstill on the Dutch front. There was a German counterattack in the Ardennes called the Battle of the Bulge, and everybody held their breath. The cold bode ill for people in the cities who had no heating. Wood-burning stoves were only obtainable at a premium. In order to obtain fuel for the stoves, many staircases were partly demolished and in some towns streets paved with wooden blocks between the streetcar rails were broken up, making it look like medieval times. Parks lost many trees.

The freezing weather brought another peril to the north. When the lakes and canals are frozen, there is no force that can keep Frisians from the ice, even those who went underground could not resist the temptation and took a great risk.

To catch the latter, the Germans dispatched troops from northern Germany to Friesland, and also being good skaters, they caught many men on the open lakes and marshes. Jenny could skate even before she could walk; her parents put her in the frame of a chair without a seat so that she couldn't fall and with that support she scrambled over the ice. Ian could not skate, which was considered a serious handicap by the Frisians, and they told him to stay behind the stove with the old women. Even Jenny had no consideration for him when she came by on skates, looking gorgeous with red cheeks and shining eyes; his ego was bruised when she avoided his advances.

"Sorry, Ian, no time for that. I have to go back with the others." He wished it would rain warm water.

There had been an alarm several times that winter, and each time Ian had been alerted in time and hid between the hay bales on the loft, digging deep down along a wall and pulling the bales close above him. There was a slight draft so he could breathe and wouldn't start sneezing at a critical moment. Moreover he had arranged with Boer Brand a knocking signal on the wall when the coast was clear. As a precaution, Vrouw Brand and Wyntje did not know where his hiding place was. Usually, when a warning of a possible search was given by a youngster, the two women quickly went to Ian's sleeping place to hide his belongings, but once there was no time to do so. Dutch vassals, always considered traitors, were accompanied by soldiers who searched the entire building and came to Ian's place.

"And who is sleeping here?" one of the vassals asked, leering at Wyntje, who had followed him. She realized the situation immediately, and without a moment of hesitation responded, "My fiancé stays here overnight when the weather is too bad to go home." The man looked at her again, then turned around and stomped downstairs and joined the others, who dismayed at not finding anybody, fired some ammunition rounds for good measure through an outside haystack, and left for another farm.

"Oh my god, that was close," sighed Vrouw Brand when she heard Wyntje's story. Later, when the signal was given and Ian reappeared, he heard of Wyntje's quick wits and before she realized what he was doing he gave her two heavy smackers on her cheeks.

"You crazy fellow," was all she could say, and then added to save her posture, "I'll tell Jenny about you!" "You may do just that, and get kisses from her also," Ian said with a big grin, and they all laughed.

It was early spring 1945 when the Allies crossed the Rhine near Arnhem and moved northward to cut off the enemy in the western part of Holland, preventing them from joining their forces to the east. At the same time, General Patton made his amazingly fast run through Western Germany to the North Sea, bringing even more disarray to the retreating German divisions.

Rumors of advancing Allied forces were rampant and some people put out the Dutch flag, which was hastily withdrawn when another German troop came through town.

It still came as a surprise when early one morning heavy tanks rumbled past the Brand farm. They all looked out of the windows, not knowing what the enemy was up to, until Ian noticed a small Canadian flag and the white star on the leading tank.

"The Allies, the Allies," he yelled, burst out of the house, and raced down the path to the road, where he stood yelling and waving like a madman.

"What on earth is he doing," exclaimed Boer Brand, not understanding the significance of Ian's excitement. His wife, composed as ever, looked at him and said, "It means that we are liberated, my dear."

And she was right: on 5 May 1945, almost exactly five years to the day, Holland was free again.

Chapter Ten

When the Allied columns went through another liberated part of Holland, they ordered the now-emerged Home Force to "clean up" pockets of resistance and people who collaborated with the Germans during occupation. There was much hatred against the latter, who were their own countrymen. Some collaborators had become that way out of conviction that it would bring a new world order, but most joined the despised NSB movement (an organization to assist the enemy in any way other than in battle) either for personal gain or for revenge.

Because they had no uniforms, the Home Force members dressed in blue overalls with an orange-colored armband. Only one day after the tank column had driven through the town and nearby village where Jenny and Ian stayed, they appeared on the streets in a requisitioned German troop carrier equipped with a loudspeaker system. It was announced that everybody had to stay where they were until the all-clear sign was given, and for those who were not from the area, a special office to issue travel passes would be opened in the town hall.

Although these measures did not give the Dutch a sense of freedom, the public understood the reasoning behind it and cooperated fully. To Ian's chagrin he could not go to The South farm and share with Jenny the joy of the long-awaited victory, but at least he could pass a message to her through a member of the Home Force that he was sound and well.

In the west the first task for the Dutch officials who came to the country on the tail end of the liberating forces was to arrange for food to the starving population. An early move in that direction came from neutral Sweden. It sent cargo planes with real white bread, which was dropped by parachutes.

Emotions ran high, on the positive side toward the Allied liberators, and on the negative side toward the collaborators who were caught and imprisoned. Rationing for the west consisted of crackers and egg powder only, a necessary approach since people's stomachs could not absorb anything heavier after being exposed to tulip bulbs and potatoes. Later the ration was gradually increased to more normal fare.

After more than a week, local travel restrictions were lifted and people were able to move around, a moment Ian used to race to Jenny, take her in his arms, and swirl her around until she was out of breath. She had received his message and they, for the first time in a long while, walked arm in arm out to the road in broad daylight.

"What are we going to do now?" she asked.

"We'll get our travel passes and go home as soon as we can, and get married," answered Ian, who reckoned he had waited long enough for that moment. After the couple returned to The South farm, the Bots family and Jenny and Ian celebrated the liberation together. They had been extremely nice to Jenny—and to Ian whenever he had felt it safe enough to come over for a few stolen hours with his love—and both felt as if they were family.

While they were gathered around in the cozy kitchen, the neighboring farmer knocked on the door, greeted them, and sat down, facing farmer Bots.

"You are a good neighbor," he began, "but I have to tell you something." Farmer Bots raised his eyebrows, and like the patriarch he was, urged his neighbor to come out with it.

"Do you remember when I had a bad case of flu some months ago and you gave me a bottle of jenever [Dutch gin, eighty-five proof] to cheer me up?"

Hearing this the two oldest sons stood up and mumbled something about checking the horses.

"Of course I remember. It was my last bottle."

"Well, when you brought it to me, I was very thankful for such a Samaritan gesture from a good neighbor until I took the first sip. It was clear water!"

Farmer Bots was motionless for a short moment, his face turning from a healthy color to deep red. Then abruptly he stood up, dropping the chair behind him, and bellowed, "Hey, you two out there, come here now." The two sons had just left but couldn't feign not hearing their dad and returned reluctantly to the kitchen. The tall farmer stood over them, his voice icy when he said to the two, "Any idea what happened to that bottle?" Seeing no way out of their dilemma, they confessed that they had a little party with friends in the barn. They were playing a game of selling cattle at the market, and with the cigars, a glass of jenever was appropriate to making a deal, so...

"Cigars? You also took some of my precious cigars?" farmer Bots interrupted, not believing his ears. His wife foresaw a heavy explosion and decided the time had arrived to interfere. "You two, get out of our sight. You will be dealt with later."

The two left hastily, and when the door closed, the neighbor couldn't hold his laughter any longer. "That is the best joke I have heard in a long time," he said, and slapped Bots on his back. "Sorry, I thought that you had played a dirty trick on a sick man." The others joined in laughter, except farmer Bots, who needed a little longer to compose himself.

"Those blasted rascals. And I didn't even miss the stuff." That settled it for the moment, and friendship restored, they talked about the future.

Soon Jenny and Ian excused themselves; they planned to go over to Wim and Cora whom they had not seen for a long time. It was good to see them again and the four friends talked about the months past. As soon as Wim and Cora could get their travel passes, they would go west to see whether their house near The Hague was still there and in what shape. Ian and Jenny told of their plans to go to their home towns in the east and they promised to write each other when postal service was restored.

Another week went by before travel passes could be obtained. Mrs. DeJong vouched for Jenny's and Ian's good conduct, and Mrs. Goes, the doctor's wife, added to it on Ian's behalf. With their own papers together they obtained the passes, which mentioned their returning home. The farewells of their respective host families and all others they had met were like partings from real family. The Brands and Bots provided the two with all kinds of food and again their one bike was heavily loaded when they went on their way. This time, there were no detours on out-of-the-way paths. They traveled on open roads, and at each checkpoint they felt good that there were such controls to catch undesirable elements. They were in no hurry, and enjoying each other's company, took their time reaching their destinations, sleeping wherever a place could be found.

Without being asked, Ian proudly declared on occasion that Jenny was his wife, and although she wasn't consulted on that state of affairs, she did not disagree, knowing full well that it would make the situation for one-night hosts less problematic. Moreover they found that the general attitude of the public had become less stiff and restrictive than before the war.

The long walk came to an end when they turned the last corner of the street where Jenny's parents lived. But there were only blackened ruins there now. Ian caught Jenny just in time, when upon seeing what once had been her parental home, she burst out in tears and almost collapsed. People living across the street came over and recognized Jenny. They told her that her parents and brother were safe.

"Where are they?" Jenny asked between sobs. They were told where her parents were staying since the fire, and Ian took her away from the sight of the wrecked house. A few blocks later they knocked on the door at the given address, which was opened by a woman. Jenny told her who she was and then heard her brother's voice upstairs. They climbed the stairs and the reunion with her father, stepmother, and brother was one of great joy.

Ian, who had never met them before, was introduced properly. They learned that the house was set on fire the very last day of the war as a reprisal for the fact that her father, who was chief engineer with the Dutch Railways, had taken part in the general strike and gone underground. They had been put in the basement with the door locked and the house set on fire. At the last moment her father managed to break open the door and they escaped through the flames and smoke.

The government had assigned the second floor of a house to them, where they were now. It was a sad story. They had lost all their personal belongings and were now living in cramped quarters. Ian and Jenny's brother went below and brought luggage and food from the bike. The food was especially welcomed with delight. Jenny and Ian had purposely saved as much food as possible for their parents and felt good when they saw how appreciative they were. "Better bringing this than flowers," whispered Ian to Jenny, who looked at him, and finding her old spirit, reminded him that she had never received flowers from him in the first place.

With so much to tell, hours went by quickly and soon it was time for bed. Now it wasn't possible for Ian to claim Jenny as his wife and he wondered what kind of arrangement would be made. Very simple: Jenny got her brother's bed, while the two young men found a place on a couch and on the floor in the living room.

This situation continued for two days until Ian, eager to go to his folks, announced that they would go to his home village, a two-hour walk. Jenny understood that staying longer in the limited space would become a strain on everybody and agreed, saying they would see each other soon. The bike was re-loaded and the two set out for their next stop. They were again welcomed with joy and the stories flowed from both sides. Ian's family had encountered the usual hardships, but they were complete and their home was undamaged. From them Ian learned the sad news that his benefactor, the government official, had been taken as a hostage, and when nobody came forward to admit to an attack on a German patrol that resulted in many deaths, he was executed together with nine other hostages from the village.

The Halls' home was as crowded as Ian remembered and although room for Jenny and himself was being arranged, the situation was only slightly better than at Jenny's parents. After a few days, the lack of privacy put pressure on everybody and one morning Ian and Jenny went out for a walk through the nearby forest to discuss their future. Both agreed that the present condition under which they lived should not continue too long.

"I promised to marry you when the war was over, and I don't see why we should wait any longer. Everybody has lost something during the war and we all have to start from the beginning, so, my love, let us make that start together."

"Oh, Ian, I would love that. Being together as husband and wife is something I have been waiting for," she said, and they embraced under the pine trees. When they returned home, Ian told his family the good news, adding that they had waited long enough—thereby cutting short any objections about the uncertainty of their future.

Now that the decision was made, the two began to make necessary arrangements. At the village hall, they were told that it would be the first wedding after the war and the mayor himself would conduct the ceremony. They talked with the minister, who regretted that their wedding could not take place in the damaged church, but smiled, saying that a proper building was available and he had another surprise for them, but wouldn't say more. Family from both sides were informed; postal service was restored, but public transportation was not yet available, which meant that not all family and friends could be present.

Nevertheless, quite a number of participants could be expected. Jenny and Ian looked at each other. What were they going to serve all the guests—crackers and egg powder? Ian had been brooding on that question for some time and thought he had an idea.

"You know the encampment of the Canadian troops just outside the village?" he asked Jenny.

"Yes, I have heard about it. But why do you bring this up? Are you going to invite an army?" she wondered.

"No, we are not that famous. But what I heard is that those troops are French Canadians, so naturally they love wine and I don't think they have plenty of it. What they do have are things like real coffee, tea, sugar, and who knows what more. I know a family in the village, from the old days, who were always wine drinkers and often gave wine parties. They also own the village hotel, although that is still closed. Maybe, just maybe, I can make a deal with them. Leave it to me."

And he went to the family and found that, as everybody else, they would love to have some of the staples Ian mentioned. Coming to the point, a barter deal was struck in good faith: Ian got several bottles of hoarded wine and would exchange that for much-desired items. Whatever he could get would be equally divided between the two parties.

Back on the bike with his bottled treasure, he went to the camp, showed his merchandise, and haggled about the exchange. He got more than anticipated and made a deal to return with more wine, hoping that his partner had more. One of the soldiers asked him whether he was a black marketeer, but when he told the reason for his action, all the men listening were sympathetic and told him there was more, under the condition that they would be invited to the wedding.

"All of you? Then we would never have enough to treat you!" Ian was shocked at the prospect.

"No, only us here and some friends," their spokesman replied, adding, "You bring wine; we give you food." Ian was welcomed at his home as a hero when he showed them his bounty. This was divided in half and he sped to his so-called partners, who were elated upon seeing items they had not enjoyed for a long time.

The operation continued until the source of it ran dry, but by that time, Jenny and his stepmother declared that a wedding dinner was secure. The women started making pastries and preparing meat and other goodies in advance of the wedding. Trips to farmers with the commodities available for exchange resulted in potatoes, vegetables, and milk. It was noticed that during the baking and frying, many people passed by, sniffing the luxurious odors.

"How are we all going to get to the village hall and community building?" Jenny asked.

Ian looked at their long list of items "to do," and told her that one farmer had taken his buggy from under the hay stack, where it had survived detection, and would be at the house on time. A wagon for hay rides and the horses were also arranged. Jenny sighed with relief. It was going to be their heyday!

Chapter Eleven

The wedding day, in the middle of June 1945, promised to be a beautiful summer day and the Halls' home was full of activity, with family and friends gathering. Most of them had not seen each other for years.

The two horses, as well as the buggy and the wagon, were festooned with flowers and waited in front of the house, their drivers dressed in dark farmers' suits. All the invitees came outside to wait for the bride to appear. Ian, who stood next to the buggy, was dressed in his Merchant Marine uniform, which was kept in his home. He was looking at the door through which Jenny would appear, wondering what kind of dress she had come up with. There had been secretive actions going on and several times when he returned from his wine expeditions he had not been allowed to enter the room.

Then there was applause and his bride took his breath away. She looked beautiful in a white dress with white flowers in her hair. She was carrying a bouquet of the same flowers and she was radiant.

Bride and groom boarded the buggy while the parents and older members of the family climbed in the wagon. The rest simply had to walk behind the carriages, which wasn't a problem since the village hall was only a mile away. Everybody in the village knew about the wedding and while the procession wound its way, many villagers joined. When they arrived at the village hall it looked as if it was a national holiday.

The wedding room was soon filled to capacity, with people spilling into the corridor. Inside, the mayor, in full ceremonial dress, was flanked by his entourage, and performed the civil part of the wedding. After signing the marriage license and receiving congratulations, the party went to the community hall where the religious part of the wedding would take place. At the entrance to the building stood a line-up of six ministers.

"Holy cow," exclaimed Ian when he saw the accumulation of clergymen.

"Not so loud," whispered his bride. "I think that is the surprise your minister spoke about." Two of the six were emeritae, one was from the village, two from Jenny's home town, and there was one who had to flee the west because his preaching was highly disliked by the occupying forces. The service was a highly spirited one and the hastily rounded up choir was jubilant. The newlyweds left the hall, followed by all the guests, and were seated at long tables outside the Halls' house for dinner.

Even Ian had not been able to barter booze, but nobody minded since a dinner with all the trimmings commanded everybody's attention. The guests offered presents, mostly heirloom pieces and items that had taken an extensive search since gift shops did not offer much yet.

"It's a pity that we could not get a photographer for this day," Jenny said, and Ian agreed. Rolls of film were nowhere for sale, and Ian had gone to the photographer in town, who wanted two pounds of butter in addition to money to come out to the wedding for photos. Ian told him he could only afford a pound of butter and there was no deal. Luckily a friend of Jenny's brother, who was an amateur photographer, had one roll left that he had saved. He was promptly invited for dinner and took shots. They all hoped it would work out.

After dinner the party continued. Somebody performed short sketches in the local folklore and there was one musician with an accordion.

The guests began to wonder when the couple was going to leave when some Canadians arrived in a weapon carrier, participated in the fun, and then announced that transportation for the bride and groom was waiting. They said the two should not walk to their mansion but arrive in the style of the times. A loud hurrah and applause accompanied this revelation and the newlyweds said good-byes. They climbed into the carrier with their possessions and went on their six-mile honeymoon trip. Housing was under government control and Jenny and Ian were happy that they could be staying for the summer months in a small cabin in the forest, instead of being packed in a few rooms in somebody's house.

The soldiers carried the luggage inside, stepped back to the entrance, stood at attention, and saluted when Ian carried his bride over the threshold. After many laughs and best wishes, including advice in French which Ian did not bother to translate for Jenny, their couriers d'amour left the pair, finally alone by themselves, in a silent pine forest. Their luck had no boundaries.

They spent the summer months in the cabin, doing what they wanted to do. Occasionally they walked to a nearby hamlet with one store, which carried the basic items for sustenance available on the ration coupons. The quality of life gradually improved, with more food and textiles available, electricity restored, and public transportation beginning to function, albeit on a provisional basis.

In August 1945, the Dutch East Indies were liberated, an event welcomed in Holland with great enthusiasm since there were many ties with the colony, established for more than three hundred years. As a result of this development, the government had begun to make plans to send troops to the Indies. It also prepared for the expected influx of patriots returning to Holland after being interred under terrible conditions in Japanese camps for more than three and one-half years.

Reading all these developments in the scanty newspapers, Jenny and Ian understood that their Shangri-La could not continue forever. Ian, especially, was beginning to feel restless. Since he had been in military service for only six months, he could expect to be drafted for overseas service, and this time maybe in the navy, his original destination. If that happened it would be advantageous for him if he could obtain his certificate for the theoretical part of the second-mate exam, for which he had to resume his study.

So one night he discussed the topic with Jenny, who looked at him with a very special expression in her eyes. Ian was not sure what to make of it. He had the impression that Jenny's behavior had been different for some time, but had put it in the back of his mind under the heading "female behavior."

"Mr. Halls, I have to tell you something," she said, and climbed onto his lap.

"Oh, yes, Mrs. Halls and what would that be?" Ian joined the pseudo-official Puritan approach between man and wife.

But he was completely taken aback when Jenny whispered in his ear, "I think we are going to have a baby!"

"A baby? You and I?" Ian stood up, holding Jenny in his arms, and whirled her around in his ecstasy, but then cautiously put her down. "I'd better be careful with you two."

They had much to talk about that night; their life and future was changing, but before continuing in that line of thought, Jenny went to see the village doctor to confirm her pregnancy—which he did.

Ian now became more determined to make the next move to continue his studies. He considered contacting his tutor in the town of Scheveningen who had helped him before. This took some doing since Mr. Wide and his wife had been evacuated from their home and now lived in The Hague. The gentleman was glad to hear from Ian and promised to have the necessary study books sent to him, so that he could start on his own.

Meanwhile the summer was nearing its end and they could not stay in the summer cabin, which was not insulated at all. So Ian applied for other accommodations and this time got a couple of rooms and shared kitchen with a family in the village proper. They left the cabin with sad feelings because this had been the beginning of so much. On the other hand, they were glad to move closer to family and the obstetrician and to have a place that could be heated. Ian received his books and from that point on their lives changed from just thinking of the two of them to getting involved in family affairs. They also paid more attention to what was happening in the world, a world beginning to pick up the pieces scattered in so many areas. Ian had begun his study with great élan and spent every hour he could spare with his nose in his books.

One day he received a notice from the Department of Defense with a request to go to town for a medical examination for the navy. Apparently the dossiers had survived the occupation and he observed that the letter was sent to his parents' address.

On the arranged day, he took the bus to town, accompanied by Jenny, who wanted to buy some baby stuff which she could not get in the village. Upon arrival in town they parted, but not before Jenny asked him if he felt nervous.

"Nervous?" Ian asked. "Me? Are you kidding!" He arranged where they should meet afterwards and then hurried to the physician's office, where he went through the program set by the navy—one that was clearly more stringent than for other branches of the armed forces.

When he was finished he was asked to give information on his present address, marital status, and related topics. Ian knew that he was back in the system after almost five years. The doctor declared him fit for duty, and told him that at the proper time he would hear from the recruiting office, but he couldn't say when that would be. Ian met Jenny at the newly opened restaurant. They were seated at a table overlooking the square and talked about their subsequent activities. Ian, who disliked shopping, was glad to hear Jenny say she had been successful in her purchases and with a smile tell him that he was relieved from that chore.

When he told her that he had passed the exam in full glory, he looked so self-important she could not pass up the opportunity to bring him back to earth.

"You big shot, better be careful because I have heard that lots of people from the farmland are always seasick on navy boats."

"The navy has no boats, but vessels," he corrected her, and thereafter they plunged into the luxury of ordering dinner. After dinner they went to the movies, something almost new to them after such a long time, and enjoyed their day in the town tremendously.

In October Ian was put on notice that he would join the navy training class in early November and after completion of the abridged course would be sent overseas. Although this was expected in one way or another, the abrupt fact came as a shock to both of them.

"How can they do that to us? Don't they know that in April we are having a baby? You must do something about it, Ian," Jenny said, putting Ian on notice that a baby was more important than naval service.

"You don't have any idea how military service works, woman," retorted Ian, and then realized a little bit late that he had been unsympathetic to her concern.

Jenny looked at him with disbelieving eyes. "You are calling me woman? Your wife, that's what I am and don't forget it!"

For the first time they quarreled and it took one full day before peace and understanding were restored. Ian found that making up wasn't so bad after all.

During the day Ian had been thinking what the next move could be and reached the conclusion that first he would go to the regional recruiting board and request a later date to join the navy; second he would register for his exam in early December.

He told Jenny his plan, and after thinking about it, she asked, "Would it be good to arrange the date for your exam first, so that you can tell the board about it? At least that gives you a better chance."

Ian agreed, and phone communications having been restored, he went to a public phone and talked with the secretary of the exam commission, who confirmed that he could take the exam in early December. The secretary had to receive the required papers within two weeks. The next move wasn't that easy and it took several calls with different people until finally he traced the right person who, after having heard his story, told Ian there might be a possibility for him to be placed on the agenda for the next hearing.

This statement sounded rather iffy and Ian did not feel completely satisfied with it. Coming home he told Jenny that he was going to the city of Arnhem where the regional board resided. He would plead his case in person. Dressed in his merchant marine uniform (for extra effect, Jenny said) he went to Arnhem by bus.

During the one-hour trip he repeated again and again what he was going to say to ensure a date would be set for his hearing. It took several hours before the board member, with whom he had spoken before, could see him. This was the opportunity to pull out all the stops and Ian gave one of his best performances.

The gentleman listened to the story, smiled, and then asked him, "Do you have a photo of your wife with you?" Ian was flabbergasted at this out-of-the-blue question.

"You mean you would like to see a photo of my wife?"

"Yes, you don't mind?"

"Well, I have only our bridal shot taken by an amateur since there was no professional photographer available."

The board member looked at the picture, nodded, and with a straight face said, "Your case will be heard on November 2." Ian thanked him with a sigh of relief, not entirely sure whether this was due to his oration or that it had been set after his phone calls and not yet confirmed. Whatever the case may be, he got a chance.

Jenny asked whether such hearings were open to the public. Ian wasn't sure, but told her that anyway they would go to Arnhem together.

So they did and found that no public was allowed in the chambers; Jenny was allowed to sit in the waiting room. Ian's name was called, he entered the room, and was seated opposite three high-ranking officers, one of them in navy uniform. His previous stint in the service, short as it had been, passed the review and thereafter Ian had the opportunity to tell them about his activities during the occupation. There were some more questions and then Ian was excused and told he would be recalled later that day.

"And?" asked Jenny, when he returned to her, and in that single word was a world of meaning.

"I don't know yet. I will be called in this afternoon to hear the decision. Let's go into town and have lunch." Under tension, they could not eat much and later Jenny could not remember what they had. They returned early to the building and time seemed at a standstill. Finally Ian was called in.

The chairman of the board took the lead: "Mr. Ian Halls, the board has considered your request. The urgency for the nation to draft military personnel, especially to serve in our colonies, is great. Consequently we can only grant any excuse in cases of serious illness or severe hardship. Your situation does not reveal either of the two. On the contrary, your wife's pregnancy is a normal and healthy condition for which we congratulate you." Here he paused for a moment. Ian felt very down, being sure his request would be denied. The chairman scanned some papers, looked up again, and continued. "However, taking into consideration your very commendable actions during the occupation, you will be called for duty on January 4, 1946. We wish you success with your forthcoming exam."

Jenny had been waiting outside the hearing room and without words looked at her husband, her heart beating wildly in expectation.

"I got two months," he blurted, and sat down. Jenny digested the news quickly and bravely looked at the plus side.

"That will give you time to prepare for the exam, and we will have the holidays together!" Ian kissed her, once more wondering how he had found such a wife.

Chapter Twelve

There were three dates which popped up again and again during their conversation on the way home: December exam, January draft, and April baby.

"You know what I have been thinking? I have just one month left before the exam and need to be with my tutor, because I can't get much farther on my own. What about calling Wim and Cora and asking them if you and I can stay with them until that time, and in the meantime, I can easily commute to Mr. Wide's?"

Jenny, who was counting every day they had left together, reacted positively to the suggestion. Again Ian went to the public phone in the village post office and called Wim at his office. Wim thought it was a good idea and said he would discuss it with Cora, but he felt sure it would be workable. They had a spare bedroom and Jenny and Ian would be welcome any day.

Two days later they had packed for their stay with Cora and Wim near The Hague, but left their other possessions in their rooms to keep the accommodations in their name. Such an arrangement was prudent, for as soon as even one room was vacated it was assigned to another party since there was no relief in sight to the housing shortage.

They arrived on a Saturday afternoon and installed themselves to everybody's satisfaction. The two women talked about sharing domestic chores while the two men exchanged thoughts about the Dutch East Indies.

"It is remarkable how your life destination, which you have planned yourself, can be changed by circumstances," Wim said philosophically. Ian understood what he meant—Wim had graduated from the Colonial Agricultural Academy, an institution preparing students to become planters in the Far East. His present government job was a far cry from his basic education.

"It looks like I will be there before you," admitted Ian, "I think it is for the good. After Japan's surrender a strong movement for independence has started and the Allied East Asia command has its hands full re-establishing order. Working on a plantation is not exactly a healthy occupation as yet."

Wim smiled, having the feeling Ian might be right. Together they made plans for Sunday. Ian had said it was going to be his only day off until his exam, so it better be a good one. With that in mind the mutually-agreed-upon decision was made to go to Scheveningen, which had special memories for Jenny and Ian. Taking the streetcar they noticed the thinned-out forest between The Hague and Scheveningen, several bombed houses, and burned-out buildings—all signs of the devastating war.

Jenny and Ian hardly recognized the center of town. Rows of houses had been torn down, fortifications had been built all over, and the once-glorious beach resorts looked drab. The November weather did not add to the scenery and soon they all agreed to return home.

"In the spring it will all be better here and then you can come again," Cora said, with the best of intentions.

Jenny looked at her. "But then Ian won't be with us," she said, biting her tongue.

"Oh, Jenny, I am so sorry. I forgot. But anyhow, you are always welcome," Cora said, and hugged her.

Ian studied without interruption. His tutor was satisfied that he had a good chance to pass the exam. He was right. Ian obtained the certificate for the theoretical part of second mate Merchant Marine without a hitch—not that it had been a piece of cake for him. There had been a lot of tension, but he made it and that was what counted.

Before returning home, Ian had an opportunity to meet with a recruiting officer of the Department of the Navy in The Hague whom he informed about his newly earned diploma. The navy man told him that a theoretical portion of a certification was not counted by the navy.

Then, after some consideration, he asked Ian, "Why don't you apply for the coast guard in the Far East? Service with them is considered military service as well." Ian was somewhat surprised about the change of subject and asked why it was mentioned. It appeared that the coast guard would accept his diploma, which meant that he could be assigned the rank of second officer instead of third officer with the navy.

"Moreover, and this may be important to you, when you join the coast guard your family can follow you as soon as things are settled there. You must, however, sign a contract for three years. When drafted in the navy, your family cannot follow. You must then gamble on how long the draft would be." The navy man handed Ian some papers dealing with coast guard service and advised him to study the contents and contact their office if he was interested.

His head was spinning when he left the office and he went into a bar to quench his thirst, but more importantly, to consider the alternatives of what he had learned. He decided to leave the subject at rest and discuss it with Jenny when they were home.

From then on things moved quickly, too quickly for their taste, but there was no way to stop it. They both felt like they were on a roller coaster, with things happening over which they had little or no control. There was one most important item they had to decide—whether Ian would join the coast guard or navy. This had to be done without delay, as the January 4 induction date was nearing.

"I have been talking with several people and no one has any idea how long the draft for service in the East may last. What some old hands, retired from the Indies, were telling me was that the developments there are beginning to resemble a guerrilla war. And if that is so, it will be a long time before it can be settled," Ian said to Jenny.

"I hear the awful word of war coming up again and again. We just went through a big one, touching millions and millions of people—and for what? Can there never be peace?"

Her last question was as old as mankind and Ian had no answer, but he knew that further stalling would take the opportunity for choice out of his hands. "All right, Jenny, I will contact the coast guard office and tell them that I want to join on a three-year contract," he decided, looking at her.

She thought for a moment, then said in a firm tone, "I love you and agree with your decision and I hope that we two can join you soon."

"That's settled. I will call right away and…," he abruptly stopped. "What did you say, we two?"

"Of course, you really don't think that I can travel before the baby is born, do you?" Jenny teased.

"Well, no, of course not," Ian tried to get out of that one, and for his own defense, added, "I don't think of our baby every day, mainly because you hardly show!" To this statement, Jenny could not suppress her laughter any longer.

"Either you need glasses or you are looking at the wrong spot. And you better go right now before I change my mind."

He didn't need more urging. He phoned the office in The Hague and made an appointment to apply in person. It was confirmed that when accepted in the coast guard it would be considered military service and the draft would not apply. The date of his assignment was to be the same as for the navy, to avoid eventual duplication. Ian wasn't sure but thought he detected a wry sense of humor when hearing the last sentence. This time he went to The Hague without Jenny, who had visited her sister and family when they stayed with Cora and Wim and now declared that traveling was no fun for her.

At the coast guard office Ian was directed to a recruiting officer who introduced himself as administrator Willems.

"Please sit down, Mr. Halls. We have talked on the phone and I understand that you are interested in joining the coast guard in the Dutch East Indies, right?" When Ian confirmed that he was, Mr. Willems told him that the procedure to sign him on would take two days and asked him whether he had accommodations for one night. Ian thought of Jenny's sister and her family and told him that it could be arranged.

During those two days, documents and other papers were scrutinized, others had to be signed, and final arrangements had to be settled. On the early afternoon of the second day, Mr. Willems, whom Ian had seen off and on when going through the paper work with clerks, called him into his office.

"Congratulations, Mr. Halls. You have been accepted in the coast guard as second officer." Then he sat down, leaned back in his chair, and went through details on coast guard duties in the Far East. Finalizing the introduction he told Ian to be in The Hague office January 4, 1946, at 0800 hours. He then handed Ian his itinerary, which read:

1/4/46
0800 hrs. Issuance of military uniform, insignia
         1st Lieutenant Army
1100 hrs. Transport to the Ridderzaal (Knights'
         Room)
1130 hrs. Swearing in as officer
1230 hrs. Return to Coast Guard office

1300 hrs. Lunch

1400 hrs. Dismissed. Free afternoon

1/5/45

0700 hrs. Report at Binnenhof, center of city

0730 hrs. Transport to Schiphol Airport

0900 hrs. Report at KLM desk, flight to Batavia.
        Check-in luggage

1030 hrs. Depart

Ian looked at the list, and after digesting the meaning, had some questions, the most important being: Why wasn't he sent as second officer coast guard? Mr. Willems smiled. "We do not have coast guard uniforms here yet. Of course, they are tropical uniforms and we don't want you to parade in short sleeves and shorts in the winter here. Moreover, the Allied Command allows air transportation for army personnel only, since there is a shortage of civil planes all over the world. You are going to be an army officer only for the voyage, and on arrival in Batavia, you will be issued naval dress." Another question came up.

"Is family allowed at the swearing in and at departure on Schiphol Airport?"

"Sorry, no family at the swearing in. It is a formality and you will find that there are civilians on board who are urgently needed in the colony who are militarized for the trip only."

All said and done, Ian took his leave from Mr. Willems. Arriving at home he had much to tell Jenny and their parents. Peter Halls, a veteran of World War I, was proud of his son and said that he would not miss being at the swearing-in ceremony.

"It is quite an occasion, with a military band playing, a grand parade, and speeches."

"Sorry, Dad. This time it is just a formality," Ian said. "No family allowed."

Peter didn't like it a bit. "Nowadays, they take the romance and glory out of everything." Jenny's father joined him and the two men started to tell each other stories of the "good old days." Nobody listened; the patched-up stories were getting stale. Ian's study over for the time being, Ian and Jenny had time for themselves again. They visited two couples living in the village who had spent many years in the tropics. Both families had returned to Holland just before 1940. They gave the young couple much information.

After one of these visits, while walking home, Jenny said, "Would the East Indies really be as wonderful as they say?"

"After years, memories become distorted. One forgets the less pleasant episodes and remembers the good times," Ian said.

"Oh boy, you are becoming a barrel of fun!"

She is right, Ian thought. How on earth can I talk about sweet memories? In an effort to save his posture he laughed, "I have read it somewhere, I think. One day when you are grey and I am bald, we'll know for sure."

The holiday season, cheerful as it was, brought with it a bittersweet feeling for Jenny and Ian. The day of their separation grew near and not knowing for how long made it worse. She would not have the support of her husband during the last months of her pregnancy and the birth. The fact that her own mother had also moved to the village made a difference to her, but still it was not the same.

The day for packing had arrived; Ian, Jenny, and her parents would all stay with family in The Hague. On the fourth of January, Ian was occupied with his duties until the afternoon. The next morning Jenny and parents took a bus to the Amsterdam airport while Ian followed his own instructions.

They met at the terminal, which consisted of a number of barracks-type buildings. The original buildings were all bombed and repair of the landing strips had naturally received first priority. What do people who love each other say and do during such last moments, Ian wondered. All that could be said was said, and when the call for boarding came through, it was a relief for everyone. Last hugs and kisses were given, tears shed, and Ian boarded the Constellation, turned around before entering, and waved. He took the impression of his wife standing there with him for months to come.

Chapter Thirteen

Ian boarded a plane for the first time in his life and was very much impressed as he was seated at the window in a club chair. The first thing he did was look at the throng of people at the barricade. He found Jenny and her family and waved. Everybody on board was waving, those on the other side of the plane leaned over and craned their necks to peer through the small windows.

Ian introduced himself to the man seated next to him. His seat mate was "Ron Vander, a CPA with a tin-mining company on the island of Billiton." Ian informed him that he was joining the coast guard as second officer. Ron smiled. "So you are a real military man, not an amateur like me. I hardly know how to salute!"

The prop engines were started, and for the last time, both looked at the well-wishers. "Look," Ron said. "There is my wife and son," pointing out to Ian where they stood. In turn, Ian explained to him where Jenny was, and Ron saw her. "She is expecting," Ron stated as a matter of fact. Ian was focusing his attention on Jenny and absorbed Ron's remark as if from a distance. Without giving it a second thought he mumbled,

"Only a little." Ron raised his eyebrows. "Explain to me how someone can only be a little pregnant?" "Huh . . . what are you talking about? Oh, sorry. I meant it only shows a little."

The engines were revved up and the plane began to move. Soon the people on the ground became smaller and then vanished when the plane turned. Ian had to swallow hard to control his emotions. They taxied for a while toward the starting point, where the machine came to a stop. Stewardesses and a steward walked through the aisle, inspecting whether all seat belts were fastened.

Now the engines were on full power, causing the plane to shake. Ian was sitting rigid, his hands on the armrests, his knuckles white under pressure. Quickly he looked at his neighbor and saw that he, too, was tense. Then they moved faster and faster and it felt to the first-time fliers like an eternity until they lifted off from the ground. They all cheered and soon became engrossed in the landscape beneath them, seeing their country from the air for the first time.

After a while they were cruising at ten thousand feet, the maximum altitude allowed during that postwar period. Seat belts were unfastened and the first daring passengers began walking around. In the late afternoon they passed west of the Alps; the sun was shining on the snow-covered mountains. It was almost an eerie sight, as if the distant mountains were on fire, which was the effect caused by the low sun rays. Everybody was silent, deeply impressed by what they saw.

The captain's voice came through on the intercom. "Welcome aboard. Our trip to Batavia will take seven days, due to the fact that we are allowed to fly only during daylight hours. A stewardess will hand you pen and paper on which you can write where you want to stay overnight: Cairo or Baghdad." He switched off, leaving all passengers in bewildered silence. Seven days? Choice of overnight stops?

"I'll be damned," said Ron. "Sounds like pre-war flights to Batavia, going from radio beacon to beacon. You got a thermos of coffee and sandwiches and off you went."

Ian nodded. He also had read and heard many stories of those early flights. The majority opted for Baghdad and that was where they landed. Imaginations were working overtime—until reality took over. The airport was far out of town. Without local currency and having been reminded of pickpockets and thieves, they all went to the airport "hotel." Its accommodations consisted of quonset huts and a larger barracks, which served as a restaurant. That was it. Plenty of flies (and other airborne objects) made the use of a mosquito net a must while sleeping.

The adventure continued with nightly stopovers in places like Karachi, Calcutta, Ceylon, Bangkok, and Singapore. Some of these cities had not seen direct war action and made visits in the afternoon and evening very worthwhile. By now Ian and Ron felt like veteran fliers, but as greenhorns, were still very impressed with the new surroundings. Ian had many moments thinking of Jenny—what she would be doing, how she would feel. The growing geographical distance between them, and the difference in time zones, made it difficult to maintain a feeling of direct contact with her. This was something that bothered him, but he couldn't do anything about it. Every time he had a chance to give mail to a returning flight-crew member, he kept her informed about his journey in brief notes.

In Ceylon, there was a request for six men to act as volunteer "slip passengers." What that meant was that a number of life rafts had to be taken on board for the next leg over the Indian Ocean. The additional weight necessitated leaving a number of passengers on the island since each plane was filled to capacity. When sufficient "slippers" were accumulated, an extra trip was scheduled.

At first there were no takers, everybody feeling too important about their future tasks to delay their arrival. However, word went around that close to Colombo was a huge navy hospital with plenty of nurses who relax on sandy beaches during their free time. The picture changed immediately, with volunteers galore.

"Let's leave it to the younger ones," Ron said to Ian, adding, "I have strict instructions from my company to arrive as soon as possible."

Ian had no such instructions but was eager to be in Batavia and begin his career. "I'll see sandy beaches aplenty, and I have my own nurse. No slipping."

From Singapore it was a short hop over the Java Sea to Batavia. Nearing the capital of the Dutch East Indies, Ian thought of what a poet once wrote: "An archipelago, like a string of gems wrapped around the equator." Poets get away with anything, he thought, while looking out of the window. In the far distance, on the island of Java, he saw the mountains and when he looked down he noticed the harbor Tandjoeng Priok. Immediately thereafter the Constellation skimmed over clusters of huts and palm trees and they landed.

"Did you see the city of Batavia?" he asked Ron.

"No, but it must be somewhere," replied Ron laconically.

From literature, Ian had the impression of a city on the coast of the Java Sea, surrounded by lush tropical forests. Now that they had landed, he was still looking for that city. Stairs were rolled to the plane, doors opened, and a gush of tropical heat came into the air-conditioned plane. The passengers, in their nice woolen winter wear, staggered over the platform to the terminal building. Inside it was only a few degrees cooler. Ian, like the others, started perspiring profusely. He took off his jacket and rolled up the sleeves of his shirt. It felt better, and now he was really ready to enter his new life. Representatives of companies, the army, navy, and coast guard were calling out names and soon several groups were formed. Ian found that there were four other passengers for the coast guard. They clustered together and the rep took their luggage stubs and pointed to a truck with wooden benches. He would arrange for their luggage and told them that their accommodation would be in the marine mess "Nautica" in Batavia.

The canvas sideflaps of the truck were rolled up and Ian got a good view when they were traveling to the city. At first there was nothing much spectacular to see, until they arrived in the center of town. It was bustling with traffic of an assortment of vehicles, peddlers carrying their wares on bamboo yokes, and pedestrians. The noise was something else—claxons blaring, bells ringing, peddlers calling their merchandise, women chattering; all this in fortissimo fashion. The scenery changed considerably when the truck left the chaos behind on its way to the outskirts of the city.

They came to boulevards fringed with palms and roomy houses, offices, and government buildings. The truck came to a halt at one of the latter; Ian had arrived.

The group was welcomed by a middle-aged lady, acting as mess chief. The single-story building was in good condition with roomy quarters, large open windows, and cool tile floors. A large living room, dining room, and covered terrace completed the pleasant surprise. Mrs. Hulscher, the hostess, told the newcomers that dinner would be at six o'clock, giving them an hour to unpack and wash up.

Ian shared a room with a colleague named Jan Kramer whom he had met during the trip over. Ian learned that Jan had been in the merchant marine before the war, was on leave when it broke out, and after liberation had joined the coast guard for the same reasons as Ian. They went to the dining room and were introduced to several other coast guard officers who had served before the Japanese invasion and were again on active duty.

A senior officer seated next to Ian looked at him. "How come you are in an army uniform?" he wondered. Ian told him the story, adding that he would very much like to get rid of the clothes and get a tropical outfit. "Well, I think that tomorrow you report at headquarters and then you'll learn what plans are in store for you."

After dinner most went to the terrace. Ian excused himself and went to his room. The bed was made and the mosquito net lowered. He looked at the contraption, undressed, and climbed under it. He was glad to be alone; his thoughts went to Jenny, who was now more than ten thousand miles away. This was going to be his life in this country for three years and he had no impression of what it looked like, but that would remedy itself soon. He tossed around, not used to sleeping without blankets and with the sounds of a tropical night. Suddenly, he awoke to the sound of gunfire, jumped out of his bed, and called to Jan.

"Did you hear that?"

"Yeah, I heard. Don't worry. When I talked with the old hands on the terrace after you left they told me that you hear it every night. Peace isn't here yet." Ian had not thought of such being a possibility in the nation's capital and wondered what it would be like outside the city.

During breakfast the next morning, nobody mentioned the gunfire, which gave Ian reason to believe that it was a regular occurrence.

A truck pulled up at the mess and the driver announced, "Headquarters." Officers, including the new arrivals, boarded for the short trip. The headquarters consisted of widely spread single-story buildings, interconnected by breezeways. Ian was ushered into the office of First Officer Werff, who welcomed him with a smile. Ian presented his papers and while Werff studied them Ian had an opportunity to observe his superior. Despite the humidity, the man was dressed immaculately in white tropical uniform and Ian envied him.

"I must say that your arrival comes as a surprise to us, and right now we are working out solutions where to place you," Werff said matter of factly.

Ian looked at him questioningly, seeing in a flash the sandy beaches and nurses of Ceylon, which he had given up. He was uncomfortable at the word "surprise." Anyway he was here and there was no way to back off, so in the meantime there were other matters which required attention.

"Sir, I am sorry to learn that I arrived here without prior notice to you, but until that is clarified there are some subjects I would like to discuss with you." He hoped he was not going too far with this statement and felt relieved when Officer Werff only asked what he wanted to discuss.

Ian told him that as a first priority he wanted to get rid of his winter army uniform, then talk about financial arrangements since he did not have the national currency (rupiahs). He also questioned whether the mess in Batavia would be his address for the time being, so he could inform his wife back home. As to the uniforms, he was told that it could take up to a week before that could be fixed. Officer Werff reminded him that the war had ended only eight months before and that textiles had not been of primary concern. There was some tension between the two and Ian found it wiser not to mention Mr. Willems' statement back in Holland.

He did not react to the information and changed the subject, which to both men's satisfaction was concluded more congenially. He was told he would be called as soon as there would be something to report, then he saluted and marched out. First thing to do was go back to the mess and write to Jenny. He went to the transportation officer and learned that it would take several hours before transport to the mess became available. It was suggested that he take a bedja.

"A what?"

"A bedja is a tricycle where you sit in front and the guy behind pedals you to your destination. Do you speak Malay?" the transport man asked.

Ian admitted having no knowledge of that language, whereupon a clerk accompanied him to the front of the headquarters. He called a bedja man, said something to him and nodded to Ian, telling him that he could step in and that the man knew Nautica. Ian enjoyed the ride, the bedja man knew his business and skillfully maneuvered through the traffic using his bell with gusto. Upon arrival at the mess, the man said something to Ian, who understood that it had to do with money. He told him to wait and went inside to look for Mrs. Hulscher and explained his predicament. She called the major-domo, who started haggling with the bedja man while Ian stood and waited. Finally, negotiations were concluded and the major-domo told Ian the fare. Everybody agreed and the affair was closed. That night he wrote a long letter to Jenny, cautiously avoiding any negative impressions he had encountered during his first day in the Indies.

Chapter Fourteen

One week went by. Ian had told Jan Kramer his experience at his first meeting at headquarters and was not surprised to hear that Jan's findings were similar. They had joined forces and paid daily visits to the head office with the purpose of becoming a pain in the butt. Their theory was that either it would get speedier results, primarily on the subject of uniforms, or that due to their actions they would lose any form of cooperation. To use his other time as productively as possible, Ian had started to study Malay and practiced it with the major-domo, who called him toean Halls (Mr. Halls).

The total population of the Dutch East Indies was more than a hundred million and consisted of many different races and languages. The Malaysian language was mostly spoken along the coasts of the thousands of islands as a kind of linguistic umbrella. For mariners it was the logical choice for communication with the local people they would come in contact with. Ian's first exercises in speaking Malay came to a sudden halt when Mrs. Hulscher overheard him talking with her major-domo. She called Ian.

"What are you doing?"

Ian told her and she tried to keep a straight face.

"My dear fellow, you should have come to me. Jatim, the major-domo, was once cook on one of the coast guard vessels. He is an excellent man for the work he does now, but being from Java, his Malay is not what you'd like to learn."

Ian was embarrassed by her remark. He had heard already that the quickest way to learn was under the mosquito net, and the looks on the faces of the informants made it clear that you were not alone under that net.

Mrs. Hulscher had been married to a planter who was killed during the Japanese invasion. Together with other women and children, she had been sent to Australia in time and had returned to Java after the war. Ian didn't suppose for a single moment that she would talk about the "quickest way" but nevertheless felt queasy.

"I will call headquarters and tell them that I have a number of new officers who urgently need to learn Malay. You will hear from me, but continue for show with Jatim. If you don't, he will be upset and feel that he has lost face—and then you are in trouble." Apparently Mrs. Hulscher had a willing ear or other influence at headquarters. Two days later a clerk came every morning to the mess and taught Malay to all newcomers. Someone with a sense of humor suggested that this move was to keep the new arrivals away from the office until it had been decided where to put them. This was quite possible since many of their ships were under repair and others, used by the Japanese Navy, had to be traced throughout the archipelago.

Some progress, however, had been made: they got their uniforms and side arms, the latter not at all a luxury under the circumstances. Ian, like the others, was glad to finally get rid of his winter uniform and to appear outwardly as a real marine officer. He looked in a mirror and talked to himself.

"Hey, man, you look pretty dandy today. Jenny, I wish you could see your husband in full glory."

At that moment Jan Kramer entered their room, looked at Ian, and remarked, "Talking to yourself, eh? I have news for you. We both are being sent to Singapore to trace one of the coast guard ships the Japs left there after the surrender."

Apparently the "office" had found a good reason to send the two of them on a search. Both received instructions to whom to report at the Royal British Navy port in Singapore. They would be looking for a minesweeper and were given more details. Jan, as engineer, was to evaluate the mechanical part and Ian, as nautical officer, the general condition and inventory of the craft. First Officer Werff, to whom they had to report, handed them the travel documents and photos of the vessel taken before the war. Ian, as deck officer, would be in charge, and Werff informed him that a telegram had been sent to the port commander in Singapore as notice of their arrival.

The next morning the two went to the airport and boarded the plane for Singapore. This time, there was no luxury Constellation, but a Dakota DC-3, the World War II workhorse, with steel-plated floor, metal benches lengthwise on both sides of the plane, and no smiling stewardesses in sight. The flight over the Java Sea was uneventful and on arrival they took a cab to the naval port. Ian presented their credentials to the commander and informed him of their mission. The port commander seemed somewhat at a loss, and told an orderly to call the port engineer. When the latter arrived, he was informed why the two Dutch officers had come. Ian observed the two men sharply and detected that the port engineer, after listening to the reason for the visit, raised his eyebrows at his superior.

The port commander coughed as if to camouflage his embarrassment.

"Gentlemen, it is getting late in the afternoon. We will arrange for your accommodation on the base and tomorrow morning our engineer will meet with you." He again called the orderly and told him to bring the two guests to one of the barracks.

On their arrival, Ian said to Jan, "I don't know but there is something amiss. Did you notice the engineer's reaction?"

"I got the impression that they didn't know what we were talking about, and to find out they shipped us off this early," Jan agreed.

"Well, let's go find the officers' club, I am thirsty." They left their quarters in search of the club. There were rows and rows of barracks and the streets between were busy with traffic. Singapore was a huge naval base and it took them some time to find the club.

Ian suggested staying there and having dinner also, thinking downtown Singapore would be like Batavia— something to steer away from. They chatted with other officers, not mentioning why they were there, and nobody asked. Time went fast, especially when listening to an endless number of jokes, a typical form of good British humor. After many cheerios, they managed to find their barracks, took a shower, and climbed under their mosquito nets. Ian had a dream of men of war attacking each other with heavy cannon fire. Small minesweepers maneuvered between the giants, trying to avoid cascading shrapnel and waterspouts. He was on one of the sweepers and shouted a command to ram a battleship, which was like a mouse attacking an elephant. Upon impact, Ian awoke laying on the floor. He sat up, remembering his ridiculous dream, and crept back in bed. Wisely, he didn't discuss his dream with Jan.

The next morning after breakfast, a second lieutenant came to their table, introduced himself as George O'Brian, and told them he was to bring them to the dock where their ship was.

Apparently they found her, thought Ian, and they followed George to his jeep. After passing along several quays where all types of navy ships were moored, George stopped, turned to Ian and said, "Here we are." Ian and Jan looked around, but could not see anything but water. "Where is she?" Ian asked. "Oh, didn't anybody tell you? She was sunk by the Japs when they surrendered. Our divers found several of them. That's why we can't bring any other vessels alongside here."

Ian felt anger coming upon him. Here they were, looking like fools while staring at murky water and nothing else. My god, what stupidity, he thought, and tried to regain control of himself. "Okay, George, there must have been some misunderstanding in communication. Shall we return to the port commander?" At no price would he even hint to somebody of another navy that one of his own would be so stupid. George understood, smiled, and told them that presumably they would like to send a telegram with their findings to their command. "You are right, George. You know how it is sometimes." Jan looked at Ian and said in Dutch, "You are learning fast and getting the same stiff upper lip as the English." Ian didn't know whether to consider his remark as a compliment and let it go at that.

George brought them to an administrative building where Ian could send a cable to Officer Werff. He first considered including some sarcasm but then thought better of it. His message read, "Located position of vessel submerged in thirty feet of water, dock 3B. Stop. Await your instructions. Stop." The message could be sent that afternoon, while a reply would take at least another day. Communications were still on a postwar basis, far from normal, and this was the best that could be done.

That evening they did not go to the officers club; there was little reason to be looked at as dumb cheese heads. Instead they went to town and were surprised to find that it looked more like a European city. Asking a policeman for a good restaurant they were directed to Albert Street. This street consisted only of small Chinese establishments. You came in through the kitchen where you could order from the great variety of meats, fish, chicken, and dozens of other ingredients hanging on hooks or placed on butcher tables. Neither had experience with Eastern dishes and they confused everybody until the Chinese chief cook promised in pidgin English to prepare an excellent dinner and pointed to stairs in the back of the kitchen.

They climbed the stairs and found the restaurant proper. The area was simple and clean—about twelve tables set for dinner. Three tables were occupied and they chose a table looking out over the bustling street. The first courses arrived and the two started with gusto. Neither Ian nor Jan knew what they were served, but they liked it all the same. They took their time when one dish after another appeared. Then a Chinese waitress came with hot scented towels, told them to lean back on the chair, and draped the towels over their faces. At first Ian thought he would suffocate but after a while he felt great and cool. He pulled the towel up at one end and looked at the other guests in the dining room, who were also leaning back in their chairs with towels over their faces. The scene was so comical that Ian could barely hold his laughter. We are playing hide and seek here, he thought. This is probably the dessert and when I look up I'll find the bill on the table. How wrong he was—they were only halfway through the meal.

The next day there was a cable for Ian. "Knew about the location but the wording 'submerged' was not relayed to us. Stop. Return first opportunity. Stop. Werff." That explained it, Ian concluded, and for good measure, showed it to George, who whistled after reading it. "Jolly funny what a missing word can cause" was his observation. Ian was sure that the message would reach the higher echelons in the port hierarchy so that the Dutch would not be made the laughing stock.

Upon their return they reported to Werff who did not touch on their mission but told them that to his pleasure he could give them marching orders. Jan was assigned to a coast guard vessel stationed on the south coast of Borneo as chief engineer. Ian was to act as second in command on a patrol vessel operating in the Bay of Batavia. He was to stay in Nautica since he would be back in port every afternoon. Both felt that this was the beginning of their career in the Far East. Mr. Werff had told Ian that the commanding officer of the craft he was assigned to also stayed in Nautica. His name was Luc Ash and he would give Ian further information. He did not recall having met him before and asked Mrs. Hulscher about him. The motherly lady smiled at him, "If you want to see him, you'll have to stay up late. Mr. Ash usually is very busy and comes home late." So Ian had started his vigil into the wee hours when an officer climbed out of a bedja, paid the man, and came up the path to the mess. Ian stood up and asked, "Mr. Luc Ash?" The officer looked at him, noticed they were of the same rank and replied, "Yes, that's me. What's up?" Ian told him the reason why he was waiting for him and was surprised about Ash's reaction to the news. "Oh brother. I am bored stiff with the daily milk run, and now we both will be bored. Welcome aboard."

Because of the late hour, Luc suggested leaving further talk to the next morning, adding that after breakfast they would take the daily truck to port and take it from there.

The trip to the naval dock took half an hour and Ian followed Luc on board. He was introduced to the two engineers and found that the rest of the crew, both on deck and in the engine room, were natives. The petty officers spoke Dutch in addition to Malay, and Ian, with his limited command of the latter, found that his start wasn't too cumbersome.

Luc called the boatswain and told him to give Mr. Halls a tour of the ship while he signed papers before they sailed. Ian could not define the type of vessel, but noticed that the boat deck, as well as the main deck, were open at the sides; officers quarters were on the boat deck and crew quarters were under the main deck aft. Stores were forward and the stern was open, probably to hoist buoys on board for repair or replacement. The radio hut was topside. Two lifeboats completed his impression from the quick tour. The boatswain suggested keeping the engine room for later, mentioning diplomatically that they would soon cast off and it would be better not to be in the way of the engineers. Ian got his drift and they returned to the bridge.

When they had cleared the harbor and course into the bay was set, Luc found time to tell Ian about this, the daily milkrun, as he called it. After passing a few small, uninhabited islands they sailed to another small island called Onrust. In the old sailing days the ships arriving from Holland after a one-year voyage had to anchor there in quarantine to be inspected before entering the port of Tandjoeng Priok. Now the island was used as a prison camp for suspected war criminals and POWs of various nationalities. Their stay there depended on the status of their cases.

Every day fresh food and water had to be delivered, and by return the change of guards were taken to port, in addition to bringing prisoners to court. "So you see, that is our duty, seven days a week," said Luc with a yawn. He told Ian that he had managed to escape to Australia after the Japanese invasion, but his wife had not been so lucky. She had spent three and one-half years in a camp and was evacuated to Holland gravely ill. He stretched himself, checked the helmsman, and invited Ian to have a beer. It was pleasantly warm with a sea breeze, the vessel steady, and the bay glittering in the bright sunlight. Life for him wasn't so bad, Ian thought to himself.

After a few weeks on this run, one evening in Nautica Luc came to Ian, took him aside, and told him that the next day he had some urgent business, so Ian had to command the craft that day. For Ian this came out of the blue and although he knew the routine by now, commanding a ship, small as it might be, was another matter. Luc looked at him, "Don't worry, you can do it. It's a piece of cake, nothing to it." And teasing, he added, "Or must I ask for somebody else to take over?" That last remark did the trick, exactly as Luc expected. "You son of a bitch, I'll show you," exclaimed Ian and both laughed.

The next day, when ready to cast off, there was a commotion on the dock. Two trucks pulled up and an unusual number of people, all women and children, climbed out, chattering in German. They clambered on board with lots of luggage and Ian went to the officer of the guards who accompanied the spectacle. "For heaven's sake, what is all this about? I am not on a pleasure trip." "They are families of the crew of a German U-boat which was here during part of the war. Somebody from the British Far East Command has promised them they could start a colony on an island in the tropics." "So, and what do we have to do with it?" "The promised island is Onrust," and he quickly turned around, shouting orders to hurry up, leaving Ian in a state of confusion. Onrust a tropical paradise? There must be a mistake, he hoped, and asked for their marching orders. These were handed to him; alas, it was no mistake. In dry official language it was stated that the party was to be settled on the island of Onrust for the time being, until a final decision was made what to do with them. The infantry officer saluted him, gathered his troop, and before leaving gave some advice.

"Have a good trip and don't lose any of them because they are accounted for!" Shit, Ian thought, what a day to take over.

During the short voyage he kept his passengers from the bridge. When they moored at the jetty at Onrust, Ian gave orders that nobody was to leave the ship and posted two sailors at the gangway. He went ashore and told the camp commander about his passengers.

"I got the information yesterday afternoon by radio and my people have been busy since, preparing some barracks for them. Of course, away from the other scoundrels." Clearly he was as unhappy with the situation as Ian, but neither could do anything about it.

"You better have some extra guards at the jetty," advised Ian. And he was right. When his passengers realized that this was their "colony," pandemonium broke loose. Several had to be carried bodily ashore, and Ian hurried to have the cargo and water delivered and the ship take off. On the way back to port, he entered in the log book the exact wording of the marching orders. Luc seemed to be genuinely surprised when he heard about Ian's special mission that day.

"Boy, you really landed something special."

"Yeah, and you told me it was so boring!"

Each day thereafter, when they landed at Onrust they noticed that the families were making the best of the situation.

Several of the members were sunbathing, laundry with flimsy clothing was drying in the breeze on lines, and there was no tumult. The camp commander paid his usual visits on board for a cold beer.

"How are our new prisoners behaving?" Ian asked.

"Well, after the first day they are doing quite well. Now it is our own guards I have to keep an eye on." Luc winked at Ian.

"You never know where Paradise is."

Chapter Fifteen

First Officer Werff looked at the sheaf of papers on his desk and sighed. He had been looking at it for quite some time and the situation presented in the papers needed to be resolved. But for some unknown reason his mind wandered to years past, instead of focusing on the present.

He was a career coast guard officer of Indo-European descent, had received his education in Holland, and spent his life in the archipelago.

When the war broke out in 1942, he had been involved in action and was interned in a POW camp on Java. Those were horrible years, but by sheer willpower he came through, albeit emaciated and with scars on his body. Many of his colleagues either did not make it or had to be shipped quickly to Holland to recover in the cool climate. But a few weeks after his return from the camp he was already in condition to resume whatever duties were asked for.

And that did not take long. The coast guard had lost personnel and vessels. To bring it back into a form of badly needed operations required exceptional efforts. Werff was asked to take care of the personnel planning; scrounging together a fleet of vessels was the task of one of his colleagues. So the two had to work closely together. Just this morning he had received the updated listing of ships at their disposal. The list looked impressive, which was deceiving since only a little more than half were operational. He remembered the fiasco of Ian Halls' mission and smiled.

"You are in a good mood," said his colleague, entering Werff's office. He passed a cable to Werff. "Just came in from our office in Australia. The four tugboats, which were ordered by our people there before the war ended, have been inspected and are ready to sail." Werff looked at him. "You've made my day. I know that we need them badly, but now I have to man them."

"Before you do that, let's go to OPS and see where the tugs are going to be stationed. That will make a difference for us." What he meant was that if the tugs were not specified as seagoing, but as harbor tugs to assist mooring ships in larger ports, there was less crew needed and mechanical requirements were less stringent than when operating at sea.

The OPS officer had it all planned: three for harbor duty and one for sea duty. Werff returned to his office, his good mood gone up in smoke. Despite knowing better, he had hoped that the four craft would be delayed, thereby easing his personnel problem. He shuffled through the stack of personnel lists, starting to manipulate names and ranks for the three harbor craft. For these he could use mostly local men, but the commanding officers were another matter.

Scanning through the medical reports of those who were sent to the motherland for health reasons, he found three who could have been recovered enough for duty in the tropics. He discussed this with the medical officer who agreed to cable them to return. When Werff told him he needed officers for the sea-duty tug, the medical officer had to turn him down. "It will result in worse conditions than the men were in before."

It sounded reasonable, and Werff realized that they were already taking risks with the other ones. Reluctantly he took a file marked "New Arrivals." To place some newly arrived engineers on the tug for sea duty would not be too bad, but to find a commanding officer was something else. Such a person should know sailing in tropical waters, performing different kinds of typical Coast Guard duties, and how to handle local crew members. He tossed names back and forth. There was a knock at the door, and Second Officer Luc Ash came in.

"Aren't you supposed to be on the Onrust run?" Werff asked him.

"Sir, I heard through the jungle drum about your predicament manning the coming tugboats," Luc said.

Werff knew that confidential information did not stay that way very long, especially in the tropics. He also knew Luc very well and wondered what reason he might have to see him without previous request.

"Sir, with permission, I would like to refer to your orders to train Second Officer Ian Halls as quickly as possible for a command post. He is ready for it."

Of course, Werff thought. How could I forget. Ian was one of the first arrivals after the war. He told Luc to sit down and both men discussed the topic.

"All right, I realize he served under your command only two months, but I will take the risk and accept your suggestion." This said and done, Werff asked Luc to send Ian to him the next morning, warning, "No jungle drum this time."

With a glitter in his eyes, he also told Luc that the following week he would send two newly arrived young third officers to Luc for their education. Luc didn't mind because he had personal reasons for remaining on the daily runs so he would be free every evening. Reasons Werff guessed but did not pursue further. Luc returned to the mess, left a note for Ian to report to Mr. Werff the next morning, and called a bedja.

Mrs. Hulscher, who wasn't born yesterday, halted him and asked innocently, "Not bad news about his family?"

Luc smiled at her; both "old" tropic hands understood each other perfectly. "No, nothing like that," and he climbed in the bedja, waving at her.

Ian found the summons, did not see Luc to ask why, and wondered what the reason could be. Nothing wrong with Jenny, he hoped. Their exchange of letters did not give him a clue; Jenny was doing fine, the doctor was satisfied, and their baby was due in mid-April. She missed him very much and wrote that she had two big jobs to do: first to have the baby and second to be with him as soon as possible thereafter. Nevertheless, Ian had a restless night; you never know what could happen in a faraway country.

The next morning he arrived far too early at headquarters and had to wait a long time before Werff could see him. Finally, he was called in. Officer Werff had observed him through the window. He was a self-assured young man, twenty-five years old, and with good appearance, without being arrogant. He felt confident he was making the right choice.

Ian saluted and was told to sit down. Werff took a paper from his desk, looked at Ian, and read aloud: "Second Officer Ian Halls is herewith ordered to assume command of the coast guard tugboat D-013 upon arrival of said vessel at Tandjoeng Priok. Expected date of arrival and subsequent sailing orders will follow forthwith."

Werff stood up and shook hands with a highly surprised Ian. "Congratulations, Ian. I have full confidence in you. Good luck with your first command." It was all so unexpected that it took Ian a few moments to absorb the news. He got a command! And Mr. Werff had called him by his first name! With the quick reaction of youth, he regained his composure. "Thank you very much, sir. I'll do my best."

Werff told him about the other officers and his crew, and details of the tugboat and her first voyage. He was to sail to the island of Seroetoe to repair the light, and thereafter proceed to the west coast of Borneo to pick up a number of sailing craft and tow them to Tandjoeng Priok. These craft were confiscated by the navy with contraband on board. Their skippers had been sent to Batavia for due legal process as soon as the bottoms with cargo arrived there. The crews had been put ashore on the island pending transportation to their home destinations. Ian would get some extra petty officers to man the last craft in tow.

"When is the D-013 due to arrive?" Ian asked.

"The expected time of arrival is in two days. You will hear from me," answered Werff, adding, "You are relieved from the Onrust run as of now."

Ian had two busy days to prepare for the voyage, arranging for sea charts, talking with the technical department, and getting acquainted with his crew and officers. But first he wrote a long letter to Jenny to let her know about his good fortune. His second in command was a young third officer called Marten Vanheel. When talking with him, Marten told him that he was a "white cockroach." "A what?" asked Ian, not knowing what that meant. He learned it was an expression for a person from Dutch parents, but born and raised in the Indies. He felt confident that they would get along with each other very well and they discussed the task at hand. The two engineers would be available at the day of arrival of the D-013. Ian had preferred to meet them earlier but understood Werff's problem with personnel shortage.

One morning while at breakfast in Nautica, Werff called him. His vessel was due in port early that afternoon and Werff would take Marten and him to the harbor. They arrived when the tug was moored alongside the dock. An Australian crew had brought her out and after the introductions the skipper wanted to know when they could return home. Apparently, he was eager to get there. Mr. Werff promised that the takeover would be done as quickly as possible.

"We need to get her out pronto, ourselves, on an urgent mission."

The chief engineer and his second arrived out of the blue and after handshakes disappeared in the engine room. From that moment on it got more hectic. Ian was surprised how many things had to be taken care of. The four officers of the tug were sitting together, discussing their various tasks. Ian gave each a listing of their assignments and they worked late hours.

Since all four stayed in Nautica, transportation was no problem. A jeep was assigned to Ian. They enjoyed the luxury of free movement. Petty officers reported for duty, which lightened the job of training the crew, arranging stores, provisions, water, and whatever parts they could get to make the navigation light on Seroetoe operational. This navigation light was important for sea traffic between the South China Sea and the Java Sea. The engineers and their helpers had their hands full getting acquainted with all the machinery.

Finally, after a week of hard work, the D-013 was ready for a trial run into the bay. Officer Werff and technical staff members from headquarters came onboard. They were looking forward to the opportunity to leave the office for a few hours and smell the sea.

Ian and Marten were on the tiny bridge and the tug's lines were let go. The D-013 gained speed when clear of the harbor. After maneuvering at various speeds, the vessel was swung around 360 degrees to check the deviation of the compass and then headed back to port. The visitors shook hands with Ian, wishing him and his crew a safe voyage. As a last word, Mr. Werff took Ian aside.

"Your sailing orders are to leave tomorrow morning at 0800 hours. Good luck and stay out of the minefields."

At daylight, which was about 6 A.M. in the tropics, all were on board. Ian felt somewhat nervous, which was quite understandable for a first command. He was heading into, what were for him, unknown waters, and whatever else would be in store for them. His chief engineer, a quiet man somewhat older than he, slapped him on the shoulder, "All right, skipper. Ready to go."

At exactly 0800 hours they cast off with three long blasts on the horn. Ian felt his skin prickle when other coast guard ships in port answered, wishing them a good voyage. Their flag was dipped when they passed the flagship of the vice admiral. The tugboat nosed into the bay and course was set to cross the Java Sea. Ian looked back, saw the shoreline in the already bright sunlight, and then looked forward.

His heart felt light as he knocked on the wooden railing of the bridge and whispered, "Here we go, Jenny. You bring me good luck." The tugboat D-013 was on her way to adventure.

Chapter Sixteen

The tug behaved very well through the waves, was easy to handle, and displayed minimum engine vibration. On the second day of the voyage the crew had settled into an easy routine. Ian observed and evaluated the petty officers and deck hands, while the chief engineer did the same with his personnel. Both came to the conclusion that, although not prime class, their crew was of good stock.

The four officers shared one cabin aft with two bunkbeds on each side, and a table and benches in the center. The cook did his best in his galley to concoct as much variety in the menu as possible. He loved working with liberal quantities of hot spices, which made Ian's palate protest vehemently.

"You will get used to it and even like it," was Marten's comment when he saw Ian extinguishing the internal fire with beer or ice water. Their mess boy was a Papoea from New Guinea, with an entirely different ethnic background than the others.

Ian talked about him with the chief, who had worked with Papoeas before.

"You can trust them completely. Until recently they still lived in the stone age—they didn't know the wheel. Due to their innocence of many material matters, there are people who regard them as children. Don't you make that mistake, Ian; they are proud adults."

Ian regarded the mess boy with renewed interest, but decided to delay learning more about him until he could be more conversant in Malay.

They were approaching their first stopover near nightfall, but could not proceed in the dark into the small bay. The chart showed rocks and reefs in the area, and the nautical almanac mentioned to "approach the bay near the lighthouse with utmost caution and in daylight only." Ian put the telegraph on slow ahead and anchored close by. As expected, the navigation light in the lighthouse did not work. Early the next morning the anchor was hoisted and they steamed slowly into the small bay. The water was clear, which made maneuvering on sight a bit easier.

Noticing the shallowing slope of the sea bottom and listening to the man singing out the depth soundings, Ian stopped the engine, let the tug drift a while, and then gave the signal "full astern." Shortly thereafter the anchor was dropped, and when it held, the engine room was signaled "finish for the day." When the engine died the silence closed in on them. Nothing ashore moved, not a sound was heard. What happened with the lighthouse personnel during the Japanese occupation? Ian looked through his binoculars but did not see a living soul on the beach.

Marten ordered the work boat lowered and waited for Ian's order to go ashore. Suddenly, he pointed to the beach. Ian trained his glasses and saw a number of men, women, and children appearing from the dense tropical forest, waving and clapping in great excitement.

Ian, Marten, the boatswain, and three deck hands, all armed because you never knew what might happen, manned the boat. In keeping with marine tradition they waited for the second engineer to handle the inboard diesel. The work boat was eased to the beach; Ian waded the last few feet to shore. From the throng of people, now silently watching, one man stepped forward with his right hand outstretched and his left hand clasped on his right wrist in local Moslem fashion.

Ian shook hands with him, both smiled, and then there was great tumult. Ian thought of himself at that moment as a historical figure greeting the locals, but with a more laudable intent than in most similar historical events.

Now the boat crew went ashore and was surrounded by the Seroetoe group. There was great enthusiasm and a cacophony of Malay and other archipelago languages. This all went by Ian, who couldn't follow what was said.

He called Marten, "Please ask the man who came in front of the others to tell his story, and you translate." In the general anxiety it took some doing for Marten to get responses to his questions, but finally the story unfolded.

Local sailing craft had seen the Japanese invasion fleet heading into the Java Sea. Other sailors passing by the Seroetoe Bay told them that the battle of the Java Sea was lost to the Allies. Fighting against the combined Dutch, British, and American fleet had been heavy but was no match against the overwhelming Japanese fleet. Although there were no instructions for the lighthouse crew about what to do, they decided to take the lenses and other vital parts of the light apart and hide them. They themselves went into the village, living there and acting as if they had not been employed by the government.

Japanese men of war passed regularly and sometimes sent a party ashore. No efforts were made to repair the light, however. They came for fresh fruit, vegetables, and to hunt wild boar and antelope. The villagers were paid in yen for the fruit and vegetables, a currency they had no use for. There was no electricity on the island, and no means of communication to inform them that the war was over. However, they had guessed as much when they noticed the flags of the ships passing at a distance. So when they saw the tug moving into the bay, the entire population of the village came out to greet them.

The people manning the light were officially employees of the Dutch government. Ian had been given special funds to give them advance money for due back pay. They were invited into the village a small distance away from the lighthouse. It was Ian's first visit in a typical native settlement and he was amazed how clean it was. There was no comparison with the slums of Batavia. All the buildings were on stilts for air flow as well as shelter for chickens and goats. Timber and palm fronds were the main building materials and many small fires were kept going to keep mosquitoes and other insects away. The only brick structures were the lighthouse and the house to accommodate the supervisor and his family.

Ian noticed that all the villagers were in rags and in his best Malay he told them that there were bolts of khaki fabric on board. The women were excited upon hearing this. Ian began to feel like a Santa Claus and was eager to get the show on the road. Declining to share the little food the islanders had, but accepting coconuts and other fruits, he organized the activities. The work boat moved between ship and shore, bringing materials for repair of the light, kerosene for fuel, and the promised fabric.

He ordered Marten to distribute the khaki and to act as paymaster for the lighthouse personnel. Some tables from the village were set up under trees near the beach for that purpose. The two engineers inspected the light; the hidden parts were dug up and appeared to be in usable condition. All in all, it looked like that light could be made operational again.

Back on board, Ian sent a message in Morse code via the ship's radio, reporting the date of arrival and his first impression of his findings. He carefully avoided any conclusion until he was sure that his mission would succeed. The chief complimented him when he read the message, "You are learning fast. Never make a promise until you are sure to deliver. We might still be missing a vital part."

Marten ran into problems when he began to distribute the fabric. He was surrounded by a throng of women, each of whom claimed to have twelve, or close to twelve, children. He called Ian to help him out of his dilemma. After listening to the problem, Ian told him to delay issuing the khaki until the next day. He invited the head (kepala) of the lighthouse crew on board.

He addressed the kepala with Marten's help when necessary and asked him, "Will you make a list of all lighthouse crew members, their wives, and children." When that was done and verified with the advances to their back pay payments, the next question was about the other non-government inhabitants of the village.

To Marten he said, "You know now how many persons you have to deal with. First issue goes to the lighthouse people. After all, the fabric is for them. If you have extra, give it to the others."

"How many yards do I give per man, woman, and child?" Marten wanted to know, looking very unhappy.

"I haven't the foggiest idea. Ask somebody from our crew. You know the total yardage of the stuff, and the rest is easy."

Obviously, both officers were on alien terrain on this matter. Ian did not feel very proud of his approach to Marten's problem but somebody had to do it and he couldn't leave it to the kepala either. When there is a shortage of something, human nature is to try to get as much as possible, fair or not. Moreover, the lighthouse repair and operation was his first priority. He gave all his attention to the progress and consulted with the two engineers. The lighthouse personnel had purposely refrained from any maintenance of the structure and building. They had acted as if they were farmers and fishermen, unrelated to the government. The Japanese had asked where the personnel were, and each time the answer had been "Taken on board a Dutch ship and gone."

Each evening after working hours, they went ashore again and took a bath in a small freshwater stream coming from the hills. This was a welcome relaxation after a day in the tropical heat. Then the four sat together, talking about their lives, Holland, and the developments in the Indies. The movement to become independent from the motherland was growing. When the Japanese occupation forces realized that they were losing the war, they sowed the seeds of hatred against the Caucasian race. Strengthened by the worldwide belief that World War II victors were to free all people, the movement became more organized, and found listening ears among the leaders of many countries. The Dutch government was very reluctant to allow independence on short notice, being concerned that it would result in chaos. Talks between the two parties had started. Due to the multitude of topics involved in drastically changing a situation that had lasted for more than three hundred years, progress, if any, was slow. Hotheads for "independence now" armed themselves with weapons from the withdrawing Japanese forces. They withdrew into the jungle and started their guerrilla actions against the Dutch.

An army division was shipped from Holland to restore order. This division was holed up in Malaysia for many weeks before being allowed by the Far East Command to replace the British troops in the Dutch East Indies. The official reason for this was to stabilize the situation before letting the Dutch division in, but more probably other politics played a role. On the island of Seroetoe, there was no trace of hostility and cooperation continued satisfactorily.

Six days after their arrival, the moment arrived to start up the light. Everybody, now more properly dressed thanks to Marten's ingenuity, gathered around the tower. The engineers and the personnel were up on the tower. The small kerosene motor rotating the lamp with the lenses was started, the lamp lit, and the revolving light was functioning. Everyone applauded and the tug's horn added to the feat. That evening there was dinner on the beach with local dances, speeches, and songs. By everybody's measure it was a jungle gala evening.

The next morning Ian sent the message to headquarters that in the following publication of the "Notice to Mariners" the Seroetoe light could be included. The anchor was weighed, and with three long blasts on the horn the D-013 was on her way, leaving waving people behind.

The trip to the rendezvous bay on the west coast of Borneo took only a few days. A westerly storm created a sickening corkscrewing movement of the tug and this accentuated a previous minor problem. The officers bathroom, located at starboard, disposed of its contents directly into the sea via a pipe with a non-return valve occasionally under the water line. The salt water had caused the valve to freeze in a partly open position which, in calm waters, presented no problems. However the rolling of the boat brought the valve above water and was then plunged back under the water, causing a strong backup into the pipes of the john.

It didn't take long to teach the users to "work on the seas": to leave the door to the gangway open and jump from the john at the moment the ship started a downward roll.

An officer standing in the gangway with his pants down, while the product at times hit the ceiling, didn't do much good for decorum.

There was a heated argument between the skipper and the chief engineer and the latter had to promise on his life to remedy the problem as soon as they arrived at their destination.

Everybody was glad when the D-013 rounded a cape and came into the calm waters of the bay. They moored alongside a primitive jetty and Ian went ashore to report to the harbor master. A native town was settled along the bank of the bay. Ian could not detect any office-like building and wondered where the office would be. He had not waited long when a European in the uniform of a harbor master came toward him. They shook hands and Ian told him the reason for his call. The man, who had not told Ian his name, nodded. Apparently he was aware of the mission.

Ian had expected that they would go to the office for the necessary paperwork but the harbor master pointed to seven sailing craft tied up in the little harbor. A local policeman stood on guard.

"I am going to tow these vessels to Tandjoeng Priok. Did you check whether any of them are taking any water?" Ian asked him.

"No, they are dry bottoms. I have the registrations here with me," the harbor master said, and patted some folders under his arm. Ian could do nothing better than to invite him on board; his invitation was readily accepted.

What a strange bird, Ian thought when they walked to the tugboat. He called the other officers and while they had a beer he observed the man more closely. He looked like he was in his fifties with grey hair and constantly shifting eyes. Ian asked him whether there were more Europeans in town.

"Only the customs officer. But he is a very uncooperative and unfriendly man," was the answer.

"Well, I'll go and see him this afternoon to get his papers on the cargo of the seven captured boats."

"Oh no, that's not possible; he will be in his office tomorrow morning."

Ian shrugged, "All right, I will go then. Where is his office?"

"In the same building as mine, at the foot of the jetty." Since the little town didn't look promising for any kind of entertainment, Ian invited "Mr. H," as he called him in his mind, for dinner.

"Thank you, but I am very busy. I will see you before you leave," and with these words he left rather hastily. Marten followed him and they talked briefly. Ian looked at the others with raised eyebrows.

"What do you guys think of this fellow? He didn't even give his name, or did I miss it?" Marten shed some light on the man. "He was in a POW camp during the war, and after liberation he was sent to this place. He was not sent to Holland for recuperation since there was a shortage of personnel. Now he is awaiting his replacement."

They discussed the harbor master further. The chief engineer thought that he had malaria, and of course, had suffered during camp years. Marten, more accustomed to local situations, found it strange that there was a harbor master, as well as a customs officer, in a place like this. And, to make matters worse, they disliked each other.

"I might go cuckoo living here," he added. After dinner Ian gave permission for shore leave for the three officers. He had paperwork to do and was eager to prepare the tow and leave as early as possible. The others were back in a very short time.

"What a god-forsaken nest," the chief declared. "Let's get back to Batavia; then we can enjoy shore leave."

The next morning, Ian and Marten went ashore to see the customs man. They found the port office, but Mr. H was not in. Adjacent was the customs warehouse in which there was an office partitioned off. They entered and both stood agape looking at the customs officer. It was the harbor master, but now in the uniform of a customs officer. He greeted them in a different voice and asked them to sit down.

"You have met that son-of-a-bitch harbor master," he began, and immediately thereafter gave a long tirade about that person. It took Ian a while to recover from the shock and he felt sick, realizing what the authorities had done by sending the man to a desolate place without any furlough.

He got his wits together and excused himself; "Mr. Marten Vanheel will go through the papers with you. I just remembered that I have an urgent matter to attend to." And with a wink to Marten he hurried back to the tug. He called the chief engineer and told him what happened.

"My god, I have never witnessed somebody with a split personality before. It was eerie."

He went to the ship's radio, sending an urgent message to Mr. Werff. While tapping the key, he hoped his message was going through since he was not transmitting on the prearranged hours. He was lucky; his message was received and confirmed. Batavia headquarters requested D-013 to remain on receiving; they would call back. While Ian was waiting, Marten returned with some additional information.

"Mr. H's name is Jan Boers, thirty-one years old, and he was sent to this post in the combined function."

"That did it," grumbled Ian. "His malnourished brain could not handle it."

Within an hour, Ian got a reply. "Situation understood. Sending replacement by Catalina tomorrow. ETA 2 P.M. Inform Boers board plane on return. Good work. Over and out. Werff." Ian went to Boers, who was still dressed in his customs outfit, and gave him the message. He saw Boer's face light up for a moment.

"But what about giving all customs affairs to my replacement? I don't care very much to do it all in a hurry—"

"Don't you worry, it will all be arranged. You better start packing. Let me know if I can be of help." Going back to the tug, he wondered whether Boers would depart as customs or as port official. Meanwhile the petty officers were preparing the sailing vessels for towing, so that they could leave right after the Catalina amphibian had taken off.

The voyage back to Tandjoeng Priok went without any problems. Ian learned that a skipper on a tugboat had to look aft as much as forward when towing. At night the light on the last craft was the sign that the tow was complete. The extra crew manning the last boat would signal when something was amiss. Finally they entered the bay of their home port and anchored near the entrance. A harbor tug took over the tow and the D-013 moored at the coast guard wharf. Ian finished the log book with "Mission accomplished," arranged crew members for harbor duty, and the four officers received transportation to good old Nautica.

Chapter Seventeen

On the way from the port to the city, traffic had come to a halt. The reason why became clear very soon. In the canal parallel to the road two small bamboo rafts floated slowly. On them were two decapitated white women's bodies with limbs and other parts tied to the rafts. Ian and the other truck occupants went to the bank of the canal. The view of the macabre sight made everybody gag and a wild roar of anger rose from the crowd.

It took a while before a boat arrived to tow the rafts away. Ian was shocked to learn from their driver that most probably the hideous crime was committed by guerrillas claiming independence. It was obvious the movement had gained strength in a short time and it bode ill for the future. Nobody spoke until they arrived at Nautica, and even the warm welcome by Mrs. Hulscher gave no relief.

The talk that evening was about what they had seen, and listening to other officers, it became clear this had not been an isolated incident. Inland prison camps guarded during the war by Japanese and Korean soldiers were attacked after the war by so-called freedom fighters. And those soldiers, awaiting relief from their duty by the British, had to wait a long time before the Ghurkas and Sihks arrived. Meanwhile, as bitter irony, the former enemy troops turned into defenders of the prisoners against the outside. By doing so, they, no doubt, saved many lives.

Ian was flabbergasted hearing all this. "Where are our troops?" he demanded. "An entire division was shipped months ago from Holland!"

"You are right," an elderly officer replied. "But that division has been holed up in some Malaysian port for reasons unbeknown to me."

Another officer asked Ian, "Did you notice the troop transport ship anchored in the bay?"

"Yes, when we came in, we noticed it."

"Well, there are Dutch Marines on board, trained in the United States during the war, but they are not allowed to come ashore. These guys are getting mad not being able to come into action while they hear about the monstrosities against our landsmen in the interior. One marine couldn't stand it any more and jumped overboard to swim to land. He didn't make it."

My god, what a bloody stinking mess, Ian thought, and aloud he said, "We were sure the war was over; does it now start all over again?"

Nobody had an answer to that question.

That night, Ian couldn't sleep, worrying that he had a three-year contract with the coast guard. Who knew how long this situation would continue? It could very well be that he would have to sweat it out that long on his own and that Jenny and their soon-to-be-born child would have to stay in Holland. On the other hand, it would be better if she stayed where she was.

The next morning he reported to Officer Werff, who expressed his satisfaction with the mission Ian had carried out. "What happened with Jan Boers? I want to visit with him."

"Can't do, he is already in Holland, on a first-priority flight."

In response to Ian's question of how a person in such a condition, having just been freed from a POW camp, could be sent to such a remote port, Werff told him that due to Boers' dual position, different departments dealt with him. Each department, reading Boers' reports, assumed that the malcontent between the harbor master and the customs chief existed between two persons. "The tropics can play tricks on lonely people, Ian."

Ian looked at his superior officer and felt a growing bond and better understanding between them. He told him about his experience the previous day. Werff shook his head in disgust.

"I don't know what the future will bring. But this morning I learned that our government has put utmost pressure on the Allied nations to allow our forces to enter the Indies and restore order. Only thereafter can the claim for independence be taken into consideration."

And with a deep sigh, he added, "And the first step cannot be soon enough."

Going back to the business at hand, Ian got his next assignment. He would be replaced as tugboat skipper and receive two days off to take care of his personal affairs such as mail. "Thereafter you will join a group of officers to fly to Manila."

"In the Philippines? What am I going to do there?" He was told the Dutch government purchased a number of Landing Ship Tank (LST) vessels from the U.S. Navy. These LST's were no longer needed, the crews had been decommissioned and were preparing to sail homeward. Countries such as France and Britain, with interests in the Far East, were purchasing the various types of war-time craft, and Holland was one of them.

The first group was going to Subic Bay where all the vessels were anchored and was to take over five LST's, prepare them for sailing, and man the last one to sail for the Indies. Also the group would receive instructions from American officers on equipment and operation of the landing craft. Other crews would be sent over as soon as the first four vessels were ready for sea. Further orders would follow in due time.

The commanding officer of the first group, Captain Bakker, was due to arrive in Batavia the next day and a meeting of the group would take place before departure, some days later. Ian used his two days off to go through his mail, the first piece being a letter from Jenny. She was doing all right and the doctor was satisfied, but the advanced pregnancy was taking its natural toll, resulting in cumbersome movement and fatigue. Her tone was upbeat, however Ian detected an underlying cry for him to be there with her.

He had a difficult moment when their mutual loneliness overwhelmed him. Before beginning to write to her, he paused for a while to contemplate his response. Letting her know that he loved her and desponded to hold her in his arms was fine and dandy, but didn't give the mental support his wife needed under the circumstances. Moreover, the time lapse between writing and receiving a reaction was such that feelings and situations could very well be entirely different.

After this rather philosophical consideration he re-read her letter and grinned when she wrote that she had completely forgotten to vote, in the first government election after five years. Consequently, she had to pay a fine for not voting. Having cleared his thoughts, he took the pen and wrote from his heart while putting his brain in gear.

He did not mention the rafts with the naked women, the papers in Holland might take care of that. Other letters from family and friends carried news from the homeland from a different viewpoint and it became clear that slowly, very slowly, the country was rebuilding. The Marshall Plan worked wonders; without it there would have been chaos for a long time.

Captain Bakker was a heavyset sturdy character who minced no words on their task. Everybody introduced himself at the beginning of the meeting. Ian was charged with the duties of junior second officer; at sea that was clear enough, but what this would entail when outfitting LST's was another matter. Captain Bakker masterfully avoided endless questions from all twelve officers on that subject by an honest and simple statement that such details could only be dealt with "on the spot."

Their flight to Manila brought them over a part of the Dutch East Indies that Ian had not seen before. Lush tropical forests, mountain ranges, sandy beaches, and a never-ending number of islands gave him a good impression of the archipelago. Upon landing at the airport in Manila they were transported to a hotel by a member of the embassy.

Their hotel was located close to the old inner city of Intramuros, and the outside of the building still carried pockmarks of shell fire. Intramuros had been heavily bombed and made a very desolate picture. During the meeting the next morning, Captain Bakker announced that he and his first officer had to go to the Dutch embassy and the American headquarters to arrange reams of papers before they could travel to the navy base in Subic Bay. Everybody was free from duty, but they were cordially invited to be back in the hotel every night.

"That sounds like a long wait," one of the officers remarked, "so let's go to town and see what's cooking." Public transportation being non-existent, they walked to the downtown of Manila in the heat. Twice a year the monsoon winds change; during such periods there is a heavy overcast sky and no wind, making the atmosphere stifling. Many streets were lined with temporary shacks, but there were bars galore and soon the group landed in one of them, thirsting for cold beer.

Ladies offering their services were having a slow day since none of the group was at that moment inclined to such activities. Or was it because no one wanted to be first, Ian wondered. There was nothing remarkable to see or do so the group walked back to the hotel for a prolonged siesta.

The days lingered on. Captain Bakker got more annoyed with the red tape he could not break through. Ian was getting edgy since it was mid-April, the time Jenny was due to deliver, and no mail was coming through. His roommate, a second engineer, wasn't much help either, being a bachelor.

There was one bright moment when they received temporary passes to make purchases in the PX store. A world of, for them, luxury items opened up and they bought everything within reach of their allowance. Finally, after weeks of lolling around, the group proceeded to the enormous expanse of Subic Bay. Hundreds of all types of landing craft were tied to buoys in the bay. Their first LST was brought alongside a wharf to facilitate working. The first officer, Mr. Boudier, made a list of duties for the deck officers. They all would be made familiar with the navigation equipment. United States Navy officers were their instructors on instruments, which none of the Dutch counterparts had operated before. Each day the engineers disappeared into the "down below," only emerging for lunch and dinner. Soaked with perspiration, they were given a separate table in the mess room.

Ian was given the additional responsibility of knowing everything about operation of the huge bow doors and ramp, where the water and ballast tanks were, and to his surprise, to fix up the sickbay.

"Why me, for the sickbay?" he asked Mr. Boudier.

"Somebody has to do it, and you earned a badge for first aid in the Boy Scouts!"

Apparently the first officer had done his homework on his officers' backgrounds. I'll be damned, Ian thought; because of the Scouts I was assigned to the signal corps long ago, and now this. I better be careful before they make me chief cook or something. At that idea, he smiled. Mr. Boudier took it as a sign of acceptance. "I knew you would understand my reasoning."

It was hard work and everyone enjoyed the moment when the air conditioning was switched on. The first two vessels were readied for sea. Officers were flown in and with Filipino crews the ships sailed for the Indies.

There was still no word from Jenny and at times Ian felt like a completely lost soul. After working hours he withdrew to his hut or walked through the base. His colleagues understood what he was going through but couldn't help him. One day Captain Bakker called him into his cabin. "Listen, Ian, I know that you are climbing the wall by not knowing what is going on with your wife. But don't become a sour note for yourself or others. Pull yourself together and be part of our team. And that is an order."

Two days later, on June 18, 1946, Captain Bakker called him in and handed him a piece of paper. Ian read, "April 18 daughter born. All well. Love Jenny."

A wave of emotions came over Ian, the penciled message shaking in his hand. Without being asked he sat down. The few words said it all; he was a father and all was well. Captain Bakker clasped his hand in a firm grip.

"Congratulations, man. I am sorry the telegram took so long; it went through all kinds of departments and finally our embassy received it and figured it out."

When he got Ian's attention, he continued. "Although the sun is not yet over the yardarm, this calls for a drink." He called for the steward, ordered two drinks, and the two seamen held their glasses up for a toast. Ian asked whether he could send a cable to his wife, which the captain promised to arrange.

"You are off duty this afternoon and tonight there will be a party ashore, so you better be prepared." Ian began feeling the impact of the message as well as the booze when he walked through the corridor to his hut. Sitting on his bed he closed his eyes trying to envision what Jenny and their daughter would look like. Now they were a family and their lives would be very different. Resolutely he took pen and paper to send a cable, mindful to put an ocean of feeling in a few words.

Wasting several pages, the final result was: "Received your cable/ am elated/ proud of you and daughter/writing/love, Ian."

He handed the cable to Captain Bakker, who would take care of it. Back in his hut he slumped on his bed, now relaxed after weeks of built-up tension, and promptly fell asleep. It was already getting dark when there was a banging on his door and loud voices were calling him.

"Hey you. Come out of your nest. Do you think you delivered the baby or what?"

Coming back with a shock to reality, Ian shouted back. "Okay you guys, be careful with a new father. That specimen has to be treated with respect."

"Hah, we'll teach you respect. Ten minutes is all you get," they said, and left with great laughter. The party was a great success with many speeches and libations. There was fraternity amongst the entire group, and when returning to the base they got the attention of the shore police.

"Will you please pipe down, sirs," the SP corporal insisted. Ian offered him and his buddy a cigar and several of his fellow officers felt it necessary to explain the occasion. The corporal waved them on, following them at a distance in the jeep. This had a sobering effect, but once back onboard, the whole thing started all over again.

The next morning everybody tiptoed around and made no waves. Ian began paying more attention to happenings around him and one day noticed that packages were thrown overboard from other vessels anchored in the bay. He asked others what they could be, but nobody knew.

"All right, after work I'll take a boat and investigate. Who will go with me?" Two crew men volunteered and they proceeded to a cluster of craft, hailing the man on watch on one of them. "Can you tell me what you are tossing overboard?" Ian asked the U.S. Navy sergeant.

He explained that the ships were being decommissioned and that the ship's stores had to be returned to the quartermaster store. But only full boxes were accepted and since they were going home, all opened boxes were dumped.

"What kind of stuff are you talking about?"

"Whatever has been opened" was the answer.

Ian explained that they were from the Indies where everything was very scarce. Would it be possible to put all the items that are to be thrown out near the gangway? They would come by every day and pick them up to help their families at home when returning. The sergeant told them to wait; he had to ask his superior. Soon after, he returned and said it was okay. If they didn't show up, all opened boxes would, as before, go over the side.

The entrepreneurs returned to the LST and asked the captain for his consent to the operation. Bakker agreed, but went even further. He ordered that the goods, whatever they were, would be stored onboard and that the third officer would keep tabs on the inventory. In addition, each officer would get an equal share in the loot when back in home port, and the "collection" was only to be made after working hours.

The following weeks brought a great variety of articles from their collection trips, from shoe laces to all kinds of canned food. A storeroom was put aside for that purpose and was soon filled. Extra space was obtained. The third officer became very popular, being the guardian of the growing treasure.

Finally, the last LST was ready to sail. A Filipino crew to help bring her to Batavia was signed on and the vessel, now named the *Albatros*, cleared the bay. Destination: Hollandia on New Guinea.

Chapter Eighteen

The routine and discipline at sea was a relief for all the officers, especially after the hectic time outfitting five vessels. A ship under sail is a well organized operation, everybody assigned to his tasks and relying on each other. A landlubber may wonder what on earth a captain is doing, and as a matter of fact, when everything is progressing smoothly, he does very little. However, seamen often are confronted with the whims of nature and it is a standing order to call the captain when something out of the ordinary comes up. Then the captain is there and takes over. Sometimes junior officers find themselves in a dilemma deciding when a situation warrants calling the captain.

Ian's watch was from 0400 to 0800, and when he took over from the senior second officer he noticed the navigation lights of another ship slightly astern from the *Albatros*. The next fifteen minutes he watched the lights closely and it became clear that the other ship was coming up fast at close quarters, following a course of interference with their own.

This is ridiculous, Ian thought. Here we are in a wide open sea, so why is this bugger chasing our tail? He decided to use the Aldis lamp and send a signal to the oncoming ship as a warning to keep off. There was no response, and the situation rapidly became uncomfortable. Changing course to avoid a collision was out of the question; the international Rules of the Sea state very clearly that a vessel being passed by another must maintain course and speed.

The next move should be to warn the oncoming ship by using the ship's horn. Doing so, all hands would be alerted and he could bet that Captain Bakker would come to the bridge right away. So, he whistled the tube to the captain's quarters.

"Sir, an oncoming vessel is approaching us too close at parallel course. I have used the Aldis lamp to alert them but there is no reaction."

"How close?" was the question from the awakened skipper.

"About one mile."

"Sound the horn. I'll be right up."

The mighty sonorous sound could awaken the entire country, but again there was no visible reaction from the other ship. Captain Bakker, in pajamas and slippers, took over the command from Ian, eyed the situation, and not noticing any change of course by the other ship, ordered Ian to use a signal flare. It looked like fireworks illuminating the sky and it was effective. Finally, the other ship became alert and changed course away from the *Albatros*.

"Well done, Ian. Next time call me earlier," the captain said, and with these words disappeared from the bridge. Ian made an entry in the log book on the happening while thinking that a skipper would give you a pat on the back and at the same time would keep you on your toes.

One of his duties, other than being on watch two times for four hours each in the space of twenty-four hours, was to run the sickbay each morning. So after his morning watch and breakfast, he opened the clinic. Two sailors were waiting for him; one complained of an upset stomach and the other ran a fever.

The first man presented no problem; when Ian had taken inventory he had found plenty of castor oil, so he gave him a very generous portion of the liquid and took him off duty for the next four hours. The feverish person was another matter because the patient told him that aspirin had not helped. In the sickbay manual he had read about the ability of the wonder drug penicillin to cure any infection. It would be several days before they would reach Hollandia and something had to be done. No way would he call the captain, he thought. I can deal with this myself, thank you very much.

Rummaging through the boxes he found the drug, as well as needles, then told the Filipino sailor to lower his pants and face the wall. The hypodermic needle filled, he jammed it into a buttock, emptied the contents, and glued a piece of bandage on the tiny wound. The sailor thanked him and walked out. Apparently his first two customers were satisfied with the treatment, survived, and told their peers about it. The following days he got more patients and they started to call him "Doc."

Captain Bakker heard about it and one day came to the sickbay. "I hear that you are working wonders here. Can I see your so-called medical notes?" Reading what Ian had written, he looked with disbelieving eyes at Ian.

"Very commendable, but will you please refrain from giving injections and passing out drugs of which you have no notion?"

Here we go again, Ian thought. Damned if you do and damned if you don't. "Captain, I have studied the manuals which I found here; everybody is happy and nobody died!" And in desperation, mixed with some anger, added, "Or shall I call you when somebody calls in sick?"

Captain Bakker, already on his way out, halted suddenly when he heard Ian's last remark. He stood still for a long moment and then turned around slowly, his face reddened. "You follow my orders, understand! And see me in my cabin at 1700," he said, and left Ian miserably behind. At 5 P.M. he knocked at the door, preparing himself for a thunderstorm on quite a number of topics, none of which were very pleasant.

The skipper answered his call. "Come in, Ian, and sit down." He was alone, relaxed, with a drink in front of him. Ian, expecting a gale force ten on the Beaufort scale, was surprised at hearing himself addressed by his first name, which could be considered a good start.

"Can I offer you a drink?"

"Yes, sir, a beer would be fine. Thank you."

After this unexpected overture, Ian waited until the other shoe dropped. But whatever his anticipation, the next move after their "cheers" came out of the blue. Captain Bakker was looking pensively in his glass.

"Well eh, I don't know how to tell you this, Ian." He was clearly searching for words. Ian looked at him questioningly. What was going on? The old man didn't know how to tell him what? He found it safe not saying anything and waited. The silence became painful.

The captain cleared his throat, made up his mind, and looked at Ian. "What the hell. I'll tell you something. Lately, I have not been able to perform very well in bed. When we are in our home port I know what to do, but all that time out in the Philippines I had no resource. Now I figured with you going through the medical manuals and having all kinds of new medications from the States, which we never even heard of, maybe you have something for me?"

Ian had to call an internal "all hands on deck" to avoid bursting out in laughter when hearing about the captain's predicament. His inner voice told him to engage his brains before putting his mouth in gear. This is great, don't spoil it, he thought.

"Well, what about it?"

"I see what you mean, captain. I haven't looked for information in that particular area, but will do so right away. I can't promise though."

"Okay, Ian, thank you. There is no great hurry, but I would like to be fit when we arrive in Batavia. Have another beer."

The important topic having been dealt with, they chatted about neutral items for a while until Ian found the time to excuse himself. The captain nodded and gave his parting shot.

"You keep this between us, 'Doc.' Take your time and let me know."

"Aye, sir," Ian said, and took a hasty retreat to his hut, closed the door, and fell on his bed, tears running down on the pillow. His laughs shook his body and it took a while before he calmed down. He hadn't the faintest idea where to look in the manuals and under what heading. After all, English not being his mother tongue and taking into consideration that government jargon does not follow indices like you find in a dictionary, it could be quite a task. Moreover, he could not afford to screw up, and castor oil wouldn't help!

They were still several days sailing from Hollandia when Ian received the medical assignment and his first efforts to find a possible cure for his captain were not very successful. Lucky for him they came into more open waters and the *Albatros* started rolling sickeningly in waves coming in from starboard quarters. The ship was in ballast, towering high above the water, and the movement increased to a wide arc, hesitated and stayed at an angle for a while, and then started rolling all over again. Sleep under these conditions was hard to come by, everybody was crusty and short-fused and the food was dismal due to the cooks fighting with sliding pots and pans. There was not a good opportunity to report to the captain on his search progress and he didn't push the issue.

Upon arrival, they anchored in Humbolt Bay near the town of Hollandia on the north coast of New Guinea. Toward the end of World War II, the town and harbor were used as a springboard for the invasion of the Philippines by General MacArthur's army. When the war in the Far East ended rather abruptly with Japan's surrender after the atomic bombs were dropped, the U.S. troops left New Guinea, leaving material behind. The *Albatros* was to load military rolling stock and distribute it to garrisons throughout the Indies.

A launch from the harbor office brought orders; the next morning before high water the *Albatros* was to beach to prepare for loading. The beach master would indicate the spot. Beaching a ship at flank speed, which is higher than normal full speed, goes against the grain and soul of every seaman. Navigating primarily consists of going from the port of departure to the destination following the shortest safe route and avoiding land and obstructions like the plague. To run a ship on shore at utmost speed is something else, and other than in wartime, it always brings excitement for the officers and crew alike.

Ballast tanks were adjusted, current and wind checked, anchor weighed, and the *Albatros* gained speed, heading directly to the section of the beach marked with flags. It was her first beaching after the war and the captain, taking command on the bridge, gave orders to the helmsman, grunting with satisfaction when everything went smoothly. The vessel tight and secured, Ian, on the fore-ship station, ordered the bow doors opened and the ramp lowered. The cavernous hold of the 4,000 ton landing ship was now accessible from the shore. A bulldozer started moving earth toward the ramp to provide an even approach for the rolling stock—weapon carriers, jeeps, tractors, and a host of other track-type, military vehicles. Loading would start in two days, when all vehicles had been moved from various spots to the beach area.

As a relief for Ian, he could now send those on sick report to the army doctor ashore. In the afternoon, the watchman told him that there was an officer to see him. Ian went to the messroom and was greeted by an army captain, "Hello, colleague, welcome to Hollandia." Ian looked at the officer and noticed the medic's badges on his uniform. Before he could answer, the doctor continued, "The crew members you sent me this morning told me that there was a doctor on board, and they spoke very highly of you. By the way, where did you study?"

Ian had to think very fast for a way to get out of the mess room where other officers were present. "Why don't we go to the sickbay; we can talk there." And they went down to the place where he had 'practiced' during the voyage.

"Here we can talk without interruption. Please sit down." The doctor looked around, admiring the instruments, equipment, and shelves with medicines.

"Well, colleague, you are very well stocked. You should see what I have to work with."

Ian found it high time to get rid of that colleague thing, and told him the situation, as well as what he had been doing in the medical field while at sea.

The doctor was aghast. "You were giving injections? And how did you know what ailments to cure with what? Good lord, you could have killed patients!"

The moment had come for Ian to defend his actions from the doctor's outburst, understandable as it might be. "Somebody had to do it, and I got the assignment." And with a wry smile, he added, "After all, I had a first aid course when in the Boy Scouts eons ago."

The doctor was astounded, unable to comprehend what he heard. Then he looked at Ian and realized the grim humor on his face. Both men looked at each other and started laughing, patting each other on the back. "Oh shit, it is a crazy world. Let's make the best of it."

Then the doctor looked around once more. "What are you going to do with all this equipment? Not operating, I hope?"

"No way; I have had enough of playing doctor. As a matter of fact, why don't you take what you need."

The doctor jumped up. "You mean that? Man, that is a godsend. Thank you!"

While the other was going through the manuals and taking the instruments out of the cabinets with loving care, Ian thought he'd better ask Captain Bakker for his approval to donate the stuff.

Captain Bakker? A sudden thought struck Ian. Of course, that was it. The solution to the old man's problems was right in front of him.

"Eh, doctor. I am having a minor problem. Maybe you can help me with that." And without mentioning Captain Bakker by name, he told the physician about an elderly man's problem. It didn't take very long to learn that he could easily obtain special local herbs which would improve the 'elderly man's' maneuvers in that area.

"You know what I will do. Give me some empty U.S. Navy bottles with blank labels. I will fill them and write the Latin name on it. There is no risk, every physician knows what it is and you will be the hero." They agreed that the doctor could take the desired books with him right now and that the next day they would exchange their wares.

The doctor left the ship and Ian went to ask the captain for his approval to donate the medical supplies to the shore clinic. The captain was ashore, so Ian went to First Officer Boudier to get his authorization. Mr. Boudier had no problem with that, and remarked that it would take Ian from the risks he was taking. Apparently word had been going around.

"You better keep it to aspirin and castor oil."

The next day the doctor came on board with his assistant, handed Ian two bottles with the magic herbs and in exchange got his treasure. Ian kept the bottles until they would be at sea again; he wasn't sure how to explain to the captain the matter of finding the medication.

The *Albatros* was loaded without problems. The lighter vehicles were taken on deck via the big platform lift and the heavier ones stowed in the hold. All lashed and secured, the ship was ready to unbeach at the next high water. Ian and some officers took the opportunity of a couple of free hours to go ashore. Walking along the beach, Ian noticed a coconut palm grove. A group of Papoeas were sitting in the shadow under the palm trees. Suddenly, Ian got a craving for cool, fresh coconut milk. He approached the group and made an offer to one of them.

"I'll give you a quarter if you climb into the tree and get me some coconuts."

The man, remaining squatted, looked up to him with a broad grin and told him, "And I give you one dollar if you do it."

Everybody started laughing and one of the officers said to Ian, "Now you know that the Yanks have been here." The men returned to the ship without coconuts.

At high tide, with the ballast tanks emptied, the *Albatros* shoved slowly from the beach, swung around, and set course to the next destination, a small island between Sumatra and Borneo, where she would discharge part of her cargo.

Time passed very quickly but there were many moments when Ian thought of his little family back home. There had been no mail when they were in Hollandia, and he was afraid there wouldn't be any at their next destination either. Their sailing schedule was clearly too confusing for the postal organization. Although not an excuse, it was understandable, since the freedom movement had exploded on many islands into a full-scale guerrilla war. The troops from Holland had finally been allowed to enter the Dutch East Indies after their prolonged stay in Malaysia. They were now holding all major cities, but penetration into the hinterland was progressing slowly, requiring more troops. Traffic between towns was only allowed in convoy with military coverage. When plantations were cleared they had to be protected against attacks by special armed guards. Quite often this was unsuccessful and the buildings were burned, the staff members killed, and the workers disappeared.

When he heard and read about these developments, Ian was glad that Jenny and the baby were still safely in Holland, and at the same time he wondered when they would be able to join him. Feeling sorry for yourself didn't help since they were all in the same boat, lousy as it was.

The *Albatros* beached on the east coast of the island of Billiton where part of the rolling stock had to be delivered to the troops stationed on the island. It was not an ideal spot to beach, and it took more than a week until an earth ramp to the ship was completed. The staff employees of the Holland-based mining company, none having their families with them yet, were quick to discover that the *Albatros'* stores included plenty of whiskey and beer. After working hours many of them found an excuse to come on board. During one of these invasions Ian met Ron Vander, his travel companion on the Constellation. Ron told him that his company had chartered a freighter with some passenger accommodations. The families of the employees were on board and the ship was loaded with urgently needed cargo to make the tin-ore dredgers and other installations operational.

"When is the ship due at Billiton, and is your family on board?" asked Ian.

"Oh yes, they are on board all right. But it is an old ship and seems to call at every port on route. They should have been here already."

Ian found the information regarding family reunions encouraging. Who knows, just maybe, Jenny and the baby wouldn't have to wait very long to join him.

One morning in mid-August when they were still unloading vehicles, Ian was called to see Captain Bakker right away. This was unusual. They had not spoken with each other very much since Ian had given him the bottles with the potency stuff. Had the captain detected that it was not the latest American wonder drug? If so, a storm was brewing.

Not knowing what to expect, he knocked on the door and after a "Come in" stepped into the master cabin. The captain sat behind his desk and pointed to a chair opposite. He ruffled through papers and then looked at Ian with a smile.

"Can you pack and be ready for the airport in one hour?" Ian eyed the captain with question marks written on his face.

The captain could not forego the opportunity to make one of his not always appreciated remarks.

"This is the first time I have seen you speechless; didn't you hear my question?"

"Yes, sir, but what is it all about, why the hurry?"

"I received a message from headquarters that your wife and child are on a rebuilt troop transport ship and the ship is due to arrive in Batavia any day now. So for heaven's sake, don't look so stupid. Get your gear and the third officer will drive you to the airport. Here are your papers. Go. Go."

Ian went full speed to his hut, his thoughts in a turmoil. Jenny and the baby almost there? And where would they stay? And, and, and . . . Throwing clothes in his suitcase, he was ready in half an hour, not bothering to inform the first officer; the captain could take care of that.

He hollered for the third officer and they climbed in a jeep, heading at high speed for the tiny airport in the center of the island. On the way, he told his driver why he was in such a hurry and the third officer grinned. "How long will you stay away? Did you get a furlough pass?"

"I don't know and I don't give a damn right now. The main thing is to see my family, and the rest can wait."

"Tut, tut. Big words. Be alert that you are not thrown in the brig instead of in a love nest."

"Shut up, wise guy. Get me to the airport and leave the rest to me."

The trip in the small plane from Billiton to Batavia gave Ian the time he needed to get a grip on the situation, for which he was not fully prepared. Within a few days he would hold his wife in his arms and for the first time see his baby. It was difficult to comprehend; it seemed so long ago since he'd seen Jenny at Schiphol Airport waving and smiling through her tears.

When they landed it was already getting dark. After collecting his luggage he looked around to see whether there was somebody he knew, but nobody appeared for him. It all was done on such short notice, and he hoped that Mrs. Hulscher had room for him in Nautica, the only place in Batavia he knew. This time he took a taxi, which he had to share with some other passengers who were going to various addresses in town. Finally, he arrived at the mess, paid the driver, and walked to the entrance. Through the open doors he could see that they were gathered around the large dining room table having dinner. Leaving his luggage on the floor, he entered the dining room and greeted Mrs. Hulscher, who was seated at the head of the table.

"Hello, Mrs. Hulscher. I arrived on short notice and I hope you have room for me."

The mess lady turned around and looked at him, not saying a word. The other officers also looked at him and Ian didn't know what to think of it. Very strange behavior, he thought. Then they all looked at somebody else, and when Ian looked in that direction, his heart began beating wildly. It was Jenny, seated between officers; his own Jenny, looking more beautiful than he recalled. She jumped up from her chair and was in his arms. They held each other, kissing and hugging under loud applause and yelling from the others. Someone shouted, "Lights out," and the scene was suddenly in the dark.

Catching her breath, Jenny whispered in his ear, "Ian, come see our daughter," and she took him by the hand and went into one of the bedrooms. There she was, a tiny little girl, fast asleep. They tiptoed to the crib and Ian, looking with amazement at their child, bent over and kissed her lightly. She stirred but did not wake up and then Ian again embraced Jenny for a long time.

The distant voices from the dining room did not disturb them. They were laying on the bed in each other's arms and there was so much to tell that hours fled. Then sounds came from the crib. Jenny rose and told him that it was feeding time.

She gave little Meagen to Ian. "You hold her while I get ready." And with twinkling eyes she saw how clumsily he held the baby, scared like the devil that her head would topple.

Jenny was breast-feeding her and Ian could not get enough of the picture. After the feeding and diaper changing, Meagen was put back in the crib, leaving the parents together with their love under the mosquito net. The mess became quiet, the tropical night with all its mysterious sounds and smells was around them and the two young people found each other. It was their world.

Chapter Nineteen

The next morning Ian went to headquarters while Jenny took care of the baby. She was having a good time with Mrs. Hulscher, who already adored both.

For Jenny it was good to relax after the rigors of sailing on an old liner ship which had been refurbished as a troop transport during the war. In fact, it was still used as a troop transport, with some cabin improvements for women and children who were joining their husbands and fathers already in the Indies. It was the first move by the government to reunite families, despite housing considerations and the guerrilla actions.

The voyage took many weeks, accentuated by a mishap which occurred when the engines stopped while cruising in the Red Sea. Floating in the very intense summer heat, catching no breeze at all and with power cut off, it became a nightmare. It took five days until repairs were made, during which time emotions ran high. All in all, it wasn't exactly a cruise and everybody on board was delighted when they docked at Tandjoeng Priok.

Families were waiting on the dock to welcome the passengers. Most were men, dressed up for the occasion and carrying flower bouquets, craning their necks to see their loved ones. The passengers looked down from the various decks to try and make eye and voice contact with their parties. Calling and shouting became so loud that nobody could understand anything that was said, but not a soul cared.

Jenny was a little nervous the morning before docking when she dressed Meagen and herself. In the eight months of their separation much had changed, and this was the moment she would present their daughter to her father. How would he look; would he have changed? And she—she had longed for him many months and now they would be together.

Standing at the railing with Meagen in her arms, she searched for Ian, but didn't see him. A sudden panic gripped her. What if Ian didn't know that they had arrived and wouldn't be here? Everything had happened so quickly from the moment she had received notification from the coast guard office at The Hague about the hoped-for, but still unexpected, sailing date. She had been assured that her husband would be informed and had written Ian right away, but she still felt uncertain. The gangways were lowered and a mob of greeters stormed on board. To avoid being trampled, Jenny found it best to stay where she was. Ian would find her, she was sure.

Passengers were already leaving the ship, voices became more distant, and still Jenny stood there with beating heart. She felt Meagen stirring in her arms, as if the baby felt her wave of emotions. Where was Ian?

Then as if from afar, she heard her name called over the ship's intercom. "Will Mrs. Halls please come to the main dining room." This was repeated several times until Jenny realized they were calling her. Quickly she went to the room and noticed the chief purser, who waved at her. She walked over to him.

"Did you call me? What's going on? Where is my husband?" The chief purser did not reply but turned around to a coast guard officer and three military nurses. "This is Mrs. Halls."

The officer took a step forward. "Jenny Halls, welcome to the Indies. Ian is at sea and doesn't know you have arrived, but he will be here very soon." And with a big reassuring and charming smile he introduced himself. "I am Luc Ash, a colleague of your husband." He then introduced his three female companions as his 'friends'. The girls said hello and took care of Meagen right away, cuddling her. Tears filled Jenny's eyes. Ian was not here; where would she go and when would he come? And why were the nurses with Luc? She collected herself, and seeing that Meagen was in good hands, turned to him.

"I remember Ian wrote about you and your daily trips to Onrust. Thank you for coming, because I haven't the slightest idea what to do now." Luc had always boasted that he was at his best with young attractive women in distress. This was an opportunity to show off and he didn't hesitate to put Jenny at ease.

"No problem at all. We have transportation at the ready and will bring you and the baby to Nautica. Mrs. Hulscher, the mess lady, has arranged a room for you."

He arranged for her luggage to be picked up and they all left the ship, heading for a waiting light truck equipped with benches. Jenny took the more comfortable seat next to the driver with Meagen on her lap. On their way to Nautica, Luc, from the rear of the truck, did his best to act as a tour guide, explaining the various points of interest when they reached the city. What he didn't explain, however, was why he had three nurses in tow, and Jenny decided she would ask Ian about the escort.

Upon arrival at the mess, Mrs. Hulscher greeted her with open arms and that made Jenny feel almost as if she were home from a long trip. Of course, Meagen received attention from everyone, including the servants. Jenny and Mrs. Hulscher established a bond very quickly, almost like mother and daughter. Since Jenny was the first family arrival for the coast guard in the mess, she got the largest bedroom, close to the dining and living areas, and soon had Meagen and herself installed.

And now, after their reunion, Jenny was on the veranda with Mrs. Hulscher and the baby enjoying coffee. Meanwhile, Ian had arrived at headquarters and was ushered to see Mr. Werff, who greeted him with congratulations on the safe arrival of his family.

"I hope that the accommodations in Nautica are satisfactory for the time being?" Ian thought of the way Jenny and Mrs. Hulscher were together.

"Oh, yes, no problem there. It is good that our daughter is very young, otherwise she would be a spoiled brat in no time!"

"Well, I am glad. As you know, your family is the first to arrive here, and proper housing is still a problem in Batavia, so this was the best solution." This matter dealt with, Officer Werff informed him that he would get five days furlough and then go back to the *Albatros,* which would then be at a second island to unload vehicles. Thereafter she would sail to Tandjoeng Priok to discharge the balance of the cargo.

"And then you will receive further orders. Does your wife speak Malay?"

"I don't think so unless she has studied it somewhat while in Holland."

Ian had a twinkle in his eyes when he thought about it. Good gracious, you don't discuss that on the first night. Mr. Werff seemed to read his thoughts, coughed, and said to him, "Off you go. I will keep in touch."

Ian did not hesitate to follow that order, he saluted and took a bedja. Arriving at Nautica, he told Jenny what his sailing orders were.

"Five long days! Great! We will use every minute of it," she declared, and then thought about Luc.

"By the way, did you arrange something with nurses?"

"Nurses? What are you talking about?"

She told him, and Ian had a big laugh.

"You know, Luc is always quite occupied with one nurse, and no doubt he found it a good idea to arrange for a sort of female welcome for you. So he probably asked her and some of her colleagues to come with him."

The five days were like a honeymoon and too soon it was time to say good-bye, although not for long. Back on board the LST, Ian heard from the other officers how they had fared on Billiton.

"They were not as lucky as you are," one colleague told him. The long exasperating journey for the families on the slow-moving freighter caused tempers to flare. The vessel was not properly equipped for carrying passengers, and accommodations were rather spartan. Many chores, such as preparing food, cleaning toilets, and doing general laundry had to be done by the passengers. The wives of company employees in the upper echelons refused to perform the more menial tasks and the ladies whose husbands were lower on the totem pole became upset. The children also became victims of the situation, not knowing to which side they belonged.

The situation drove the captain crazy, and after talks with the parties involved led nowhere, he ordered the purser to make up a list of tasks to be done by rotation of the women regardless of employee ranking.

He had called everyone concerned to a meeting, announced his verdict, and added the warning that if he was not satisfied with their performance, he would send an explanatory radio message to the president of the company in Holland.

With a smile he finished, "So, ladies, it is up to you all to make life onboard bearable. I don't want to hear any more complaints and the purser will report to me if there are still problems. Thank you for your consideration."

When the vessel finally arrived in the roads west of the island, the first joy of reunion changed quickly into remembrance of what had happened. There was much complaining about that demanding trip. The employees had quite a task on their hands soothing their wives' feelings of animosity against others in the small community. So his colleagues told Ian he was lucky, although late, to see his family in harmony.

It took them only a couple of days to deliver the rolling stock to the army and then the *Albatros* sailed for Batavia, their final destination. The third officer, who had worked diligently under direct orders of the captain, had recorded the inventory of the bounty they had collected from the U.S. ships in Subic Bay. He was now bombarded by the others questioning what each share was going to be.

Captain Bakker had instructed him to divide whatever there was equally among the officers, including himself. Never before on board a marine vessel was there such a popular third officer and he was lucky to be able to refer to captain's orders whenever another officer tried to obtain priority for special treasured items. Lists per person were issued to each participant and became the focus of discussions in the mess room.

Some tried to exchange unwanted articles on their lists for other items. With his newfound authority, the third officer turned down each approach.

"If you fellows don't like canned vegetables or shoe laces, that's too bad. Change it with somebody else when your stuff is ashore. But not now."

That settled it, and when the *Albatros* docked, there was no dispute on that topic since they all were eager to go ashore after their long stay in the Philippines.

Meanwhile Jenny had, on occasion, talked with Luc who still resided in Nautica and when she learned that the *Albatros* was due to arrive in port, she asked him whether she could go to the harbor. Luc looked at her.

"Okay, I'll try and fix transportation."

"But this time, no nurses please." Both laughed, understanding each other perfectly.

When the day came, she noticed a senior officer climbing out of a jeep, asking for Mrs. Halls. It was First Officer Werff, whom she met for the first time. He told her that the *Albatros* was due to arrive any moment and he would take her to the port. Meagen was quickly bundled up and they left. On the way to the harbor they had a good conversation and Werff told her about his family.

The *Albatros* was moored when they arrived and Jenny, assisted by Werff, came onboard. Ian, who was finishing up on the fore-ship, noticed her and Meagen waiting aft, and after last instructions to the boatswain, came to them. They embraced, he cuddled their daughter, and led them to his hut. Shortly thereafter he was called to the captain's cabin, where he found the skipper and Mr. Werff. Captain Bakker addressed him.

"Ian, the *Albatros* will stay in port for another three weeks, and during that time you will be the officer in charge. Thereafter Mr. Werff twisted my arm by telling me that he needs you for another job. I don't like to let you go, because you know the ship and have carried out your various duties very well."

His last words were accompanied with a wink. Both understood what he meant.

"Thank you sir. I am sorry to leave the *Albatros*." Then he turned to the personnel officer.

"Can you tell me what the other job is?"

Mr. Werff told him that the commanding officer on a patrol vessel stationed on Billiton had to be relieved for health reasons.

"You will be the next commanding officer. You and your family are to fly to Tandjoeng Pandan on Billiton when the *Albatros* is ready to leave. Housing will be arranged." Not fully comprehending what it all entailed, Ian took his leave and told Jenny the newest development. They had many questions in their mind and no answers.

"Anyway, it is a promotion for me and from what I know of the island, there are no guerrilla actions there."

Jenny looked at him and mockingly saluted. "Yes, commanding officer, sir, at your orders!"

Ian shared his daily travel to the port with others, including Luc, who seemed to have a never ending contract for the daily Onrust run. Each afternoon Ian returned to the mess; his duty was considered a soft job.

Jenny busied herself during daytime studying Malay and being coached by Mrs. Hulscher on how to run a household in the tropics.

Two days after the *Albatros* had arrived in port a truck pulled up in the Nautica driveway. The third officer stepped out and asked for Mrs. Halls. She was feeding the baby, so Mrs. Hulscher came to him and asked what his errand was. He explained to her that it was Mr. Halls' share of the goodies from Subic Bay. She assumed that Ian was sending his belongings ashore and told him to put it in the corridor to the Halls' bedroom. He looked at her and shook his head.

"Can't do, lady. There is too much."

Jenny had finished feeding the baby and came to them, asking what was going on. When it was explained, she said to go ahead and put the stuff, whatever it was, in their room. The third officer went to the truck, and four coolies jumped out and started to carry a great assortment of cartons to the room. The two women were speechless.

"Wait a minute, young man," ordered Mrs. Hulscher when she saw the continuing flow of packages.

"Well, I told you what it was," the third officer informed her, somewhat brusquely, and told the coolies to carry on.

Soon the walls were covered with packages, stacked six feet high. "Good heavens, I have no idea what this is. Ian hasn't told me." Mrs. Hulscher was clearly upset, so Jenny added, "And I am going to ask him in no uncertain terms for an explanation when he comes home tonight."

Ian got a cool reception when he returned that afternoon and Jenny asked him to come to their room, while Mrs. Hulscher hovered somewhat behind. He stepped into the room and stopped, seeing the spectacle. Then it dawned upon him that he had clearly forgotten to tell both women. Oh brother, he thought, how am I going to get out of this one. There is a storm brewing and this looks like a mess. He turned around to face the music.

"It is all my fault. I had so much on my mind that I completely forgot to tell you. Moreover, I had no idea it would be so much."

Jenny, feeling Mrs. Hulscher's presence, was forced to keep up a very determined reaction.

"You see what you created: a mess here. Mrs. Hulscher won't tolerate it. Get rid of the stuff, whatever it is."

The mess lady had, in her heart, already forgiven Ian and interrupted. "Now, wait a minute you two. I see that this, what you call stuff, is mostly canned food. I also know that on Billiton there is still rationing and not much to buy other than the basic essentials. So, as an exemption to the rules of the house, let it stay and ship it to the island as soon as possible. You'll need it there."

Both Jenny and Ian were surprised at the unexpected turn of events and Ian expressed their appreciation. "Thank you very much. I will have it all packed and shipped before we leave." They both went into the room and when they looked at the heaps of packages with their bed and Meagen's crib next to them they couldn't contain their laughter. Mrs. Hulscher, who wasn't far away yet, heard them and smiled. Those two will go a long way, she thought.

By now, more families were arriving and the mess became crowded. The housing in Batavia was still a problem and many houses were divided to accommodate more than one family. Air conditioning was non-existent and subdividing a house meant that the natural air flow was disrupted. The effect in the tropical heat was predictable and the demand for fans skyrocketed. Although they didn't know what it would look like on Billiton, Jenny and Ian began looking forward to leaving.

When that day came, they bade farewell to Mrs. Hulscher and went to the airport. The plane to Billiton and a number of other islands was, as usual, a Dakota. There were no seats, just metal benches alongside with indents for your behind. And, of course, there was metal flooring. The plane took off with Jenny and Ian sitting close but not next to each other; Meagen was in a baby basket on the floor at Jenny's feet. They were about half way over the Java Sea when, with a bang, the cabin door flew open. A great surge of wind resulted, and to her horror, Jenny saw the basket begin sliding toward the open door. She screamed and managed to stop Meagen just in the nick of time. The steward rushed to the door and a crew member came to help him. They were unsuccessful in closing the door and cordoned the opening off with ropes.

Ian took Meagen in his arms, exchanged seats to sit next to Jenny, and comforted his stricken wife by holding her tight. The passengers were all shocked and the steward told them to keep their safety belts on, not to move, and to hold each other. The pilot announced that they were flying at minimum speed low over the water and that there was no immediate danger. The next half hour seemed to last forever until they finally landed on Billiton, which was the first stop. At the small primitive airport they were greeted by a gentleman who was the combination customs officer and harbor master. This one looked healthier than Jan Boers on Borneo, Ian noticed.

They went to the town of Tandjoeng Pandan, half an hour drive. Jenny had overcome the shock of almost seeing their child fall out of the plane and paid attention to the surroundings. They told the harbor master what had happened on the plane.

"You were lucky, indeed. I hope the rest of your stay with us will be a good one."

Their accommodation was a roomy house, which they had to share with the coast guard engineer stationed there. The situation was not ideal, but not bad either, and within a short time they had settled in the little town. Ian set out to sea to patrol the straits between Banka and Billiton, while Jenny went through the adventures of taking care of a growing baby, running a small household, and getting used to having domestic help. Food and clothing were still rationed, with only the basics available, and when "the Philippines collection," as they called it, arrived, they realized what a treasure it was. The cans were mostly in the same size, all painted dull green with the contents in small black lettering, which started to fade in the tropical humidity. So when they invited friends for dinner, it was always fun to decide what they would have. They stayed away from the everyday monotonous fare. A can was shaken; if there was liquid it could be any kind of vegetable, but if it was dry, it was anybody's guess. Such dinner parties became well-known for their hilarity.

According to veterans, life was almost the same as it had been before the war on outposts like Billiton. There were a couple of hundred Europeans in Tandjoeng Pandan, consisting of people who worked in government branches, mining, and on shipping companies' staff, as well as in a smattering of other private enterprises. The military were stationed in the center of the island.

Ian found that for the first time in many years his life was almost, but not quite, settling into a routine. He captured some smuggling craft, patrolled around the two islands, and was on good terms with the harbor master. Family life was great, especially when measured on the basis of being a marine officer without extended stays at sea. At times he wondered how long this could last; he didn't wonder too long. They had been on Billiton less than a year when another order arrived.

Chapter Twenty

The harbor master handed him the message from Mr. Werff without any comment, but watched Ian to see his reaction. Ian read it and then asked him, "Where is Tandjoeng Pinang?" All those tandjoengs, which is Malay for cape, made it confusing for him.

The harbor master smiled and told him that it was the capital of the Rhio Archipelago, a large number of smaller islands south of Singapore. "Why do you ask?"

"I am being transferred to that place as commanding officer of a minesweeper stationed there," replied Ian without too much enthusiasm.

The harbor master raised his eyebrows. "Congratulations, Ian. It is one of the most desirable locations for a coast guard officer."

Ian learned that, although it was part of the Dutch East Indies, the going currency was the Singapore dollar instead of the rupiah. Also, it was a free port like Singapore, meaning no import duties and plenty of imported goods and appliances at low prices. In short, a choice assignment!

In the message Mr. Werff had said that a letter with more details would follow. By now Ian had evaluated the background information and realized that again the transfer was a promotion to a more livable area with command of a bigger ship. He rushed to Jenny and told her the good news. They looked into an atlas to find out the exact location of their destination. Ian, remembering his first short stay in Singapore, found that Tandjoeng Pinang was not far from that big city, so maybe they could go there occasionally.

Jenny was elated hearing all this.

"Can I buy clothes there for Meagen and myself?" she asked, thinking of the rationed textiles and lack of clothing shops on Billiton. This question was out of Ian's range of knowledge on such matters, but he said that no doubt there was such a possibility.

"I'll get some more information soon from headquarters."

Within a week, the orders arrived. His replacement would arrive in a month's time and thereafter he and his family would fly to Tandjoeng Pinang to take command of the coast guard vessel *Rian*. Ian would report to the harbor master there. Sailing orders would come via the latter, who carried a navy ranking. So this time there was no combination customs officer and harbor master, Ian thought. Included in the orders was a short handwritten note from Mr. Werff.

"Ian, you performed very well with your command. Therefore, I do not hesitate to give you a larger vessel with a more important mission. Again, good luck and relay my best wishes to Jenny. I am sure you three will like it there."

During the weeks waiting for his replacement they got additional appetite-whetting bits of information from friends who had been there. One evening when Ian was in port, they discussed the move and looked at each other.

"Let's not go overboard. It all sounds so damned nice that it is too good to be true," Ian said. But then he stood up, took Jenny in his arms, and danced around the room while singing a popular tune. His voice awakened Meagen, who started to cry. He took her up and the three rolled around on the floor.

Panting from all the acrobatic excitement, Jenny suddenly remarked, "I wish our parents could see us right now."

"Oh boy, don't get homesick, my love," Ian replied, and there they were sitting on the floor, trying to picture their parents and other family in faraway Holland.

"Okay, that's enough. We'll celebrate this moment with your homemade egg brandy," Ian said, and got up to get glasses and the bottle. Looking into each others' eyes over the rims of the glasses filled with thick yellow liquid, they toasted each other, the baby, family, Werff, and the whole bloody world.

His replacement arrived with his family, who were all glad to get out of Batavia, and they camped for a few days together with the Halls. The transfer of the command didn't take long. Jenny donated the last remaining cans of the Philippines treasure to the colleague's wife, belongings were packed, and with a farewell to friends, they went to the airport. This time the plane they boarded was a Catalina amphibious. Tandjoeng Pinang had no airport so they had to land in the bay.

After a scheduled landing on another island they headed for their destination. Peering through the porthole-like windows, they saw the town below. There were hills, a military encampment, a European quarter, and extensive areas with native buildings. Then the Catalina swooped down onto the bay and taxied to a mooring amidst gushes of water.

Ian took Meagen and they climbed into a motorboat which brought the passengers to the jetty. The harbor master, a well-proportioned, jovial gentlemen, welcomed them.

"Hello, glad to see you. My name is Dick Fransen, but call me Frans, please." Not a bad start, thought Ian, and introduced Jenny to him, apologizing that Meagen didn't smile at him.

"Don't worry about that; it will change when she is growing up."

Jenny liked the man at first sight, mainly because he didn't show off his seniority and was more casual than the harbor master they had met before. They walked to the shore and entered the harbor office where Frans called for iced tea.

"Too early for a drink," he grumbled. Turning to Ian, he continued, "I told you that I was glad to see you, and that is a fact. Your predecessor on the Rian had to leave rather unexpectedly and we have a busy schedule here. As a matter of fact, the *Rian* should sail tomorrow."

The last words were accompanied with a teasing smile when he noticed the reaction on Jenny's face. She tossed the ball in his court by remarking, "Why not tonight?"

Ian felt somewhat uncomfortable about the sparring between the two, which was more like establishing the lay of the land. But Frans took the challenge in good humor.

"Okay, lady, that's one for you. Now maybe you'd like to see your accommodations?"

Jenny smiled sweetly. "It happens that I thought about that, too."

After a short walk they were shown a brick house. Housing was still in short supply, necessitating that the house be split to accommodate two families. Nevertheless, their half was pretty comfortable, and Jenny told Ian so. When parting, Frans told them that he had arranged for the servants to come the next day and present themselves. Hearing the plural of the word, she asked, "How many servants are you talking about?"

"Well, I think three or four. I'm not sure. They sort of come with the house." And with that he left the young couple, asking Ian to see him the next day.

As was usual at that time in the Indies, houses owned or requisitioned by the government were fully furnished to avoid employees having to ship their furniture and other bulky possessions all over the archipelago. Everybody traveled light. They were still unpacking when a clerk from the harbor office came with a cash advance of Singapore dollars.

The next morning Ian went to the office. Frans called his driver and they went to a small dock where the *Rian* was moored. It was a larger type of minesweeper than he had commanded before, and he liked the appearance. With a feeling of pride, he stepped on board and was greeted by the petty officers, who were introduced by Frans. He got a cursory tour of the ship for a first impression; there would be plenty of time for all the ins and outs later.

After returning to the port office, Frans gave him an outline of his duties. The main item on his roster would be guarding against infiltration of guerrillas from the big island of Sumatra into the Rhio Archipelago, the east coast of Sumatra being very close. Secondary items included placing the *Rian* at the disposal of the governor and other officials when not occupied on more urgent missions; transporting troops between the islands; and taking bunkers in Singapore. The secondary activities were new to Ian, and the last one intrigued him especially.

"Why taking bunkers in Singapore, which is outside the Indies?" he wondered.

"Well, I'll tell you later. At the moment your bunkers are full and the ship ready to sail." Then looking at a planning board, Frans continued. "Tomorrow morning you and I are expected to meet the governor and his staff. Thereafter I'll introduce you to the army garrison staff. The Royal Dutch Navy has an operating base on our island, one hour sailing from here. One day you will have to go there and introduce yourself. They know you have taken command of the *Rian*." His secretary brought him telephone slips and papers, and looking at them with a weary eye, he sighed and dismissed Ian.

It was lunchtime and he walked the short distance to his home to see how his family was doing. Jenny saw him coming, fished Meagen from the playpen and greeted him rather formally. Ian was surprised but did not ask why the formality. Instead he took his daughter, who was more than one year old by now, and tossed her high up in the air. She loved it and made all kinds of happy noises. Ian took her on his arm while Jenny whispered in his ear that there were two ladies inside with whom she had gone shopping. Aha, Ian thought, there hasn't been any time lost. The two women were the wives of other coast guard officers; one was married to the engineer stationed ashore and the other to an officer commanding another minesweeper, also stationed in Tandjoeng Pinang.

Jenny told him about her tour of the town under the guidance of the two women. "This place is much bigger than the other one where we were. And you should see the view from the hill. It's beautiful. Islands as far as you can see. And the shops are unbelievable . . . crowded with merchandise like before the war. Chinese own the shops and they all speak English. And, and ..." They were all laughing at Jenny's enthusiasm when they were interrupted by a little woman dressed in Javanese clothing. "Oh, I forgot, Ian. This is Fia, our cook. Her husband is Anjoeng, who cleans the house. And then we have a Chinese amah who does the laundry, and her daughter Amoy. I don't know what she does. And isn't it nice, Fia speaks Dutch." You rascal, thought Ian, you have it all nicely arranged on such short notice. In his heart he admired her and compared her still rosy European appearance with the seasoned tropical complexion of the other two.

After a while the two ladies took their leave and the Halls family had its first lunch in the new house. Ian told her about his experience that morning, going lightly over the patrolling part and the fact that the jungles of Sumatra were close by. The day she learned about the situation, which officially was called a "police action" but in reality was a vicious war, would come soon enough. And although they didn't touch much on the subject, both knew what was going on in general in the Indies and that worldwide the resistance against colonization was gaining strength.

The next morning Ian was introduced to a host of functionaries in various departments, from governor to the lower echelons; the military; and the heads of the local Chinese community. Having satisfied the exigencies of protocol, Frans and Ian went to the Chinese restaurant, which functioned as a clubhouse for the European population. They settled in easy chairs in the cool room and enjoyed a beer. "We now have gone through the official hoopla, and you are officially recognized."

They had lunch in the clubhouse while talking about the town and its inhabitants and in general about the waters in the archipelago.

After lunch, Frans rose. "Let us go to my office and discuss your itinerary; it is nobody's business and listening ears are everywhere." In the office Ian got the call sign of the *Rian* and the hours receiving and transmitting radio messages were permitted. Frans pulled out a number of detailed sea charts and together they went over them. "There is a maze of channels, and my assistant has marked all those which have sufficient water under the keel for you to navigate." Ian looked at the markings and noticed that there was not much open sea; it would be mainly navigating on sight. The *Rian* was not equipped with radar, which precluded sailing on dark nights.

"I'd like you to cover the territory for two weeks as your reconnaissance. Call at the various military outposts on the islands to get acquainted with the officers. Some are interesting characters." Frans' last words were accompanied by a broad grin.

"Is there anything special about my crew members I should know about?" Ian asked. He had noticed he was the only European on board.

"They are all natives. Your second in command, as well as the petty officers, are well qualified for their job, and your second knows every spot where you can go and anchor for the night. The entire crew is trustworthy."

Two days after this discussion, the *Rian* left the harbor. Jenny and Meagen were on the pier waving good-bye. The *Rian's* top speed, at fourteen knots, was not bad for a minesweeper rebuilt for patrolling and carrying passengers.

Ian was now fully conversant in Malay, which was a necessity since only his two engineers spoke Dutch. Jalim, his second in command, was a man of few words but knew his business. Part of their swing around led very close to the densely overgrown east coast of Sumatra, and although there was no sign of life or building in sight, Jalim suggested taking the covers from the ship's guns and holding them on standby. Ian agreed and the gun crews manned the pivoting platforms.

As before, Ian found it remarkable that one part of the population was fully devoted to the Dutch cause, while the other part was fighting against it. Then he remembered that during the occupation by the Germans one couldn't trust his own landsmen, not knowing whether they were collaborators. The situation in the Indies was not exactly the same, but being so close to guerrilla-held territory meant that he had no choice but to trust his crew. It would be easy for them to overpower him and 'join the other side' with a highly valued prize. Putting these thoughts aside, he scanned the hostile coast.

Before nightfall, they reached an island close to the coast of Sumatra, navigated through a narrow channel, and came alongside a primitive wooden dock. Sentries of the garrison helped with the mooring lines and as soon as the ship's telegraph was on "stop" three army officers came on board, saluted the flag, and introduced themselves to Ian. They were seated on the sloop deck behind Ian's cabin, and the mess boy came topside with bottles of beer, which were greeted appreciatively by the officers. Lively talk followed, giving Ian a clear understanding of life close to the enemy, with no entertainment to speak of.

Ian looked at the trio. These three could very well be the characters Frans had mentioned. After another round of beers they stood up and invited Ian to come with them and have dinner. They had to walk through a forest and climb up a small hill on top of which were the simple garrison buildings, surrounded by a palisade of pointed bamboo poles. The sentry at the entrance asked for the password before letting them in.

The first lieutenant asked the sentry, who snapped to attention, if all was quiet and when this was confirmed they went to the officers' quarters. Another round of libation was followed by an excellent dinner of rice with numerous side dishes, all very spicy. After coffee, Ian made a move to leave, but was halted by Captain Jon Hartman, the garrison commander.

"What is your hurry, man? Somebody stowed away in your hut?"

The other two joined in. "Yeah, there must be something hidden on board. We must search the ship."

Ian envisioned the spectacle of such a drastic move and had no intention of letting it happen. "Okay you guys, under one condition. I will have the right to search with my men the entire bloody compound."

"Wow, spoken as a true saltwater hand. Let's forego the searches." With those words the three toasted the Dutch Coast Guard and its servants. Ian fell in with toasting the gallant officers of the Royal Dutch Indies Army, KNIL for short.

A feeling of companionship was established, and they asked Ian to tell about his time during the war in Holland. He went briefly through that period and his escapades and when he finished there was silence. The three army men, who had spent years in Japanese POW camps and were drafted into service right after liberation, had not been in Holland for a long time. They envisioned the conditions of life there and in their minds reminisced about their own entirely different and horrible experience.

"But at least you were among our own people," Jon remarked.

"That is right," admitted Ian. "But after the Germans came it didn't take long to learn that you could not trust anybody whom you didn't know. There were your own landsmen who helped catch others who resisted the enemy forces. The collaborators were comparatively small in numbers but wielded great power under the German umbrella."

"We were worlds apart," Captain Jon put their thoughts into words and then cited Kipling: "East is East and West is West, and never the twain shall meet."

The first lieutenant broke the somber spell and told Ian about what he called a minor problem they had encountered not so long ago. Being lonely in this place they had arranged with a local fisherman who regularly called at Singapore to bring from there three nice Chinese women. This was done, with only a small variation: the man brought four ladies instead.

"The bugger apparently reckoned one as reserve," the lieutenant grumbled, and continued. "We had some misunderstanding amongst our three how to divide our entertainment, and it resulted in a melee where the *Rian* also became involved, and . . ."

Here he was interrupted by Jon. "There ensued some shooting and it happened when the *Rian* was here. They thought that we were attacked and started firing their guns over the hill. We believed that the *Rian* was attacked, and it took us a damned long time until it was settled." Ian could not hold his laughter, and soon the others joined. "But what is your minor problem?"

"Your predecessor and I agreed to enter the happening in our log books as an enemy attack without casualties. However, our Chinese guests, when they returned to Singapore, made waves and accused us of harassment. We don't know whether they went to our embassy in Singapore and we haven't heard anything since." It was agreed that if Ian heard of the affair upon his return to Tandjoeng Pinang, he would let them know.

Meanwhile it was growing late and this time he wished his hosts goodnight.

"Come onboard tomorrow morning for a real breakfast" were his parting words. That night there was no shooting and all was quiet. Ian was up early and ordered breakfast prepared for four, which sent the cook scurrying. At 0700 hours, the three guests promptly reported for duty, as they called it. The gusto with which the excellent breakfast was honored did not deserve to be considered 'duty'. The other lieutenant, who was not so outspoken as his two superiors, surprised the others by asking Ian if he had heard of the Tandjoeng Pinang amateur theater group? Ian hadn't, pointing out that he had been there only a week. "Why do you ask?"

"We have been digging a hole for a swimming pool and now the cement has been poured. Within a month our pool should be ready. For the official opening with ribbon cutting, etc., we thought we would invite the group and give a performance. The pool, by mutual consent, will be named 'The Virgin.' And that creates another minor problem." His face was a picture of innocence, which made Ian uncomfortable.

"You fellows are full of minor problems, it appears. What is it this time?"

"Well, how do we find out who is a virgin? Because that is the one to cut the ribbon and make the first splash."

Jon looked at his junior man admiringly. "Very well put. Can we find one virgin from the theater group?"

They talked among themselves, mentioning names of unmarried females, and there were not many candidates. Ian expected that this topic, with all its far-reaching implications, could be discussed for hours.

"All right, my friends, I have to leave you with your headaches and imagination. Don't expect me to go search for your virgin. And now you are cordially invited to leave this bottom; we sail in half an hour."

They parted as good friends, and the *Rian* was on her way to another settlement. Ian thought about the three officers he had just left behind. No doubt they were characters and no doubt excellent men on hard duty who had the need to blow off steam occasionally, otherwise they would go bonkers.

The *Rian* continued the sweep through the archipelago. Ian had the opportunity to become familiar with the waters and was confident that there would be no problem completing the balance of his three-year contract in this area. By now he had served half his time. Ian had radioed his day and time of arrival at the home port and found Jenny waiting for him on the jetty with Meagen. As always, the reunion was great and Ian noticed with satisfaction that his family was doing very well.

194

Chapter Twenty-One

Life in town was more active than they were used to on Billiton. There were parties given by the government and the military, card games in the club house, tennis, and swimming. Jenny had a good time and Meagan was growing up to be a very healthy and good-looking girl. She was, her parents felt, only a little bit spoiled. Whenever Ian was in port, they got invitations for private parties and soon had several friends. "Not too many," Jenny said. "Otherwise you hear too much or give reason to others to talk about you."

"You are a very wise woman," noted Ian. "You have learned your lesson on what to do and not to do. As long as I am your number one!"

"Well, I'll think about that," she teased him, adding, "Don't forget I am very attractive and you are often at sea."

That reminded him of a story he had just heard and he told it to Jenny.

"There was a young couple, he was a traveling salesman and she was feeling very lonesome. It didn't take very long until she became involved with another man. One late afternoon the salesman returned home days earlier than expected and they promptly made love to celebrate the occasion. He took her out for dinner and afterward they went to bed. The telephone rang. She thought, Oh my god, it may be him, but her husband was already in the living room and took the call. After agonizing moments for her, he returned to the bedroom. 'Who was it dear?' she asked, pretending not to be too anxious. 'Oh, somebody from the coast guard,' he said, getting into bed. 'The coast guard? What do they want calling us?' 'Well, a guy asked whether the coast was clear.'"

Jenny had listened with laughing eyes and in the end naughtily added, "Luckily we don't have a telephone." After those words they rolled around on their king-size bed, talking and laughing until Meagen started to call. During breakfast the next morning, a clerk from the governor's office came to the door, asking for Mr. Halls.

"Yes, I am Mr. Halls."

In rapid Malay the clerk told him that he had a message from the governor and handed Ian an envelope with the governor's seal. Ian thanked him, opened the envelope, and pulled out a letter. Still standing in the doorway, reading the message, he didn't say a word and sat down.

Jenny looked at him. "Aren't you going to tell me what it is, or is it very top secret?"

Ian put on his most serious expression, looking at her, and when he saw that his wife was almost going to explode, he grinned at her. "My darling, we are invited for dinner at the governor's mansion tomorrow night."

"Tomorrow night? I haven't heard there was a party. And I have nothing to wear."

Ian wisely didn't react to that typical female outburst and decided to leave for his ship and talk with Frans to ascertain that he would be in port that night. He bent over her and whispered in her ear. "Talk with Fia, maybe she knows what kind of dinner and how formal it is. Servants always know more than their masters."

Passing the port office on his way to the *Rian*, he dropped in and told Frans about the official invitation.

"Don't worry," Frans told him. "The governor's secretary asked me to keep the *Rian* in port for a few days. So it looks like you and Jenny will be the only two invited."

Ian wasn't sure how Frans arrived at that conclusion but took his word for it, still not knowing why they were asked. Well, whatever, he thought. It could do no harm for a young officer to meet on a more personal basis with the big boss.

Coming home for lunch, he told Jenny what Frans had said and she smiled sweetly at him. Not knowing what to think of that, he asked, "You smile like Mona Lisa. What is the reason behind it?"

"I only did, as a faithful, loving, caring wife, what you suggested. I talked with Fia." Apparently she had the same information as Ian, but with some additions concerning the dress.

"It is not a gala party, and I found something suitable to wear." When he heard that statement Ian sighed with relief. In his heart he was very proud of his wife and she had never given him any reason not to be. As additional information, Jenny told him that the governor's wife was in Holland because of poor health and that his niece was running the household for him. So that night, there would be the four of them.

The evening was a very pleasant one. The young couple was immediately put at ease by the governor, an aristocratic man with a refreshing sense of humor. His niece was a charming hostess and the conversation flowed easily. The mansion, like all old colonial houses, was very spacious with large open windows and high ceilings. It was situated on the water's edge with a magnificent view of the bay and the waters beyond. They were seated on the patio with their after-dinner drinks, enjoying the beauty of the tropical night and the bright stars.

When it was time to leave, the governor said, "Ian, I am glad you could be with us tonight, and I am sure we will see each other more frequently."

When they returned home, Jenny asked what the governor meant by his last words.

"At first I couldn't figure out why we were invited for dinner, but now I understand that he wanted to know us better." There must be another reason to it also, thought Jenny, but did not discuss it any further. She checked Meagen and thanked Fia for baby-sitting.

The next morning when Ian was on board the *Rian* talking with his chief engineer, a clerk from the port office came with the message that there would be a meeting in the office at 1400 hours. It sounded rather official, and when Ian entered the office he found several people gathered there already. Frans introduced him to the regional navy commander whom he had not met before, and thereafter Ian greeted the others. He noticed the army major and his adjutant; the lieutenant governor with one of his assistants; and for the first time, his colleague, the commanding officer of the other coast guard minesweeper stationed in Tandjoeng Pinang.

Frans chaired the meeting, letting the lieutenant governor begin.

"Recent reports from our people throughout the Rhio Archipelago and part of east Sumatra indicate that the guerrillas are gaining in strength. The possibility that they will soon try to infiltrate into our area is very real. The population and the industries in our region have to be protected against acts of sabotage as well as armed intimidation. This, gentlemen, requires a plan of action to be executed without delay, encompassing our civil service, the navy, coast guard, and the army."

At that moment there was a knock on the door and the chief of police entered, waved to everybody, and sat down. After this brief interruption Frans continued the meeting.

"This morning there have been separate meetings among the various services, and now we are gathered here to inform everybody on the general picture. Major, will you start please."

The major stated that several divisions had been sent from Holland and that the KNIL was now at full force. Rhio had received more troops and the time had come to give more assistance to the small garrisons holding several towns on islands close to Sumatra, as well as on Sumatra itself. The army lacked the sea transportation to do so. Next came the navy commander, who explained that the largest ships under his command were corvettes, suitable for patrolling the Straits of Malacca. Some smaller craft were used in more congested areas. All told, he felt confident in their ability to keep the situation under control for the time being.

Frans explained that the coast guard had two minesweepers and six Higgins craft, small unarmed boats with very shallow draft, which could carry up to eighteen men. The lieutenant governor closed, saying the police force had been put on alert. The governor's office would act as central command post and all actions would be coordinated there.

The functionaries dispersed and Frans asked his two commanding officers to stay.

"Your bottoms will be used mainly for troop transporting whenever needed. Exception, to a degree, will be the *Rian*; she has more cabins and therefore is more suitable to be put at the disposal of the civil service. Gentlemen, keep your vessels at the ready so that you can sail on short notice. Thank you."

"I figure that you should go to Singapore for bunkering, so that you are ready for the next mission," Frans told Ian. "Your second, Jalim, knows the procedure. For your information, you may expect that several wives of dignitaries will take the opportunity to go shopping, and I am afraid my wife will be one of them." Then he gave Ian more details, such as that usually the *Rian* would stay for two nights at anchor near the navy pier, and that he would get diplomatic mail to hand deliver to the Dutch Embassy.

On a more personal basis, Frans handed him an envelope with money. "This is for emergency, if my wife is spending more than she plans, but don't tell her."

Oh, brother, Ian thought. Now I am becoming a guardian of a number of ladies and I have to act like the smiling captain on a cruise ship.

"Can I go also?" Jenny begged when Ian told her the story.

"For heaven's sake, women on board is bad enough, but no way babies, too."

"Do not worry, sailor. I heard about it from the wife of the shore engineer. She is not going this time and would love to have Meagen for a couple of days, so, can I?"

Women, Ian pondered. At times they are a royal pain and hit you in the soft underbelly, and at other times they sing as sweetly as a nightingale. No wonder Adam ran into grave trouble in Paradise.

"Okay," he gave in, for lack of a reason not to. "But I have business to attend to, so you are on your own."

"I won't be alone. I'll go together with some of the other ladies I talked with."

When the *Rian* was ready to sail, several husbands, whose wives were also going, took Ian aside, gave him the same message as Frans had done before, and handed him envelopes. Although this was done in a covert way, Ian doubted the women were unaware of the 'emergency' funds. He put the stuff in a small safe in his hut, went to the bridge, and told Jalim to give one blast on the horn as a signal that they were leaving. There were eight passengers, including Jenny, and after they said hello to Ian they gathered on the sloop deck, talking a mile a minute during the five-hour trip.

Proceeding slowly inside the breakwater near the navy pier, the *Rian* was followed by fast-rowing Chinese in their sampans. Their small boats served as water taxis. The *Rian* anchored, the gangway was lowered to water level, and the rush was on.

Jenny also was in a hurry to get ashore and gave him a fleeting "see you later" and jumped into a sampan. Ian eyed the little flotilla and wondered whether some would stay in a hotel or come back on board. He also wondered when his wife would re-appear.

Some crew members asked permission to go ashore, and he asked Jalim to make a list for shore leave. An oil barge was ordered for the next day and Ian decided to go ashore himself to deliver the diplomatic pouch at the embassy. When he returned on board, there still was no Jenny. Late in the afternoon she and three other ladies arrived, carrying packages and claiming that they were very thirsty. The other four stayed in a hotel, they told him.

That evening they all went to the newly opened, first high-rise building in Singapore, the Cathay, which included a movie theater. The film *Gaslight* was shown. The air conditioning in the theater, a novelty at that time, was set way too low and the four women were shivering in their light dresses. Ian had the time of his life when they came as close as possible to him for warmth. The next day the ladies decided to take in more educational sights and visit the orchid gardens, the Tiger Balm Park, and even a museum. Ian was impressed with such outpouring of noble intentions. He couldn't go himself but wished the adventurers a good time.

Departure was set for the following day at noon sharp and he heard his passengers talking about a last roundup shopping spree. Most probably that would be the time for the envelopes, he reckoned. Jenny had bought clothes and female things for Meagen and herself, and was elated being in Singapore. There were only two requests for a loan, one by Frans' wife, who winked at him knowingly when stating that she was sure it wouldn't be a problem. Shortly before noon, with the engine on standby, Ian looked toward the navy pier to see whether two missing women were coming. At noon he ordered the gangway hauled and the anchor weighed.

Jenny came rushing to him. "You can't leave them here. Wait. I am sure they have a good reason for being just a little bit late."

"Time is set; no excuses."

"But the weather has become nasty, with rain and wind."

"Don't give me a weather forecast, Jenny. I'm aware of it." He didn't tell her that he had ordered only that the anchor cable be shortened, so that it would take only a moment to weigh the anchor. Finally, almost half an hour late, the pair came in sight, waving and calling. There was no time to lose, he had to enter the unlit narrow channel to Tandjoeng Pinang before dark, so he ordered the anchor weighed, steaming dead slow ahead and put a rope ladder over the side.

The *Rian* started moving slowly, and the sampan rower worked madly to deliver his passengers alongside. Even within the breakwater the waters had become choppy, the sampan couldn't speed up and Ian was forced to stop the engine. Finally the two women clambered up the ladder and immediately Ian ordered Jalim to put the telegraph on full ahead, leaving the sampan in the wake. From astern there was shouting.

Jalim ran aft and came back to the bridge. "Sir, the sampan oarsman hasn't been paid yet." Ian cursed under his breath, yanked the telegraph back to stop, fished a ten-dollar bill out of his pocket, and told Jalim to go aft and hand it over. Meanwhile, he had to go slow and stop, to avoid colliding with other anchored craft and keep the rudder responding. Again back on full ahead, the *Rian* had cleared the breakwater and course was set for home port.

Lucky we have a while when the current is with us, and then dead tide, so there will be no current. What fun with such a party on board, he thought grimly. But then he found his sense of humor, told Jalim to take over, and went to the mess room where his passengers were gathered. Packaging materials were strewn all over, and with great gaiety, everybody was showing everybody else what was bought. When he entered there was a sudden painful silence. The two later arrivals stood up, uncertain how he would react.

"We are so sorry, sir. We had a hairdresser appointment, but it took much longer than said, and then we couldn't get a sampan, and . . ."

Ian raised his hand to stop the flow of words. Looking very sternly, he said, "I am afraid I have to charge each of you a fine of $200 for having delayed a coast guard vessel for more than an hour and exposing said vessel to grave dangers of collision in congested waters."

Their mouths fell open and wide-eyed in panic they looked wordlessly at him. Then he grinned.

"Okay, this time it will not be reported. I am just joking. But next time, be there promptly." He winked at Jenny, who responded with a big smile, and before returning to the bridge, he added, "By the way, you can call me Ian."

A short while later Frans' wife came up to the bridge. "You really have it made, Ian. You could be a diplomat, and be certain the word will go around. On your next trip to Singapore you may expect even more passengers!"

"Oh no," exclaimed Ian in disgust. "Next time, we'll keep it secret." The lady smiled knowingly and returned to the mess room.

They just made it before dark and the various husbands and children were there for welcome. The envelope business was taken care of the next day to everybody's satisfaction.

Chapter Twenty-Two

A KNIL colonel with his detachment had arrived at Tandjoeng Pinang by packet-boat and the *Rian* was scheduled to transport the troop to the Sumatra mainland. The destination was not disclosed. A special army radio station was installed and the cabins occupied by the colonel and his staff. Frans handed Ian sea charts of the Sumatra east coast and told him that during the operation the ship's radio was not to be used. The colonel would be in command, but Ian, as skipper, was responsible for the safety of his crew and ship. In combinations like this, there is a fine line between responsibilities and duties, as both men knew. As if reading his thoughts, Frans could not do better than to express his full support of Ian.

"You will see that the colonel is reasonable and I trust that you'll keep your ass clean! Your sealed orders will be handed to you just before departure; open them when out of port."

That night Ian had to stay on board, which was a strange situation being in home port close to but separated from his family. Jenny understood what was asked of him. When he was leaving her and Meagen they clung to each other speechlessly. Words were unnecessary between them.

It was still dark the next morning when the troops came on board, occupying every available space on the main deck. Ian noticed that there were no heavy weapons in the outfit, but did not pay further attention. Gear and food were stowed in the forward hold and at first daylight the colonel told Ian they were ready to leave.

As he followed the channel to open water Ian opened his orders. He had to follow a course which did not lead directly to the town on the east coast, but in a roundabout way, obviously to mislead enemy eyes, which could be everywhere.

The colonel came to the bridge. "I have ordered my men to lay low during daytime. When we get close to our destination, there will be no cooking fires. We'll live on rations."

"Aye, sir. What is your preferred time of arrival?"

"I am told it will take less than forty hours to reach the destination. Correct?"

Ian told him that he knew about the routing and the destination. He would check and report to the colonel.

When he had gathered the requested information, he sent a sailor to the colonel with the message that he was ready; he did so purposefully to make the point that he was the skipper. The colonel came to the bridge and suggested that they go down to the mess room and talk out of earshot from the petty officer and the helmsman on the bridge. Ian told him that his crew was trustworthy and that he preferred to remain.

The colonel looked at him and smiled. "Okay, young man. I see your point." Then he turned more serious. "It is your head you put at risk if there is a leak. But this is not the time to start nit-picking; we have to pull this off together." Ian felt relieved it was settled and the two went to the charts.

The colonel explained the plan of action. The town they were heading for was located at a wide sea strait protected from the weather by a number of small islands. There had been a contingent of troops there, which were apparently overrun by the enemy and never heard of since. The plan of action was to approach it from one side, staying four to five miles away, drop half of the soldiers, then turn around to open sea and repeat the maneuver from the other side. That part of the operation had to be concluded before daybreak.

It was close to full moon, which was helpful for navigating with all lights off. The colonel showed Ian some aerial photos of the town and surroundings. There were no beaches anywhere and the coastline was overgrown with mangrove.

He called Jalim and brought his second up to date on the plan. Jalim confirmed that he had been there before, and after looking at the photographs and the chart said that, weather permitting, it could be done.

"How close can we come to the shore?" asked Ian.

"Pretty close; there is plenty of water and the bottom is mainly mud."

The colonel grunted with satisfaction and when Ian asked him how he would get his two parties ashore the answer was "By rubber dinghies. We will use your lifeboats to bring all other gear and food ashore when we have re-taken the town."

Toward dark the *Rian* was closing in on the coast near the entrance to the sea strait. The dinghies were inflated and ready to be pushed into the water from the low stern. It would take three trips to the shore to land half of the company, with two men in each to row back to the *Rian*. All lights were extinguished and the *Rian* moved inland at slow ahead. Everybody onboard was silent, commands were whispered, and tension was building.

Ian had placed Jalim forward to pilot the ship close to the shore when nearing the first drop-off point. Hours went by and it was close to 2300 hours when Jalim signaled to stop the engine. Ian used the speaking tube to the engine room since the ringing sound when using the telegraph could be heard quite a distance over the calm waters.

Soon the *Rian* was dead in the water, a grey ghost with only the sound of an occasional revolution of the propeller to keep her steerable. The moonlight filtered through high clouds sufficiently to guide the first party into the mangroves. Their path through the phosphorescent water was illuminated, but that could not be avoided.

Each landing party disappeared without a sound into the jungle, not even making a clatter of weapons. And then Ian realized that only the officer and his subalterns had pistols; all soldiers carried their klewang, a typical KNIL weapon like a machete. Ian shuddered when the significance dawned upon him.

The two dinghies returned from their last trip and were hauled on board, and again at slow ahead, the *Rian* returned to open water, rounded two islands, and moved cautiously inland. This time it took a while longer to find the second drop-off point.

"Damn it, man," the colonel whispered to Ian. "Can't you speed up? We are getting behind schedule."

Ian, with his eyes on Jalim in the bows, didn't even turn around, but hissed, "Shall I use the searchlight or the ship's horn?"

At the estimated four to five miles, the engine was stopped again and the landing maneuver repeated. This time the dinghies remained ashore. Ian turned to the colonel, asking curtly, "Now what?"

"Move slowly to the side of the strait opposite the town and hold the ship in that position at first daylight, but not before," the colonel said, and with these words he went below to his radio operator.

Ian felt he had to say something; he called Jalim to the bridge, instructing him to stay out of sight of the town. He went to the colonel. "Sorry, sir, but your remark came at a very inopportune moment."

The colonel, somewhat more relaxed now, looked at him. "Okay, let us both forget it. I was on pins and needles, too." Thereafter he spoke softly to the operator and turned to Ian. "For your information, each group has a small hand-held transmitter, and when the two parties meet, we'll get the signal that the town has been encircled from the land side."

The next phase for the troops would begin at daylight to avoid calamities amongst their own, the colonel continued explaining to Ian. A small town like this is in the dark, and we know that there are only three buildings with one single generator power source. That is where the enemy troops are supposed to be, according to an infiltrator we sent there who returned alive. Also, according to that person, there were no survivors when our people were overrun, so there will be no mercy. Hearing all this, Ian again felt a cold shiver.

It is crazy, he thought. For five long years, we at home have done what we could to become free again, often at great risk of life, and now we are on the other side, fighting those who want to be free. If that creates a big mess, as our government rightly states, well so be it. Then it is their own bloody mess. When you burn your behind, you've got to sit on the blisters.

Back on the bridge he noticed that it was almost five o'clock and within an hour it would be daylight. The cook had no fire, so no coffee was available, and there was no appetite for cold food. At the right moment they arrived opposite the town and Ian kept the *Rian* in position, not knowing what to expect. He didn't have to wait long; the colonel came to the bridge.

"The two parties made contact more than an hour ago and will begin the attack in—," the colonel began, then looked at his watch, "—eleven minutes." Slowly the town became visible in the growing daylight and they and other crew members observed the dwellings through binoculars.

The waterfront appeared deserted, no boats were tied up. The wooden planking of the wharf was in disrepair and the simple one-story buildings along the wharf looked dilapidated. The three taller buildings were coming into focus more clearly and that was the area everybody was looking at. The silence on board was occasionally disturbed by the sound of the main engine and the propeller wash, to keep the *Rian* in position in the tidal current.

The ship's heavy gun was manned and trained on the wharf area and the machine guns were at the ready. There was, however, no chance they could use them on the town; this would endanger their own soldiers. But it was more as a measure to be ready in case boats were used to escape. Minutes passed and then the colonel in a low voice loaded with tension said, "Now!"

At first it seemed that nothing happened but then pandemonium broke loose. Doors were kicked in, women screamed, men yelled, and in a flash the murderous room-to-room fighting began in full force. The observers on the ship could not follow the action in the melee. Some people ran to the wharf as if to jump in the water, but seeing the *Rian* with its guns trained they ran back into town.

The colonel paced the bridge and stopped suddenly when shots were fired. Then he went down to the mess room, calling the radio operator. "Any message?"

"No, sir, they are too busy, I figure."

"Call me as soon as they come through," he said, and went topside again.

It felt like an eternity but, in reality, it was less than two hours later when one of the officers ashore came on the radio, reporting, "Mission accomplished." The colonel asked Ian if he could bring his ship alongside the wharf, but Ian told him he would first lower a lifeboat and check whether there were submerged pilings or other obstacles. The colonel nodded understandingly and asked if he could go ashore in the boat. Ian left Jalim in charge on board, called the boatswain and some sailors, and navigated to the wharf. The colonel climbed aboard and Ian ordered the boatswain to cast off and let the boat float along the wharf. The whole construction was a rickety affair and the boatswain grumbled, "When we tie up alongside, the whole thing might collapse." Ian agreed and they went back to the *Rian*.

"We will anchor close to the dock and use our two boats to bring their stuff ashore as soon as we get word from the colonel," he told Jalim. "Meanwhile send one boat back to shore and wait there for whomever wants to return."

While the ship was kept on station, he called the mess boy. "Run to the cook and let him make a fire very fast. I want coffee and chow for everybody." Although they had not been directly involved in the fighting, the strain on him, maneuvering in the dark and taking chances with his command, was now broken and reaction set in.

Steaming black coffee and a hearty breakfast helped him over the hump and his personal welfare improved even more when he filled his pipe and relaxed in a chair on the boat deck. His mind wandered on how Jenny would feel under the circumstances without any radio contact between the *Rian* and port office. He was yanked back into their present situation by Jalim.

"Sir, when are we going at anchor? This continued maneuvering to stay in position is driving everybody up the wall."

Ian eyed his second in command. The man was right. "All right, Jalim, call our boat. I will go ashore myself and see the colonel."

Going into the town he noticed that there were no civilians in the street. When he saw one of his own soldiers, he asked where he could find the colonel. The man pointed to one of the main buildings, and going there he met the officer who had led the first party ashore. Ian told him that he wanted to anchor close to the wharf, but only when it was safe to do so.

"If you expect that guerrilla reinforcements might come to try and retake this place, my ship at anchor will be a sitting duck."

The lieutenant shrugged as if he couldn't care less, which Ian could understand when looking at him; it surely had not been a picnic. "The colonel is very much occupied right now. I'll tell him that you will anchor close by," the army officer said, and walked away.

Ian was just a little bit pissed off by the rebuke and decided to take things into his own hands. Back on board he ordered the crew ready to anchor and when that was done put the engine room on standby, ready to go at a snap. The anchor watch was doubled and the rest of the crew sent off to quarters.

They stayed there for three days, ferrying the army's belongings ashore. A Catalina landed in the straits, taking the wounded to a military hospital. A small boat arrived with some replacement troops and heavier gear. A section of the dock was being repaired with the help of men from the population who had not been involved in the fighting. All in all, the small town started to resemble normal life. On the fourth day, the colonel and his adjutant returned to the *Rian*. He declared the situation under control and asked Ian to bring them back to Tandjoeng Pinang, a request which Ian was obliged to honor.

They would arrive in the afternoon of the following day, and on that morning the colonel lifted the radio silence order. But that was under the condition that Ian could only inform the harbor master of their estimated time of arrival; the latter would know whom to contact. The ETA message was sent and receipt confirmed.

Nearing the pier at Tandjoeng Pinang, Ian noticed a small crowd on the pier, mainly consisting of army personnel. But between all the camouflage uniforms he saw two and a half white spots, being Jenny, Meagen, and Frans. Crew members saw their relatives and there was much waving. Ian was surprised to see so many families of the crew members, which was unusual. The answer came when he heard the chief engineer, who was on deck for a short while to catch some air, remarking to Jalim that it was payday.

A strong offshore wind made it necessary for Ian to swing the *Rian* around and approach the head of the pier with speed, to avoid drifting away from it. He ordered the helmsman to steer close and judged the right moment to put the telegraph on full astern. The engine was stopped but didn't respond to astern. Everybody looked up at the *Rian*'s bridge, the officers on the pier saluting the colonel, and with amazement they all saw the ship sail by at only a few feet distance. Fleetingly Ian saw their eyes open wide in surprise. He wasted no time, yanked the telegraph on half ahead, and again turned the ship around for another approach. He took the speaking tube to the engine room and gave the chief a dressing down in such terms that even the colonel, within hearing distance, was very impressed. The second approach was executed more cautiously but still at fair speed and this time the engine responded.

Quickly the gangway was put out to the jetty and the waiting people were coming up to the boat deck, Frans first.

"That was a hell of a performance," he called loudly, knowing full well what had happened. The army officers, headed by the major, saluted the colonel and there were handshakes and congratulations. Ian looked around and then saw Jenny with their daughter still standing on the pier. He rushed down and jumped ashore. Meagen saw him and put her open arms to him. "Daddy, daddy!" Jenny could not hold her any longer but Ian caught his daughter just in time, hugging and kissing her. After a while, Jenny tapped him on his shoulder.

"Hey, you two! Remember me?" Then it was her turn to participate in the festive welcome, not caring if anyone was looking.

"Come on board, love," Ian said, and went ahead with Meagen on his arm. The military and Frans were still on the boat deck and when the trio arrived everybody was introduced to Jenny. The army staff were getting ready to leave. The colonel turned to Ian. "Thank you for your cooperation. You did a fine job." He saluted, turned around, and left, followed by his subordinates. Frans was also ready to leave, but not before making a remark.

"I have never been exposed to the sight of a ship passing at two feet from a waiting crowd, and at that high speed. Thank heaven you reacted so well." And he went down, whistling. Ian, as usual, didn't exactly know how to interpret the remark.

From the pier Frans turned around and called to Ian. "Before I forget, go easy on the chief. It isn't his fault the engine slipped up. It has happened before. Didn't I tell you?" Ian held the railing, his knuckles white, and would have gone after his boss, but for Jenny who held his arm. "Forget it, that's the way he is. There is another person I have to talk with you about."

That other person turned out to be his own daughter. One morning Jenny had dressed her up to go for a walk but first had to make some arrangements with Fia. Meagen used the opportunity to walk off by herself, and when Jenny came into the house, she was gone. Jenny and Fia ran into the street, calling her, and checked the Chinese shops nearby, but no Meagen. Alarmed, Jenny went to the police station. The sergeant on duty sent two men on bikes to search, and told her to stay at home, just in case. Jenny couldn't stay inside with thoughts of kidnapping or other calamities in her mind, and stood in front of their house.

Then she heard a child crying; around the corner came a man with a soaking wet Meagen in his arms. He was on the pier going ashore when he saw her wading from the beach toward deep water. He ran to her and here she was. Jenny held her close. "What were you doing there?"

"I was going to daddy" came the reply.

Ian was listening with a mixed feeling of anxiety and fatherly pride. "Thank god that man saved her," he said, looking at his daughter. He asked Jenny, "Who was that man, and what did you do?"

"I, of course, thanked him and offered some reward, which he refused to accept, saying it was Allah's will."

Ian kissed his two women and they were leaving the ship when he turned to Jenny and asked her to wait a moment. He disappeared into the engine room where he found the chief surrounded by his helpers. Ian went to them and addressed the chief engineer. "I apologize for chewing you out earlier. I just learned that something like this has happened before. You are not to blame. Tomorrow we will discuss what can be done."

The chief's face lit up as if a burden had been taken from his shoulders. They shook hands, and Ian joined his family on their way home, safe and sound.

Chapter Twenty-Three

There was typical weather for a month when the monsoon turned from a westerly to easterly direction or vice versa. Usually it meant a heavy overcast sky with sudden short downpours accompanied by strong winds, which die down thereafter. The *Rian* had cleared the straits between the islands of Bintan and Singapore, and was heading northeast into the South China Sea.

It was the biannual trip of the ship, chartered by the government to call on the Anambas and Natoena islands, which were part of the Rhio Archipelago region. Ian had found a quiet spot, sitting on a bollard near the bow, where he could catch a light breeze while within calling distance from the bridge. It was close to midnight; at times there was a break in the clouds and moonlight filtered through, casting a cold light over the long swell of the sea. The noise of the engine was, at this time of the night, the only dissonant sound on board.

Preparations for the three-week trip had astounded Ian, who had no idea what to expect. One day before departure a great number of stretchers had been delivered on board, plus lots of luggage, and even furniture.

"What on earth is all this for?" he had asked Jalim, who told him that it was mainly for the police force group who would relieve the one on the islands for a six-month tour of duty. But the real spectacle started the next morning when the clerks and servants of government officials arrived at the crack of dawn, followed shortly thereafter by the police group with their wives, children, goats, chickens, and kitchen utensils. The pier was crowded not only with passengers and their belongings, but also relatives and friends saying good-bye. Ian couldn't believe his eyes; a clerk of the port office had given him a listing of his passengers, but that was a far cry from the invasion he witnessed now.

The listing he looked at was already impressive by itself: the governor and his lieutenant; a physician and two assistants; a dentist plus assistant; two officers of justice; and two police officers with, innocently and deceivingly added to the list, a platoon. No word of families, clerks, servants, and the menagerie. He quickly estimated the crowd at close to a hundred and promptly became alarmed. Jalim was standing next to him, looking from the bridge down to the turmoil on the pier. He watched the face of his skipper, understanding very well what was in his mind. "Don't worry, sir. It is always the same twice a year. You'll get used to it."

"But where are we going to put all the people and animals?" Ian asked in despair.

"They all find a place eventually. Only when it rains it becomes a problem."

Ian had the impression that Jalim was amusing himself at his skipper's expense, and decided that life was too short to bother.

"Okay, Jalim, you are in charge of the passengers and their belongings. See to it that the goats and chickens stay downwind." He left the ship with the notice of departure at 1000 hours and walked to Frans' office. The latter asked him innocently how things were going. At that moment Ian had no words and marched out.

Going home for breakfast he used Jenny to blow off steam, telling her the situation. There was no understanding of his hurt feelings in that quarter either. Jenny broke out in laughter and could not stop, tears in her eyes. She even rubbed salt in the wound by promising she wouldn't miss coming to the pier herself. Anger and self-pity rising, Ian burst out, "It's a mess. Cooking in shifts, water rationing, maybe even pissing in shifts, and . . ." Then he realized he was acting foolishly and joined in his wife's laughter.

Well before sailing time they walked together to the *Rian* and Jenny found the whole matter quite hilarious, warning him to at least keep his bed to himself. Shortly before ten o'clock, a cavalcade of cars and jeeps came on the pier with the listed dignitaries. A warning whistle sounded, good-byes were said, and the *Rian* was under way, miraculously with everybody on board.

Now it was late, but Ian had no urge to turn in, thankful for the moment of peace and quiet. He was reminiscing about the happenings of the past weeks. After his return from the military operation to recapture a town, it was decided that some repairs of the *Rian* were necessary. One of which was to avoid another mishap during maneuvering. It had taken over one week, during which he fully enjoyed family life in all its facets, not the least of which was being involved in nighttime diaper changing.

When repairs were finished, Frans had informed him that he would bring the amateur theater group to Captain Hartman's garrison for one weekend, to perform for the troops. Frans also mentioned that the official opening of a swimming pool was one of the planned festivities. With a shock, Ian recalled their 'virgin' problem, but all had gone well. One of the group was a young female secretary and when she was asked to cut the ribbon and name the pool, she had agreed to do so, telling Hartman and staff, "What's in a name?" and that the rest was none of their business. She had made the plunge and all got wet inside and out. That trip had been a jolly good one with lots of jokes and stories.

Ian steadied himself against the ship's movement, leaving the forecastle to get to the main deck. He had to maneuver cautiously in the semidarkness to avoid stepping on people who were sleeping on mats spread out in every available space. Reaching his cabin he looked at his bed and smiled that nobody had claimed it, as Jenny had warned him.

The third morning after their departure the *Rian* closed in on the first inhabited island of the Anambas group, anchoring close to the shore. There was no protection from the swell, and only those officials who had some business there would visit the village. The work boat was lowered, bringing the first people ashore. The dentist and his assistant with their manually operated drilling equipment would go on the second trip. The work boat returned and the boatswain brought a message for the dentist. One of the villagers had been his patient half a year ago and suffered from a toothache ever since. Raving mad from the constant pain he was preparing to come on board.

The dentist felt uneasy. "Is he a tall guy? Is he armed?" he asked the boatswain, who found the situation very interesting. Both questions being affirmed, the dentist turned to Ian.

"On second thought I don't think it necessary for me to go ashore. There is nothing I can do for him right now."

Ian kept a straight face. "That is your decision. But what would you suggest I do when your patient takes a canoe and climbs on board?"

There was no suggestion, but the dentist kept a wary eye on the land until late in the afternoon when the last party returned and the anchor weighed.

Next stop was the main island where an adjunct to the governor called 'the resident' resided and where the police force was stationed. The town was located at the end of a deep bay, surrounded by steep hills.

Ian had tried to contact the resident by radio but there had been no answer, so when they rounded the cape and the town came into view, he used the ship's horn to announce their arrival. At first there was no movement around the little jetty but within half an hour, while the *Rian* was getting as close as possible, people moved around. Tying up at the jetty was out of the question, so again they anchored and lowered the boat. The first trip carried only the governor and his lieutenant; the latter had informed Ian that protocol dictated this arrangement.

All others on board followed the proceedings from the ship. The resident had alerted the police, who had formed a line of official welcome for the governor and his lieutenant. The sloop moored alongside, and the governor and his assistant came up on the jetty. The resident stepped forward to greet the governor, and when he got close came to a sudden halt. Through his binoculars Ian noticed that, without shaking hands, a rather lively dispute between the two civil servants took place. Abruptly the governor turned around and boarded the boat, with his aide following him on his heels.

Back on board the *Rian* the governor took Ian aside and told him that he had given his resident two days off, before he joined them visiting some other islands. Meanwhile the police group could install themselves in their accommodations in town; the returning group would be picked up when they came back to drop off the resident.

Ian and his passengers didn't know what to think of it, but the activity of ferrying the police force was a welcome distraction, especially when the goats and chickens got their turn. After dinner they all gathered as usual on the sloop deck to enjoy the evening. The governor was aware that nobody had asked him why the resident was not with them, and felt that some explanation was called for. He turned to Ian, who had the least amount of tropical experience. "Do you know what a durian is?"

Ian had not the foggiest idea.

"A durian is a large tropical fruit with a soft meaty interior. The taste is like coffee with sugar and whipped cream—in one word, heavenly. But the smell is worse than raw garlic and lingers for days." Here he stopped and looked around. It dawned upon some of his veteran officials what had happened on the jetty and they had trouble containing their laugh.

During the following discussion on the topic, Ian learned that, when on duty, civil servants were forbidden to eat the fruit on pain of forced furlough. The lieutenant governor then told the others that the resident had expected them several days later and since the durians were in season, had gorged himself with the fruit. Now they all snickered and grinned, knowing full well the position of the resident. After a while the governor joined in.

"When he comes on board, please do not make it too difficult for him. After all, he has to sweat it all by himself for six months."

Two days later the resident came on board. He was in his late thirties, officially a bachelor, and a likable fellow. Other than his durian appetite he had only one peculiar streak. He told his listeners that every living thing was held together by vibrations. That was no problem as long as you didn't eat something with the same vibration sequence. If you did you would simply fall apart and that was it. He quarreled endlessly with the chief cook about a number of ingredients not for consumption. The cook would not take the intrusion into his domain any longer and the resident had to prepare his own meals.

The *Rian* toured several populated islands and everyone was occupied with his specific line of work. The governor and his staff dealt with government matters, the physician and assistants saw patients who couldn't survive on local drugs. The dentist was careful in his approach and pulled teeth in great numbers, avoiding drilling and root canal procedures.

The officers of justice had a special task on Great Natoena Island. Just before the war in the area broke out, a Russian freighter went off course in bad weather and wrecked on its coast. Most of the crew managed to save their lives and landed on the island. In addition to the natives, there was a detachment of KNIL soldiers on the most northern outpost in the South China Sea. Equipped with a strong radio transmitter, they functioned as a vanguard listening post. The message of the shipwreck was received at headquarters, but when the Japanese invaded the Dutch East Indies some days later, nothing was heard from them again.

The resident said that each time when he came to the island in one of his local small craft, the population fled into the interior, so probably there were no Dutch or Russian survivors. When the *Rian* anchored and the men went ashore, the village again was deserted. They found one old man who obviously could not move fast. He was interrogated and it came out that at first the three different parties on the remote island lived a peaceful existence, forming three separate villages. However, tension reared its ugly head, sometimes for minor reasons. The real difficulties started when native women became the target, then shots were fired and people were killed. Finally the original villagers survived and the Russians and Dutch were buried. The old man brought them to a small clearing in the woods; there were no markings on the graves, and the digging took time.

None of the *Rian*'s crew was willing to help, so the servants were collected and they separated the remains using the metal uniform distinctives. Packed in gunny sacks and small wooden boxes, the tragic bones were placed in the forward hold to be taken to Tandjoeng Pinang. This aroused a dispute among the *Rian*'s crew members, which went so far that the chief engineer asked for a word with Ian. He liked the calm, knowledgeable man, and anticipating that it would be important, asked him into his hut, out of earshot of the passengers.

Superstitious seamen believe that when there is a clergyman on board you will get stormy weather, but carrying dead bodies on a ship spells disaster, especially when murders are involved. Crew members had learned what had happened and consequently were very unhappy with having the remains on board. They had asked the chief to act as their spokesman and urge the skipper not to take the bodies on board. Ian had to think fast. He could either use his authority and tell the crew that it would be done as ordered, or give in and refuse to take the human remains on board. Neither of the two alternatives was satisfactory. Then he saw a solution to the dilemma.

"Chief, I understand your point. However, we do not have dead bodies but only some bones. The souls of these persons have long since left, and the only, but important, reason we'll take what is left to Tandjoeng Pinang is to give them a proper military burial. Only then will their spirits come to rest."

Ian realized that by making such a statement he was treading on a slippery path. The chief looked at him pensively, considering what his commanding officer had said. Personally he was inclined to accept the reasoning, but wasn't sure how the other crew members would react.

Seeing the man's hesitation and unwilling to argue any further, he continued, "We will do as I said. I make you one promise: if we come into a real dangerous situation, I personally will arrange a burial at sea." The chief understood that it was final and felt relieved.

"Thank you, sir, for your understanding." He saluted and went to the crew's quarters.

The governor had stayed onboard while the other officials were occupied on the island. His personal servant had told him about the crew's reluctance to have dead bodies on board, and knowing that Ian was not a so-called 'old tropic hand,' he asked Ian if he could be of help. Ian, glad he could discuss his decision with somebody who knew the colonies in all its facets, told him what he had done. The governor nodded.

"Well done. You, of course, have no intention of having a sea burial." It was not a question but a statement. Ian was sure that if push came to shove, he had somebody who would back him up, and said so. "Of course, Ian. I shall be there."

After some short stops at other islands, they arrived back at the main island and dropped off the resident, whose tour of duty wasn't over yet. The returning police group, with followers, came on board, carrying with them several sacks. Ian asked his mess boy what they had in the bags. The mess boy said with a broad smile that no doubt they were durians. He called Jalim.

"Inform everybody that if I smell durian, the whole harvest goes overboard. I don't care where they stow the fruit, as long as I don't smell them."

It was time to weigh the anchor and the *Rian* was homeward bound. The weather, which had cooperated for weeks, turned nasty on their way back and the ship worked heavily in the high seas. Most of the passengers were seasick and had no interest in their surroundings. Ian took long hours on the bridge, and at times, even he had trouble steadying himself. After two long days they entered the Singapore Straits and came soon in calmer water. People who were so sick that they wanted to jump overboard felt better as soon as the rolling and pitching movements of the ship subsided. There were even some brave people who talked about food, but when they smelled fried eggs the idea was quickly abandoned.

Ian had radioed their ETA and received the request to, if at all possible, arrive at 4 P.M. Arrangements for receiving the fallen soldiers with military honor were made for that time by the army.

Adjusting the speed to comply with their request and placing the boxes on the main deck, the *Rian* approached the jetty. It looked like half the population of the town had come out. The guard of honor presented arms, and the roll of drums covered with cloth were accompanied by the sound of trumpets when the boxes under the national flag were slowly carried from onboard to a weapon carrier on the jetty. All stood at attention until the vehicle and the guard of honor were off the long jetty.

The usual melee followed and it took awhile before Ian discovered his wife and daughter, trying to come on board against the human current. Since he could not leave the bridge before his passengers had left, he sent the mess boy down to coach Jenny and Meagen topside. Like always their welcome was as though he had been away for months. Meagen was now a beautiful girl of a year and a half, very independent and spoiled by the servants, whom she could wind around her little finger. This didn't work at all with her mother, who controlled the daughter with a loving but firm hand. So now the little lady tried it out with her daddy and was rather successful.

After their embrace, Ian looked closer at his wife and got the impression that something had changed. When they arrived at home, Jenny leaned close to him and told him that she was pregnant.

"That is what I thought when looking at you, my love," he said, and took her in his arms. There was joy and happiness in the small Halls' household.

Chapter Twenty-Four

By a stroke of luck the Halls were able to leave the partial housing and move into an old wooden house owned by the government. The nice thing was that they didn't have to share it with others and it had a yard. The move was simple and presented no problems.

"Finally, we are on our own," exclaimed Jenny when they walked hand in hand through the rooms. Fia and Anjoeng had packed their belongings and installed themselves in the servants quarters, detached from the house. Next to their quarters were the kitchen and shower, which was not a shower actually but a tiled room. In the corner was a concrete cistern with water. With a small bucket you splashed the cool water over your body, and for the children it was a delight to be there. Doors and windows were opened, mosquito nets hung above the beds, china and other more valuable items placed in the dresser and cabinet, and presto, the move was accomplished.

Ian had to go on patrol quite frequently and caught several boats with illegal cargo, which were towed to Tandjoeng Pinang for prosecution. He even captured a rebuilt motor torpedo boat, used for arms smuggling. The MTB was hidden in a small cove and could not escape to open water, otherwise her far faster speed would have made her untouchable. The time had come that the *Rian* had to go to dry dock for its annual repairs. The nearest dry dock in the Dutch East Indies was in Batavia and that was the destination. Ian had arranged for Jenny and Meagen to go with him and stay for the duration of the overhaul in a navy mess in Bandoeng, a town south of Batavia high in the mountains on Java. The repairs took six weeks during which Ian once flew to Bandoeng for a week, enjoying the cool air with his family.

Upon their return home they found that the town had not suffered any calamities and the population was as vibrant as ever. This was confirmed with the arrival of a highly placed official from Batavia who came to inspect something. His position in the government hierarchy required that he had to be treated with distinction. Since a prolonged stay of such a guest can be exhaustive for a small group of local officials, the lower echelon of government officials were asked to share the burden, and in turn, entertain the privileged guest. Frans and his wife were the organizers of one such evening, heading a group that included Jenny and Ian.

The party started with a one-hour tour around some islands in the bay on board the *Rian*, followed by drinks and snacks on the large patio of the Fransen home, which was located near the top of the hill. For dinner the entire group went to the Chinese market square; alcohol was plentiful and the party became animated, partly because nobody adhered to any form of protocol. Darkness fell, the dinner was over, and Frans observed it was time for some kind of different action. He stood up and announced that everybody should find a place in the few vehicles available and follow him.

Frans' wife, who apparently knew what he had in mind, tried to dissuade him from his plan, but to no avail. The group of more than twenty people climbed into the vehicles, and followed Frans out of town to a rubber plantation. Not many in the party knew that the only fresh-water pool in the area was located there. When they realized what his idea was, the ladies protested; no one had a swimsuit and skinny dipping was out of the question.

Frans had arranged the vehicles in a circle facing the pool with headlights on for illumination. As master of ceremony, he declared that the ladies would swim in their bras and panties, and the men in undershorts. The guest of honor said he would use his sleeveless pullover, and pull his legs through the arm openings. He abandoned that idea when Frans asked him what he would do with the opening through which he put his head. With great enthusiasm the group swam and splashed around in the pool, and the last one to leave the water was their guest. They looked at him and all started to laugh when he went under water, came up again sneezing and coughing, and went under again. "He is quite funny," most laughed.

Jenny, who was more alert, shouted, "He is drowning!" and jumped in the pool. Two men followed her and together they swam him to the side, where he was dragged onto land. He was breathing heavily, he sputtered a little bit, and looking around him uttered with a trembling voice, "This is a jolly good party!"

Frans, who as chief host felt very responsible for the well-being of their guest, was relieved when the fellow talked. He ordered a fire made and soon everyone gathered around it to dry their improvised swim outfits. Someone started a song with others following, and soon there was a scout-like campfire atmosphere. It was very late when the party returned. The following morning Frans was asked to see the governor.

"I don't know and don't want to know what in God's name you have done with our guest, but he keeps saying that it was the best time of his life. And now, get out of my sight!"

"Yes, governor. As you order," he said, and marched off. The governor watched him leaving the building, and seeing that Frans' shoulders shook in suppressed laugher, smiled, and turned to his desk.

Life was not only fun. The war, which still was called "police action," intensified. Its impact was mainly felt in the bush and on plantations; there was no grace period. During one of his patrols near the Sumatra coast Ian received a request by radio to go to a fishing village on an island near the coast. The village was in a strategic location and a small garrison was holding that position, albeit with some difficulty. Ian, being close to the village, was asked to go there and see whether the *Rian* could be of help. When he arrived, he talked with the commanding officer, a first lieutenant.

Ian invited him on board and offered him a cold drink, then heard the sad story. The island was, for the greater part, controlled by guerrillas and his troops were outnumbered ten to one. So all they could do was to try to hold the center of the village and its direct periphery. At nightfall the troops had to withdraw into the rambling garrison quarters and expand again when daylight came. This jigsaw movement, carried on for many weeks, was a headache for his men and a greater problem for the population. The shopkeepers had no choice but to change the Dutch flag from their shops to the independents' colors when darkness fell, thus serving both sides. This standoff situation had one somewhat brighter side; the guerrillas, as well as the troops, needed supplies, and consequently, the shops were not ransacked. "You don't kill the goose that lays the golden egg," the lieutenant added with a dry sense of humor.

"I wonder what I can do for you." Ian remembered vividly the action in which the *Rian* had been involved, with a contingent of the army. "To me it sounds like a request for the navy and marines."

"I asked for such support but the navy could not help, being fully occupied in other areas which needed it more urgently." There was a moment of silence while both men evaluated the possibilities for a solution.

Ian broke the silence. "Either you receive more troops or I take you all onboard and you abandon the place." It sounded harsh but the army man had to agree.

"You can send your own message through army channels, but since I was asked by my superiors to see what I can do, I will send my opinion as I just stated before. You agree?"

"Okay, I don't like it, but there is no alternative."

The reply came quickly. "*Rian* to stay in position. Assistance will arrive tomorrow morning, instructions are with leader of that group." And as an afterthought it was added, "Please inform the commanding officer."

"Tomorrow morning? Where on earth are they coming from?" That was a good question to which they had no answer, but anyway it was good news. The *Rian* left the small dock and anchored at a short distance and Ian, doubled the anchor watch. He had no taste to become part, or worse, victim, of the nightly hide-and-seek game.

Early the next morning he came alongside again. The night had remained quiet, following the usual pattern of events, and there was no sign that the enemy had listened in on the radio. Either they had no radio on the island or were not aware of the ship's wavelength. Hours went by and every moment the lieutenant became more nervous. He paced the dock back and forth, and like Ian, trained his glasses on both sides of the straits. Maybe they were sending his colleague, the commanding officer of the other minesweeper stationed at Tandjoeng Pinang, with troops?

His thoughts were interrupted by the sound of a plane. Friend or foe? Did the opponent have any planes? If so, the *Rian* had no anti-aircraft guns and couldn't do a thing. Apparently the lieutenant had asked himself the same question and barked an order to his men on the dock to take up positions on the shore, out of sight. At the same moment Ian had alerted his crew to stay under cover, whatever good that might do.

The plane came in low over the water.

It was a Catalina of the Royal Navy Air Force. "It is one of us," Ian yelled at the lieutenant. "Do you have a boat?" The army had a motor launch used to patrol around the island, which was at the ready. The amphibian landed in the water and taxied toward the dock. The launch approached the plane when it had anchored; a hatch was opened and a number of soldiers stepped into the launch.

The lieutenant and Ian were on the dock. "I counted twelve men. Are they my assistance?" the lieutenant asked with a bitter tone in his voice. The launch docked and the dozen men marched single file to the waiting men. At the head of the small troop was a gigantic major, followed by a sergeant major and ten privates. The major ordered halt and introductions followed. A faint smile was on his lips but not in his eyes.

"My orders are to take over the command of the garrison as long as we are here." The lieutenant was still not over his dislike of the so-called assistance, but was outranked. There was another surprise coming.

"We are going to have some sleep. Call us at 1800 hours, and have food prepared. You are in charge until that time. Please have one of your men show us where we can rest." The major handed Ian an envelope, saluted the two dumbfounded officers, and the small group marched off.

When they were out of earshot the lieutenant turned to Ian, eyes blazing. "This isn't real. I am hallucinating. My saviors have come here for a nap!"

"I agree, it sure looks funny. Let's go on board and see what my orders are. Maybe they are sending me a canoe for help." Ian ordered a neat gin for both, which went bottom up, and opened the envelope. He whistled when he read his instruction, and then looked at his compatriot.

The orders were straightforward. Major Renne and his men are a highly specialized group, trained in night operation. Ian was to cooperate to the fullest with the major's plan of action and coordinate the *Rian*'s employ with the aforementioned officer. No radio contact unless with the major's consent.

There was not a 'for your eyes only' stamp on the orders, so he handed it to the lieutenant.

"I have heard stories about this group. If half of them are true, we have it made." Clearly he saw the situation differently now than before. "Why don't you come to me at 1800 hours and have chow with us. Maybe you and I will hear more about what our roles will be."

Promptly at six Ian was at the barracks, consisting of a row of low buildings in a poor state of maintenance. His host welcomed him in his office. The major and his group were preparing for whatever plan of action and a meal would be ready soon. While waiting, Ian looked around the office. There was not much to see. The accommodation had a Spartan look with only the bare necessities.

The major came in and closed the door behind him. He was dressed in fatigues and jungle boots and made a formidable appearance. "My men and I will leave right after dinner and will return at first daylight. Possibly your sentries won't recognize us on our return, so we'll arrange a password." Then he continued, explaining that none of the lieutenant's soldiers should go outside the compound and whatever they heard outside, no shooting. After their return the lieutenant was to take charge again and extend his presence into town as before, but no farther.

Then he turned to Ian. "And you, sir, no gunfire either unless I ask you for it. Patrol the straits at irregular intervals, but stay between the island and the mainland."

"What do I do at night?" Ian asked.

The answer came without hesitation. "You patrol at night as well and can use your searchlight whenever necessary, and when completing a sweep, go at anchor. Stay away from the dock."

Further instructions for Ian were that he should make his presence known. When noticing people leaving the island, he had to hail them and search the boat and the people for weapons. If they were fishermen, they would let them go. If weapons were found, take the boat and the weapons and deliver the people to the lieutenant for interrogation. "We need to gather as much information as we can on the situation on the island. And now, let us enjoy a meal."

After the simple dinner they witnessed the group's departure. Faces and hands darkened, they slipped out of the compound and almost immediately were lost in the dark.

The two officers returned to the barracks, where they entered the lieutenant's office. Ian had a question and then realized that he didn't know the lieutenant's name. "Sorry, we have been so occupied that I don't know your name. Mine is Ian Halls."

The other man apologized. "Mine is Cor Heugel." That item settled, the two men talked briefly about Major Renne's group out there in the jungle.

"Did you notice that their only weapon is a dagger?" asked Cor.

"Yes, and I know what that means. I also noticed that they were holding hands when they left."

Cor nodded. "During operations in the dark, requiring close combat, they use touch signals."

Far from being a coward, Ian was glad he was not tramping around out there right now.

"We'll learn soon enough how things are developing. I'll go onboard and start patrolling the inside coastline of the island."

This mode of operation went on for three days and nights without changes in the situation as far as both Cor and Ian were concerned. Cor told him that each morning the silent group returned, tired and dirty, and above all, very hungry. On the fourth morning during breakfast, the major asked Cor to signal the *Rian* to come alongside and ask Ian to see him.

When the three officers were together, Major Renne told them that the first, what he called "phase," went satisfactorily. Cor and his men could now maintain their presence during darkness, so there would be no more night retreats.

"Give the merchants one night to get used to it, but if they still fly the enemy colors at night, it will be considered an act of treason and will be dealt with accordingly."

Then he turned to Ian. "Your patrolling was effective. But from now on you can expect attempts by the enemy to flee the island to the mainland. Be alert and fire only when you must."

After this oracle, he yawned. "I think it is time for a nap. Keep up the good work, men."

The island was about twenty miles long and three miles wide, and Ian doubted whether he could be successful preventing who-knows-how-many guerrillas from crossing the straits, fleeing from something at which he could guess, but didn't want to think about. As he expected, he did not encounter the expected exodus and somewhat dismayed received a message from Cor that the major would like to see them. It was the sixth day after the major and his small group had arrived.

This time the major was in full uniform, which was a surprise to both of them. He started with a brief matter-of-fact observation, namely that there were no more enemy troops on the island. Secondly, he said that he would strongly suggest reinforcements and two more motorboats so that future infiltration would become very risky for the infiltrants. Thirdly, he thanked both for their cooperation and expressed high regard for the lieutenant in staving off the lugubrious risk of being overrun. And lastly, he handed Ian a message in which a Catalina was requested to pick him and his men up this afternoon. "And herewith your radio silence is lifted. I'll now write my report. Thank you, gentlemen."

The two remaining officers fell silent after hearing the surprising news, contemplating the events. After a while, Cor came up with a suggestion. "Could we at least arrange a guard of honor to see them off?"

"I don't know if Major Renne would appreciate it, but yes, let's do it. We know the ETA of the plane."

When the Catalina streaked over the water, settling deeper, and taxied to the dock area, the major and his jungle fighters marched single file to the dock. Then he saw the two rows of men, one in khaki, the other in white, standing at attention, their officers at the flanks. He called a halt to his group, saluted the two officers, and then something unmilitary happened. The major, with a voice like a bullhorn, ordered, "At ease," turned to his group, and said with a smile, "Shake hands, everybody!" It was a remarkable moment of fraternity, with no regard for rank or age.

The Catalina left, and the *Rian* was ready to leave also. "Cor, when you come to Tandjoeng Pinang, you will be very welcome at our home."

The *Rian* cast off and was on her way to home port.

Chapter Twenty-Five

At home, Ian found that Jenny was carrying signs of her pregnancy. She was easily tired in the often oppressive heat, but in her usually realistic way declared that it all was part of the experience. Her servants took the burden of any kind of heavy work, which included Meagen. This little one, who stole everybody's heart, was growing up as a vibrant girl and enjoyed life to its fullest. After each trip, Ian found something new in her behavior and was astounded by her choice of words, not only in Dutch, but also Malay. Young as she was, she could command the servants, who good-humoredly obeyed. She was chubby, but not fat, and looked like health eternal. Jenny sighed when telling Ian about the day Meagen had come from outside, smelling terribly.

"Meagen, where have you been and what did you do?" After more prodding, Jenny discovered that she had been in the yard, found a dead snail, and had been fumbling to get the snail out of its shell. Another day Fia found her in the street, drinking rainwater from the ground. Since she didn't get sick from these escapades, the doctor declared that this child had an enormous immunity. Otherwise, she was very particular about cleanliness and dresses.

"Your daughter is a walking contradiction in terminology," declared Ian when Jenny related the stories.

"Ha, now it is my daughter when you hear something like that," Jenny reacted but could not hide her smile.

"It is already hard enough to keep her under control with the servants, but oh boy, when daddy comes home! You are like putty in her hands." Then she threatened, "One day I will tie her to a tree in the backyard." Ian found it better to abandon the topic of their daughter. "All good news from home, I hope?"

Ian went to the office to report to Frans about the action on the islands and the amazing Major Renne and his group. Frans nodded. "They are really something and I would rather dine with them than fight."

"Will Lieutenant Heugel get the requested reinforcements?" Ian wanted to know.

"Yes, they are already under way."

On a more personal note, Frans told him that he and his wife were keeping in close contact with Jenny.

"She is holding out very well under the circumstances, but she hates it when there is radio silence, not knowing whether you are all right. Well, that goes with the territory. Nothing we can do about it."

Discussing the *Rian*'s schedule, Frans told Ian that within a few weeks he should go to bunker in Singapore, to avoid getting low on fuel when more special operations might come up. Meanwhile, he was to continue patrolling. Ian had, after completion of his twelve months at sea, received his certificate of second mate merchant marine. He was now senior second officer and in an official letter from First Officer Werff was offered service on one of the LST's. Discussing this opportunity with Jenny, they both preferred to stay where they were. Jenny loved the old house they had for themselves, and with the end of her confinement only a couple of months away, didn't want to move to another location.

Answering Mr. Werff's letter, Ian wrote that he was very appreciative of the offer but felt that he was of more value to the coast guard in his present position. "Do you think Mr. Werff will buy it?" he asked Frans, who was reading his copy.

"Hank and I are good friends. I will give him my opinion in a cover letter and keep you here." It was the first time Ian had heard the given name of Officer Werff.

As if continuing on the subject, Frans remarked, "You are now in the third year of your contract. You are not a coast guard career officer, and honestly, I don't see you as a merchant marine man either. What are your plans, if I may ask?"

That was a good question, Ian thought. He had not given it much consideration because it seemed so far off, and moreover, his life until present had so often been dictated by situations over which he had little or no control. But this, indeed, was different, and he and Jenny were going to give it some serious thought. Nevertheless, he was thankful to Frans for bringing it up, although Ian was surprised about his remark concerning the merchant marine, his dream of many previous years. Frans took the silence at face value and changed the subject.

Meagen's birthday in April was not far off, and neither was the due time for the second child, expected in early May. Ian didn't like the idea of confronting Jenny with important decisions right now; she had enough to deal with already. Better to wait until after their second child was born. They had until January to make up their minds which way to go. His next patrol could be arranged so that he would most probably be at home on Meagen's birthday. They had purchased presents already, such as clothes, which the little lady loved, and a tricycle. Jenny had invited a number of children Meagen's age for her birthday party, so that was arranged.

What Jenny didn't know was that Ian had ordered a new, bigger refrigerator; this one would run on kerosene as its energy source. No more would they have the headache of power outages, which happened frequently, and the system would run silently. Ian had figured that for a growing family you would need more stuff to keep cool and the old, small refrigerator would not do. He was lucky that there were no sudden emergencies which called for his assistance, and he was home on Meagen's second birthday. Jenny was getting heavy and Ian could do the lion's share of entertaining the crowd of little critters.

The party started early in the afternoon. Meagen was excited about her presents and Ian was exhausted when the show was over. It had been an exhilarating day for everyone concerned and the two parents looked proudly down on their first-born, who was already half asleep when her head touched the pillow.

"I envy everyone who can fall asleep that easily," said Jenny, who lately tossed around and around.

"Soon you will be able to do so, when you have no more ballast."

"Ballast? Is that how you consider it? How in heaven could I have fallen in love with such a brute?"

"Oh, very simple. You fell for my charm and irresistible personality. Moreover, ballast is something heavy in sailors' terms."

"You are a conceited, inconsistent male and if you don't come to bed with me right now, I'll divert you to the couch."

They did not have a couch, and both chuckled when installing themselves under the lowered mosquito net.

"I am cockeyed with fatigue," declared Jenny, and before he fell asleep Ian heard her murmuring 'ballast' from far away.

The month of May had arrived and the *Rian* was scheduled to go to Singapore for bunkers, this time without Jenny. Using the radio when in port was not allowed, and Ian had arranged with the embassy to be notified immediately when Jenny went into labor. Due to the possibility that he would leave Singapore on short notice, his passengers were informed that they ran the risk of not finding the *Rian* in the roads. Consequently, there were only a few shopping-happy ladies on board. Ian had not been there when Meagen was born and was determined not to miss it this time. He arranged to take fuel in the shortest time possible and when he arrived in Tandjoeng Pinang didn't see Jenny on the pier. Alarmed, he ran to their home and found her sitting in an armchair knitting something small.

"Oh, Ian, I didn't know you would be so early," she whispered in his ear when he bent over to kiss her. "And it is already late in the evening—how could you find the channel?"

"There were two guiding lights on which I could navigate," answered Ian, admiring her for her maritime understanding. "I think Frans had arranged for it, so I owe him one." Relaxed that he had made it in time, he felt his stomach growling and rummaged in the old refrigerator for food. It reminded him of the new, big one, waiting to be delivered when Jenny went to the hospital.

They sat there for a while, content to be together again. It was getting close to midnight, but Jenny wasn't sleepy. "You know, a funny thing happened this morning. I hammered a nail in one of the corner posts to hang a picture, and then the nail fell out, leaving a small hole, and some kind of grainy stuff came out." Ian didn't know what to think of it and told her he would check it in the morning. He did, using a hammer and pounding lightly on the beam. It sounded hollow, and at one spot, the hammerhead went through the paint into the wood. Alerted, he tested other beams and boards with the same result. "Must be bloody ants," he grumbled. "The whole house may collapse any moment."

He called Jenny and Meagen and told them to go outside, and then told Anjoeng to run quick to the manager of the government workshop. When it was explained to Anjoeng, the man ran off. "We better wait outside," Ian said to Jenny, and explained what he feared had happened. "I may be wrong, but this house is hanging together on its paint."

Within the shortest time, the manager and some of his helpers arrived. "That servant of yours gave me a shock, telling me that the house had collapsed." He went inside, drilling holes, and concluded that of the single-story dwelling, only the two bedrooms were safe. They would be back with beams to support the structure temporarily. Thereafter part of the roof and the dining and living areas would be torn down. After all that good news, the manager asked Ian, "Do you have somewhere to go in the meantime?" knowing full well that it was a redundant question, but you never knew.

The answer did not surprise him. "No, not on such short notice. Moreover, my wife is due any day and I don't want to go into the hassle of packing and moving right now." They discussed any alternative and came to the conclusion that if a big tarpaulin was pulled over the roof of the damaged area, the house could remain livable to a certain extent. Ian and Jenny opted for that solution so they could stay where they were. The only one who loved it was Meagen, running around in what she called their tent.

Two days later, toward evening, Jenny told Ian, "You better alert Dr. Sie Dwong. I think I am going into labor, the contractions are about five minutes apart."

Ian was up in arms. "Can I leave you alone for a moment? Why didn't you tell me before? Is that why Meagen is with friends?"

Not waiting for an answer, Ian ran to the doctor's house, not far from where they lived. He knocked on the door, praying Dr. Sie would be home. He was, and told Ian to bring Jenny to the little hospital. Since he was one of the few to have a telephone, he would alert the nurse to prepare for the confinement. Returning home he found Jenny ready, took the bag, which had been ready for several days, and walked her slowly to the road. Their house was seventeen steps below the road and when they reached the last steps, Jenny asked to sit down to catch her breath. They sat together, looking at the velvet sky and stars. Then Jenny looked down on their 'tent' and they held each other and started to laugh.

"We are nuts, sitting here like forlorn lovers. And on our way to the hospital to deliver a baby!" It was not a long walk and Jenny was taken to the delivery room, leaving Ian pacing the corridor.

Dr. Sie arrived, nodded at him, and went into the room. Shortly thereafter the nurse told Ian he could come in. Jenny looked pale and was obviously in pain. Dr. Sie was at her bedside and when Jenny let go a subdued scream, he told her, "Don't scream, Chinese women do not utter a sound when having a baby." He reached for his pocket and took a cigarette. Jenny looked at him with fire in her eyes. "I am not a Chinese woman and I will scream or yell when I want. And if you light that damned cigarette, I will kick you out of here myself." Wow, Ian thought, and that is coming from my wife, who smokes and inhales deeply to her toes!

Dr. Sie found no words, put the package back, and attended to her with a kind of awed admiration. It became a long night and near daybreak Jenny delivered the baby, complete and crying. "A boy, oh love, we have a son!"

Ian was jubilant, the long night forgotten, and overwhelmed by all he had witnessed. After having noticed all the manipulations which accompany the care of mother and child, Ian sat at her bedside and together they felt very happy in their renewed parenthood.

"I am tired now and want to sleep. Please tell our daughter and friends."

Ian kissed his wife. "I'll be back soon," he said, and walked in the early morning to their home, descending the steps two at a time. The servants congratulated him on their son, and Fia made him strong black coffee. Before taking a shower and relaxing, he went first to their friends who had taken Meagen. Entering their house, he took his daughter in his arms and told her that she had a baby brother and that mommy was very happy.

"A baby brother? I always asked for a little sister; did you forget?"

That was a complication Ian had not thought about, although the determined little girl had told them on every occasion that she wanted a sister. The lady of the house smilingly came to the rescue when she noticed Ian's dilemma, embracing Ian. "I am so glad for the two of you; congratulations." And then turning to Meagen, she said, "I am sure that a brother will be a lot of fun. You can play with him, and when you grow up, he will protect you like a big brother." That was something Meagen had to think about, and their friend looked at Ian. "And you better go home and take a nap. I will have Meagen dressed up when you two go to the hospital this afternoon."

The afternoon visit went very well, considering the girl/boy complication. Meagen looked at her brother cursorily and then climbed in bed next to Jenny, who pulled her close. The news that Jenny and Ian had a son went around in the small community very fast and often Ian and Meagen found visitors in Jenny's room. Their son was named Peter and as such officially entered in the population register. Frans accompanied Ian to the registrar, acting as witness. On their way back, Frans remarked, "You are lucky that you aren't a Papoea."

"What is that supposed to mean?"

"According to their custom, when a woman is in labor, the husband goes to bed next to her and moans and groans and screams as if in pain until the baby is born. The idea is that by doing so he takes the pain away from his wife." Ian's first reaction was that such a thing was ridiculous, but then realized there might be something to it for people who not so long ago lived in the Stone Age.

The work on the house went very fast and when Jenny and Peter came home, the tent was gone. It still smelled of paint but that didn't bother the Halls a bit. Ian would go to sea with the certainty that his family was all right and well cared for. With great pleasure he thought back to the moment when Jenny saw the great, new refrigerator in the dining room.

It was at the end of May when he came home from one of his trips that he and Jenny had a long talk about their future. He told her what Frans had said about not being a coast guard career officer or a merchant marine man. Jenny was not surprised to hear what Frans had said and asked him what he thought about it.

"As far as the Dutch Indies coast guard is concerned, I think he is right, because it will mean that we will always stay in the Indies. I don't think you and I are ready for that, not with the coast guard."

Then they discussed the topic of the merchant marine. Jenny had a very good understanding of his desire to sail worldwide, especially during the occupation years when there was no place to go.

"It is your life and if you are happy as a deck officer in the merchant marine, so will I be. However, it will be different from what you have been doing now."

Always a good planner, Ian came to the next hypothetical question. "If neither the coast guard nor the merchant marine, what would we choose: to stay here in this area or to go back to Holland?" And as a second thought he added, "Staying here depends very much on how the situation will develop; independence will be obtained, but the question is when and under what conditions would we be able to stay." It was getting late and Ian concluded, "Let us both put on our thinking cap and talk about it later. And now, mother of my two children, off to bed."

Life went on, the *Rian* was involved in several other military missions in a war which continued seemingly without end. The Dutch held more cities and towns and controlled the coastal areas of most islands, but the steaming jungle and settlements deep inland remained under guerrilla control. The inhabitants of Tandjoeng Pinang were not directly confronted with the situation other than troop movements passing through. It was almost like another world.

It was during one of his stays in the home port that Ian heard about a government official whose short-term contract expired and would not be renewed or extended. This was nothing special but for the fact that this gentleman functioned as shipping agent and airline agent, on behalf of the government. The reason for such activity by an official was simple: there was no civilian in Tandjoeng Pinang to do that work. Moreover, most passengers and cargo were government business, so the temporary solution was not far-fetched.

Ian didn't give it another thought, preoccupied as he was with family and work. But the next morning when he went to his ship he found that the jetty was almost filled with stacks of baled rice. There was a freighter anchored in the roads, discharging the rice into lighters, which were towed to the pier, the bales were stacked on the pier and loaded onto trucks, one at a time. Working his way to the *Rian*, he asked Jalim if such cargo arrived regularly. "Yes, sir, and not only rice but also general cargo, arriving by scheduled steamers calling here." Then he noticed the official supervising the activity as the person who would leave his post soon.

An idea came up: would it be possible for him to start that business after his term with the coast guard ended? He went to the man, whom he had not met before, and started talking with him. Yes, the man said, he was leaving in six-months time and as far as he knew, no replacement was arranged. "It is not a government job, and a civilian should do it." Asking further, Ian learned that in addition to handling incoming and outgoing cargo, he rented a tugboat and lighters from the harbor master. No, he was not acting as airline agent; that was done by the port office. Ian thanked the official and instead of returning to the *Rian* he went straight home.

"Jenny, I'd like a cup of coffee and want to talk with you."

Not being used to such a formal approach, her first reaction was "What is wrong? Has something happened?"

"No, my dearest, nothing is wrong," he said, and told her what he had learned on the pier. "What would you think if I told you that there may be an opportunity for us to start our own business?"

"You mean asking to become shipping and airline agent?"

"Exactly. I haven't the slightest idea what kind of income it would bring, but that can be found out."

They looked at each other and by mutual understanding agreed it would be worthwhile to find out and apply to the shipping and airline companies to be appointed as their agents. "Before that, I'll talk with the governor and with Frans to obtain their backing. After all, they are involved right now."

Frans was surprised hearing Ian's plan. "I never thought about that, but I will be glad to get rid of the airline work, which is a burden for us. You have my full support." Thereafter he asked the governor and informed him what he had in mind, provided the governor would agree. As a real diplomat the governor hedged at first, telling him that he wasn't sure and wanted to know how Ian could handle the significant government cargoes.

"I understand that, if your idea works out, we have to pay you for your services?"

Ian had done his homework. "But then you will not have that person on your payroll, and I probably will agree to a special government tariff."

The governor smiled. "Already becoming a businessman, Ian? All right, I like your approach. When the shipping company contacts me, I'll inform them that you are the right man for them."

So far so good, Ian thought, and thanked the governor. As he was leaving he was called back. "Ian, don't forget to talk with the major. The army has even more business in that field than we do."

Ian had to sail soon and time to do the groundwork for his plan was running short. So, without prior appointment, he went to the major's office. A sergeant at the reception desk was reluctant to let Ian through. "The major is occupied right now and I don't know whether he can see you later."

Ian decided to cut through military performance. "I am the commanding officer of the *Rian*, and as such have participated in several army operations with a colonel and with Major Renne. It is imperative that I see the major." Then seeing that he was putting undue stress upon the sergeant, he added. "Sorry, I can't wait. I have to sail tomorrow. Please do the best you can."

The sergeant nodded. "I understand, sir. As soon as the major is free, I'll announce you."

While waiting, he heard the loud, angry voice of the major, and at times the more subdued voice of the minister. Oh boy, Ian thought, those two are at each other's throats again. It was no secret that both men disliked each other to a high degree. In church on Sunday mornings, the minister, militarized with the rank of captain, included in his sermon various sticky remarks about the army and more particularly the major, however without mentioning names. In his pulpit once a week he was inviolable, but each time thereafter was called to report to the major. There was one good thing about the situation: the church was always full. Apparently this moment it was the major's turn, and the sergeant coughed nervously, looking at Ian. Both smiled with understanding, and the painful silence was broken by the minister marching red-faced out of the office. The sergeant rose to salute him and went to the door to announce Ian, but Ian quickly said to give the major five minutes to calm down.

Those five minutes appeared to be the minimum. Ian was announced by the sergeant, who softly closed the door after Ian had entered. The army officer stood at the window looking outside. Clearly he was still agitated. Without turning, he said,

"Yes, what do you want?" A hell of a start, but being inside, there was no retreat.

"Sir, I appreciate that you can see me on such short notice." The major was surprised to hear these words, turned around, and recognized Ian as the commanding officer of the *Rian*. He regained his composure. "Please sit down. You have been quite helpful to us. What can I do for you?" That second sentence sounded a lot better in Ian's ears and with aplomb he delivered his plan.

The major listened attentively and when Ian was finished leaned back in his chair. "We have one captain, one lieutenant, and some enlisted men in what we call our transport department. If the shipping and airline company appoint you as their agent, that's fine with me. You'll have to work closely together with my transport officers."

"Thank you for your kind words. I wished to inform you before contacting the companies."

"Good strategy, sailor. Good luck."

That evening letters were typed on a borrowed typewriter to the head offices of the two companies in Batavia in which Ian expressed interest in acting as their agent in Tandjoeng Pinang and asked for details if the interest was mutual. "It will take weeks, if not a month, before we can receive an answer, if at all. Moreover, if we get only one positive response, there is no deal. We need both," Ian declared.

"Do you realize there are three ifs in what you are saying?" They both realized it was a shot in the dark, and even if the three ifs turned positive, they still didn't know whether the income would be sufficient to make a living.

Chapter Twenty-Six

The first reaction came from the Royal Packet and Navigation Company (KPM) when Ian was at sea. Jenny opened the letter, anxious about its contents. Scanning through it, she was relieved to find that the gist of their reply was positive. Ian's expression of interest in acting as their agent was sent to the KPM office in Singapore, being within its jurisdiction of the region, for follow-up. Mr. Halls would hear from them shortly.

Leaving the children with Fia, she walked to Frans' office, eager to show a good friend what she assumed was a good start. Frans agreed. "I know the KPM director in Singapore. He is a reasonable man. When Ian is back, I'll give him some pointers which he might use when negotiating."

She looked pleadingly at Frans. "When will Ian be back?" "Oh no, lady, you are not going to twist my arm to disclose to you military secrets! He will return next week and I forgot already that I told you."

A clerk from the post office brought her the message that the *Rian* was due to arrive in the afternoon and Jenny took her two children to the jetty, by now a familiar place for her. When the *Rian* was swinging around to approach the jetty she noticed that Ian and some crew members wore bandages. Alarmed, she called out to him. "Ian, what happened?" He waved at her but did not answer, being occupied with bringing the ship alongside. As soon as that was done, he jumped ashore and embraced his family. "Nothing serious, we got some wood splinters from enemy fire. Don't worry, no doctor needed." Meagen looked with respect at his bandaged forehead and arm, and her lips started trembling. Quickly, Ian took her on his arm and they went onboard. Reassured, Jenny took the KPM letter from her purse and without a word showed it to Ian. A broad smile lit his face when he read it. "Well, that's a good start. Did you hear from the Singapore office?"

"No, but don't forget we get mail only once a week." After having given final orders to Jalim and the boatswain, the 'Halls crowd,' as Ian called them, traversed the sloop deck. Jenny then noticed that both the work boat and the lifeboat were heavily damaged. She wanted to say something, but Ian shook his head not to talk about it. Passing the port office Ian waved to Frans who responded in the same manner. Aha, Jenny thought, Frans knew about it via the ship's radio, but didn't tell me. At home Ian became the center of the servants' attention when they saw the bandages. Jenny wanted him to see the doctor, which he stubbornly refused. "You were a nurse, so I have the best service a man could want." Then he told her that they had been involved in a combined action of the navy and the coast guard and that a navy doctor had treated him and his wounded crew members. That was all he wanted to say and Jenny did not press the issue. She wished with all her heart that her husband would succeed in his plan and stay ashore.

Weeks went by without receiving any news and their hopes sank into low gear. Once a week a Catalina of the Royal Dutch Airlines (KLM) landed, or rather 'watered,' at Tandjoeng Pinang on its schedule from Batavia to Singapore, and returned the next morning on the way back coming from Singapore. Still there was no news, neither from KPM nor from KLM.

"Maybe next week" became a standard expression which sounded more hollow each time. The next day, when the plane returned from Singapore, a KLM steward went to the *Rian*, asking for Mr. Halls. "The port manager told me I could find you here. I have a letter for you." He handed Ian the letter from KLM.

Ian thanked him and opened the letter when he had left. The contents were practically identical to the KPM message. They also referred the matter to the KLM office in Singapore. The difference was that the Singapore office manager invited Ian to come to his office at Ian's convenience for further discussion. So far, so good, he thought. It would be very nice indeed if KPM would ask the same, but that would be too much to ask for. While he was busy with his paperwork, he heard somebody coming up to the bridge, and assuming it was the shore engineer who was supervising the repairs on board, he called out to his mess boy for another cup of coffee.

"Good morning, sir," a familiar female voice said. With surprise he looked up and saw Jenny standing in the doorway. She was holding something behind her back. "I have a surprise for you."

"And I have one for you," he said teasingly. "Let's hand our surprises over simultaneously." He got a letter from KPM, and handed the KLM message to her. KPM Singapore informed Ian that they would send somebody from their office to Tandjoeng Pinang to talk with him, at his convenience.

"Our chances are getting better all the time." Both were excited about the program. When Jenny was leaving, she said, "If it is convenient for Mr. Halls, would he join us later for lunch?"

"Mrs. Halls, I wouldn't miss such an invitation at any cost."

From that moment on, events proceeded at a roller-coaster pace. He informed Frans about the latest developments, and both worked on a long-term schedule, covering Ian's last three months with the coast guard. Of course, there always was the possibility that something urgent could come up, but other than that, the only sure thing was the forthcoming biannual trip for the government to the Natoena and Anambas islands.

The Fransens had become good friends with the young family and Frans liked the idea of those two succeeding in their efforts. He called on Ian the next day. "The shore engineer tells me that within a few days the repairs on the *Rian* will be complete. I think that right after, you need bunkers." Ian understood what he meant: that would give him at least a day off in Singapore to visit the KLM office.

Playing the same game, he remarked, "Good idea, I almost forgot." At the post office he sent a telegram to KLM announcing the date for his visit. This time, Jenny didn't want to leave the two children with others, so she stayed home.

The discussion in the KLM office was very cordial and resulted in an official written offer. Ian played it safe and told them that his acceptance would depend on whether he could make a deal with KPM. The manager smiled. "I appreciate your situation. You can't make a living on our agency alone."

It was later in the afternoon when he left the KLM office. As long as I am here, why not see the KPM people, he thought. He took a taxi and entered the office, many times larger than the airline's and far more official. Must be big business here, he thought, and asked for the director. "Do you have an appointment?" the attractive Chinese girl at the reception desk asked. "In a way I have," replied Ian with fingers crossed, and showed her the letter. "I think the director is with the general manager right now. I'll try to find out if he can see you." She took the telephone and after a while told Ian, "Both the general manager and the director would like to see you now."

After introductions there ensued a general discussion on shipping specifics in the Indies. The director started to talk about more details, while the general manager observed Ian's answers and attitude. It was getting late and the director asked what Ian's immediate plans were. Was he free for dinner tonight? Yes, that could be arranged. He was asked to wait outside for a moment, and left the two men alone.

They looked at each other, and the general manager said, "Go get him. I am sure he is the right man for the job."

"I agree. I will go there as soon as possible, before he eventually decides something else." The dinner that night took place in a very exclusive club. Ian had the impression that Mr. Venema, the director, wanted to observe him in these luxurious surroundings. He learned a lot about the shipping company in general. Mr. Venema asked him when he was heading back to Tandjoeng Pinang. "Tomorrow at noon," answered Ian.

"Can I go with you?"

"No problem, but be prepared for a number of shopping-worn ladies on board."

"Fine. I'd like to stay for some days, talk with you and with important shippers. I'll stay with friends."

On arrival, he passed by the port office and found Frans still working. "I have a job for you on short notice. A government official has arrived with his family and servants to replace the man on the island of Karimoen." The hurry was due to the fact that accommodation of that family with children and baggage in Tandjoeng Pinang presented a problem. Oh shit, Ian thought, and told Frans his predicament. "What? You have Venema here? That son of a gun? We were together in the same camp during the war. I'll take care of him until you are back. If you leave tomorrow morning you'll be back within three days."

Greatly relieved, Ian went home where he found his family at dinner. This time Jenny had not come to the jetty. "You'll get spoiled if even on short trips we are all on the pier to welcome our master," she joked. This remark did not meet with Meagen's approval.

"Mommy is very naughty," she declared and turned to her brother for understanding. "You think so too, Peter!"

"You little pest," exclaimed Ian, fishing Peter from his crib and holding the two on his knees.

"But we all love mommy, and therefore, you may give her this," he said, and put Meagen on her feet and gave her the KLM offer to hand to Jenny. "That is the beginning," he said, and then told her about Mr. Venema.

That evening they had much to talk about, and when in bed, Jenny snuggled close to Ian. "Oh I so hope that it will all work out," she whispered and nestled in his arms. The next morning he noticed Mr. Venema in Frans' office. Before he could say anything, Venema said good- humoredly, "This man here is threatening me if I dare to leave before you return. Don't worry. I have enough to do in the meantime." That was nicely arranged and Ian took off with his passengers, promising himself to make it a fast turn-around. When he approached home port he noticed that this time his clan was waiting for him, to everybody's delight.

The meeting with Mr. Venema in their house went very well. First they thought it better to send the children for a walk with Fia, but then decided not to. "After all, we are not meeting in an office, but in a home."

The business details went smoothly and they were surprised to learn the potentials. It was not a gold mine, but with the proper approach and determination offered a fair living. In conclusion, Mr. Venema handed Ian a standard agent contract, unsigned.

"This is what we would like to offer you, with amendments, particularly to the special situation here. Study it and tell me your decision tomorrow morning." Ian noticed that it was an open ended agreement and the date to start was set as February 1, 1949. His contract with the coast guard ended on January 5, so that gave him some time to make arrangements and set up an office. An office? And housing? They had clearly overlooked that 'minor' detail!

"Uh, Mr. Venema, we may have a minor problem. We'll have to vacate this government-owned house, when I leave the government service." Venema was clearly surprised, and then chided Ian. "Sorry, I assumed that you knew that KPM owns an office with living quarters annexed to it in Tandjoeng Pinang."

When he saw their questioning eyes, he continued. "As per one of the amendments, the premises are yours to occupy as long as you are our agent."

That evening Ian and Jenny made calculations and after a lengthy discussion the decision was made. They would go ahead with the opportunity. The die was cast. Unable to sleep, they held each other close, knowing that it was a far-reaching conclusion for their future.

"During the wartime we made decisions at a moment's impulse, but now with two children, it sure is different," Ian said. In the semidarkness came Jenny's voice. "Together, you and I will make it."

The next morning Mr. Venema came to their house, sat down, and looked at them inquiringly. Ian told him that he accepted the offer, and both signed the papers and shook hands.

"Welcome on board, I am delighted. You will get reams of documents and I shall send one of our men to you for a week to get you started."

Preparing to leave, he told them that the governor had agreed to vacate the office, and the family who occupied part of the house would move into the dwelling in which the Halls lived now. Apparently he had felt pretty sure that Ian would accept the agency.

Before leaving on his last trip into the South China Sea, there was quite a lot to do: confirming to KLM that he was accepting the agency as of February 1, 1949; sending a letter to Mr. Werff, informing him that he would stay in Tandjoeng Pinang after the expiration of his coast guard contract; and meetings with the governor and major informing them of his activity as agent, which would be confirmed by the companies concerned. Other topics could be dealt with after his return.

Now he was ready for the last two months in coast guard service and wondered whether he could say good-bye to the seven seas without second thoughts. But then he knew that his family was most important to him, and moreover, he would still be close to the ocean and air operations. Jenny, Meagen, and Peter were on the pier to see him off for his four-week voyage. "Okay, sailor, come home safely. Thank god, I'll not have to say that many more times." On the command "fore and aft, let go" the *Rian* gathered speed and was soon out of sight of the small crowd on the jetty.

Chapter Twenty-Seven

Upon his return from the Natoena and Anambas islands trip, Ian had one more month in government service to go. Due to increasing demand for weapons, ammunition, and cigarettes by the guerrillas on Sumatra, smuggling of those contraband items from Singapore and Malaysia became more lucrative. Payments were usually made in tea, rubber, tobacco leaves, and coffee. Imports and exports were illegal when not covered by permits issued by the Dutch East Indies government. Consequently, the two coast guard minesweepers were heavily engaged in patrolling the coastal waters, while the navy operated mainly in the Malacca Straits and beyond. Frans told Ian that he had no choice but to include the *Rian* in the heavy schedule.

"Sorry, fellow, I can't give you a leisurely finish of your contract. Your successor is due to arrive only shortly before you sign off."

Well, I have to bite the bullet, Ian thought. Clearly Mr. Werff still did not have much extra personnel. Ian had received a personal letter from him in Twhich Mr. Werff congratulated Ian on his new endeavors and expressed his regret that Ian would not extend his contract or join the coast guard as a career officer.

"Well, I am not going anywhere, and am always prepared to help my successor out when needed," Ian told Frans.

"I knew we could count on you. Thank you," Frans said in appreciation. So within two days the *Rian* was out on patrol again, stopping craft to inspect their cargoes. One morning they noticed a tugboat towing two lighters, and set course to intercept. When it became clear to the tugboat crew that the *Rian* was heading for the tow, they slipped the hawser and pulled away full speed, leaving the lighters drifting. This maneuver fueled Ian's suspicion; he ordered full speed and went after the tugboat. It was a wooden affair and no match for the *Rian*, but clearly the tug skipper was determined to avoid a confrontation. The tugboat didn't show colors, which meant very little anyhow since all native craft carried several different nationality flags.

Ian was surprised that it took them so long to overtake the tugboat. Getting nearer he ordered the machine guns manned as a precaution. Jalim and he were keeping the tug in view through their binoculars. Suddenly Jalim called, "Look, the tug falls apart!" And then Ian also noticed that boards were loosening from the bow, opening the boat. The water gulped in and in seconds the tug dove at a steep angle into the waters, showing her stern briefly, then disappeared completely.

It all went so fast that they almost overran the spot where the tug had disappeared. Ian yanked the telegraph to slow ahead, shouted to the helmsman to give full port rudder, and coasted the *Rian* around to see whether there were any survivors. He stayed around for quite some time, but there was no sign of life, only some flotsam and jetsam in the area. Jalim gave Ian his opinion on what happened.

"I think that because of the high speed the vibration caused the curved boards on the bow to loosen." Ian nodded. After the war there was a shortage of local craft and lots of boats were built in a hurry. Shoddy workmanship and use of green lumber resulted in a product that could not be classified as seaworthy.

They left the site of the tragedy and went looking for the abandoned lighters, which were drifting aimlessly. With the *Rian* alongside, the lighters were inspected. Their cargo was a smelling mess of semi-dried little fish called terassi, which are used as an ingredient for spicy pastes in the Indies cuisine. However, the moisture content had to be controlled, which wasn't done in the lighters; hence, the fishy smell. Even Jalim wrinkled his nose and asked Ian what he was going to do. "I will make an entry in the log book. We'll tow the lighters to home port. Pay out the hawser as much as possible to keep the lighters far out."

It was the correct decision. Human lives had been involved and although none could have been identified and neither could the tugboat, there was always a possibility that relatives of the tug crew might report them missing. Leaving the lighters drifting would present a danger to ships if the lighters were in shipping lanes. The *Rian* could only proceed at low speed and despite the long hawser there occasionally came a whiff of the pungent aroma to the *Rian*. "It smells" came the polite understatement of the mess boy.

"It stinks" was the curt reply from Ian. There was nothing he could do about it. "Shortly, we can alter course and get into the wind."

All hands on board were glad when the *Rian* entered the channel to Tandjoeng Pinang. The towline was shortened and since they had no spare anchor, Ian had to bring the *Rian* with the lighters alongside the jetty at dead slow into the current. It was a tricky maneuver but went well. Having radioed the situation to the port office, he was not surprised to see Frans waiting on the pier. When ship and barges were tied up, Frans stormed to the bridge with a face like a thundercloud.

"Are you out of your mind to bring this, this . . . ." In his agitation he could not find the right words to blow off steam.

"This is terassi, and old timers always assured me that cured terassi enhances the palate. This stuff is curing." Ian tried to keep a humorous atmosphere, but to no avail.

"You turn around right now, let the barges go in deep water, and sink them in some god-forsaken spot outside navigable waters," Frans fumed.

Ian had never seen him so uptight and decided to take a more official approach, thereby hiding his annoyance. "Sir, I entered the mishap in the log book. I hereby deliver the two lighters with cargo to the harbor master of Tandjoeng Pinang. Further orders will be carried out only when in writing."

Frans looked at Ian as if he had been punched in the stomach. Then realizing the validity of Ian's reaction, he gave a parting shot. "Tut, tut. Since when are we talking like that to a superior? And what happened to a cold beer when the aforementioned superior welcomes one of his stubborn underlings after a dreadful voyage?"

"Aha, that's more like it," Ian said, and called for beer. Whatever happened to the lighters, Ian did not know and neither did he ask, but two days later they had disappeared and were never heard of again.

His successor arrived and Ian took him on board for a last short patrol. Back in port he collected his gear, stepped ashore, and saluted the *Rian*. He would see the crew that night; Frans had arranged for a men-only, 'farewell-to-arms' party for them in the Chinese restaurant. Frans' wife knew about the arrangement and had warned Jenny in advance.

"My dear, you better close the hatches and tie up secure," she said in sailor's fashion. "It is going to be a long night, with speeches and drinks galore. When our sweethearts return home in the wee hours, pretend to be fast asleep." How right she was.

The next morning the children awoke and as usual when Ian was home, climbed in their parents' bed, filled with energy. Jenny, still half asleep herself, whispered to them, "Shh, daddy is still sleeping. He has a nail in his head." Meagen looked shocked and Peter, looking up at his big sister, also put his little hands at his mouth, mimicking her. Meagen, not understanding that it meant somebody had a king-sized headache, went looking for the nail. Ian stirred at the commotion, mumbled some incoherent words, and slept. Jenny hastily diverted their attention by promising to bake some real Dutch pancakes and they left him in peace.

Life was different from then on, and the entire family loved it. The days were filled with family life, which was a luxury not experienced before to such an extent. There was work aplenty to prepare for February 1, the day when the combined operation would start: moving into the KPM building, outfitting the residential and office sections, arranging with the port office to charter the government-owned tugboat and lighters, studying the flow of KPM and KLM documents, and another zillion items. Money they had saved dwindled rapidly and since there was no bank in Tandjoeng Pinang, there was no possibility of drawing on a bank account. Hunting for bargains in town, they succeeded in purchasing some used items: a typewriter, a small safe, and a bascule, the latter to weigh airline passengers and luggage.

Letters of introduction of the new agency had been sent from the Singapore offices to all customers on Bintan island and on February 1, 1949, Ian and Jenny proudly hoisted the KPM and KLM flags on the poles in front of the office, next to the Dutch national colors. Jenny had, in a short time, acquainted herself with the ins and outs of the business, and the two stood in the office, each holding a child. "Here we go, darling. Again as before; for better and for worse," Ian said.

The office was filled with bouquets of flowers from Malayan, Chinese, and Indian merchants; from the government offices; and from friends. Refreshments were on tables to welcome well-wishers and soon the place was crowded. Meagen and Peter were allowed to partake in the festivity and had the time of their lives. Although no business transpired on opening day, they were off to a good beginning.

The promised KPM man, Max Dront, had arrived and proved to be highly valuable for the week of his stay, going through all details. One evening, having dinner at their home, he talked about the days passed.

"I understand you two will run the agency together?" When this was confirmed, he continued to give his opinion on the operation of the dual agency. "I don't know how busy you will be for KLM, but I think that very soon you will need two people: one who will prepare the Bills of Lading and talk with shippers, and one who will deliver papers to customers."

As for the former, Max had traced a Chinese man in town who had done this kind of work before and suggested Ian talk with him. Most of the private shippers were Chinese and they preferred to deal with a landsman. As for the other, they needed an "oppas" who could do odds and ends without taking Jenny's and Ian's time.

"There are no telephones on the island and everything has to be done by verbal or written messages." Ian and Jenny looked at each other and Max understood the situation. "I have looked at the scheduled ship movements via Tandjoeng Pinang this month and can assure you that the two men I talked about are essential for a smooth and efficient operation, and that's what you and we want."

Ian talked with Oei Pheng Hui, the man who had previous experience, and found him willing to work for him. As for an oppas Ian went to the port office and told the secretary what he was looking for; could the secretary suggest someone? Within a day a young Malay presented himself as candidate for the job and handed Ian a note of recommendation from the secretary.

That settled, the first action came when the weekly plane from Batavia arrived, moored on the buoy and opened the hatch-type door. The motor launch, chartered by Ian from the port administration for these occasions, came alongside to take passengers, luggage, and cargo to the pier. There was no problem since the launch crew had done this before when the port manager acted as KLM agent. There were only a few passengers for Singapore, the last stop on the route. Early the next morning the plane would return to Batavia with four stops, including Tandjoeng Pinang.

Ian and Jenny were up and around before daybreak, checking all the documents that might be necessary. The army transport officer handed requisition forms for six military passengers, their allotment for that route to Batavia. Tandjoeng Pinang's total allotment was for twelve passengers and more than six had already assembled in the office. Jenny had issued numbers in order of arrival at the office and wrote tickets while Ian was busy weighing the passengers and their luggage. This was needed for making up the "stowage plan," an inventive form related to establishing a required load center of the plane. Passengers had no choice where to sit; their location was determined by their weight.

The bay waters were smooth and the plane was on time. The captain checked the plan, signed for approval, and soon all were onboard. Ian remained on the jetty to make sure everything was all right, gave a thumbs-up sign to the pilot that the bay area was clear of boats, and the plane took off. It had been a hectic couple of hours and their first act as agents was completed without problems.

Chapter Twenty-Eight

Ian steered his small motorboat toward the spot where the river flowed into the bay, about half a mile from the pier. At that point there was a tiny island by the name of Bajan, and he banked his boat on its beach. He had an appointment with Frans, who would meet him later on Bajan. When Ian had asked to see him here, Frans had sputtered, "Why there? Isn't my office good enough?" Ian had replied that he had a very special reason for asking Frans to see him there, and to whet his appetite, had added, "It is important for you and me." Seated on a tree trunk he looked over the bay and let his thoughts wander, reminiscing about his time in Tandjoeng Pinang.

It was five months since they had started the agencies and they had done very well. Jenny was his right hand and liked the work in the office, which included meeting with people. To lighten her housework burden, and here Ian had to grin at the word "burden," Fia was now promoted to in-house servant, which included taking care of the children. Another cook was now stationed in the kitchen under Fia's supervision. Meagen went to nursery school and Peter, now eighteen months old, was doing great. The business had flourished and was growing, despite the still-continuing conflict, or maybe because of it.

Living in a small town without a newspaper, with no phones, and no local radio station, it was difficult to fully comprehend what was going on in the world, even in the East Indies.

It soon had become clear that the two lighters from the port office, which he used to haul cargo to and from the KPM ships calling at the port, were not sufficient. The ships had to anchor in the roads, about two miles from the port, because of their draft. One day he had met with an elderly Dutchman who apparently was well-off financially. They talked about business in general and then he asked how Ian was doing.

"I learned from Pheng Hui that you, at times, are short on barge capacity?" Andries Pott asked Ian, who confirmed it. "If you are considering adding tonnage capacity, maybe I can help you," Andries continued. The discussion went on and some days later they made a deal: Andries would provide three large barges and a tugboat, and Ian operate that fleet. Profit would be shared fifty-fifty and a handshake concluded the deal. It had worked very well for both parties.

Another thing that had worked out very well was his arrangement with the local Chinese longshoremen gangs. Through his man Pheng Hui he had arranged a simple agreement when ships had to be handled—so many tons of cargo in or out to be discharged or loaded within a number of hours or days, depending on the tonnage, at an agreed upon price per ton. Ian had made the deal with the three heads of the kongsi. They had to arrange for the number of longshoremen needed to stay within the allowed time. It worked like clockwork, with minimal administration, no tax matters, and not even a listing of names. It followed the well-known rule of "no cure, no pay," which meant that when there was no work for the KPM agents they looked elsewhere or went fishing.

Andries and Ian had called their venture the "Rhio Stevedoring and Lighterage Company" without any fanfare.

Having excess barge capacity, he found additional work between islands within the archipelago.

He was interrupted in his thoughts by the sound of the port launch. Frans let her run onto the beach and stepped ashore. "Well, here we are. What's cooking?" No doubt he was intrigued about this rendezvous and couldn't make head or tail of it.

"Have a seat," Ian invited him, making a place on the trunk.

"Is this a government-owned little knoll?" he asked.

"Yes, it is."

"Nobody using it?"

"No." And then Frans' patience wore thin. "For crying out loud, are we here playing hide and seek? Come out with it, man."

Ian decided the charade was over. "With your approval I am going to ask the Dutch East Indies Government for a ninety-nine-year lease on Bajan." Before Frans had an opportunity to interrupt, Ian continued. "I plan to build a shipyard here for repairs and maintenance of small vessels. It is the only place in the area with deep water to the beach."

Frans digested the information, which to him came out of the blue. After a while he wanted to know "Why, with my approval?"

"Very simple. You issue annual certificates of seaworthiness to all craft registered on Bintang. The craft settle in the mud and only at low tide can you inspect them to check the hulls. Now they come here, winched high and dry, ready for inspection."

For heaven's sake, this fellow is on to something, Frans thought. No longer do I have to tramp around in the mud, often in the night. Half won over to the idea, he asked again, "But what do you need my approval for?"

"Because I am willing to take that rusty pram of yours from your shoulder. You know that LCT, tied up at the pier." The LCT (Landing Craft Tank), a small sister of an LST, was found there after the war, engines dismantled, and corroding away. And then he told Frans he would push the LCT at high tide onto the beach at Bajan with two tugs, tie her up, and use it for some machinery and lumber, needed for repairs, instead of building a workshop and store.

"Aha, but the LCT is government property and if I agree, you'll have to pay."

"Seven hundred fifty dollars as is. And if you let that bucket sit there much longer it will sink and that will become a real costly affair to salvage."

"You son of a bitch, you have it all figured out, eh?" There was admiration in his voice. "And when does his majesty wish to conclude that deal?"

"Tomorrow, under proviso that I get the lease for the island, and when I told the governor about my plan, he was all for it and promised expediency to complete the papers. So do we have a deal?" Frans stood up from the trunk and padded along the beach, contemplating the issue. Ian's plan incorporated a two-fold advantage; better and more convenient inspections and getting rid of the useless LCT. And if the governor was for it, why should he not be?

He turned around and shook hands. "Okay, it's a deal. You are really something, Ian. The only thing missing with you as a businessman is slanting eyes." And their laughs rolled over the bay waters.

Ian got the lease on the island, paid for the LCT, and inspected the landing craft more thoroughly. He wanted to lighten her as much as possible so that it would rest as high as possible on the beach. On the island laborers had dug a small inlet so that the LCT would be on an even keel, close to where the slip was going to be. Finding that there was still fuel in the tanks, he asked the manager of the local utility plant if there was an interest. There definitely was, also for the lengths of armored wiring on board. The two bronze propellers found a buyer in Singapore and Ian had already saved several times his investment in the craft.

Through Pheng Hui he found a native who had been a ship's engineer, signed him on as his yard manager, and sent him to Singapore to visit shipyards for rails, a winch, dollies, and other items (preferably used) needed to construct the slip. The engineer sent him a telegram with the details and together Ian and Jenny calculated that they could handle seventy percent of the total price. Ian cabled back his price and after the local custom of haggling back and forth, purchase was concluded at seventy-eight percent of the initial asking price.

Meanwhile the agencies and the lighterage operation required full attention; Pheng Hui needed help with the shipping operation and the administrative work; and the load became heavier, so two more people were hired in the office. Jenny was now able to take Ian's place when he was out of the office, either on board ships or on Bajan. For the slip yard, he had the manager, machinists, and carpenters on the payroll. The ex-LCT was firmly secured and looked like a real shop with a generator, lathe, drillpress, welder, and lumber. The wharf was ready for business.

Chinese New Year meant a day of entirely different activities, as Ian found out. Frans had informed him that on that day you start with visiting the captain of the Chinese population, offering him a happy and prosperous new year. Thereafter you visit the lieutenants, followed by important Chinese merchants and kongsi leaders. The captain and lieutenants were not military ranks but indications of a form of civil authority amongst the Chinese.

As a good friend, Frans picked Ian up and before leaving he warned Jenny that it was going to be a long day. So the two walked over to the house of the captain, who welcomed them under his roof. Ian had expected that all Chinese dignitaries would be there to receive the well-wishers, but the scenery inside the spacious house was quite different. On the front gallery a large number of chairs were placed in horseshoe fashion, one leg near the entrance and the other end at the exit. Several guests were seated already at the beginning of the line and when Frans and Ian arrived they moved over to make place for them. Others coming after them got the same courtesy and that resulted in moving to the rate of new arrivals. When you reached the end, you left. Interrupting the procedure and leaving before one reached the last chair was considered very impolite. During this version of musical chairs, champagne and Chinese snacks were served. Voices in different languages mingled with Chinese ding-ping music and Ian enjoyed every minute of it.

The procedure continued more or less the same during the day, but the next Chinese host served brandy, the following whiskey, and so on. That was, by itself, no problem and to be considered a nice and friendly gesture, and you could always politely avoid a second drink, right? When asking Frans how to handle the booze onslaught, he was told to take only little sips. This was obviously a good idea but for the fact that even after a tiny sip, the host servants filled the glass to the rim right away. At the end of the line, you always ended up with a full glass. Champagne was not too difficult to finish off in one long gulp, but brandy and whiskey were another matter. Again, Frans came to the rescue. "Just before leaving, you put your hand around the glass so that your host cannot see whether it is full, and graciously dump the whole business in the basin near the exit." The contents of the basin already smelled like a distillery despite the addition of some kind of refreshing liquid.

They had made three rounds, walking from one place to the other, and it was time to take siesta during the heat of the day. Both men walked as if in a daze and Ian, who lived closest to the Chinese quarters, found his home and disappeared with a "see you later," leaving Frans to climb the hill. Jenny had arranged for a quiet siesta time and woke up her husband with strong coffee. Soon he was back on his feet, continuing the visits of dignitaries and merchants. It was a hell of a day, with the positive side that he met a great number of people and got better acquainted.

The work went on with a high degree of efficiency to local standards, but was never dull or routine. One day Ian was on a trip to the Shell Oil tank park on the island of Samboe to conclude a deal transporting oil products in drums to Tandjoeng Pinang. Pheng Hui was out on a KPM ship in the roads. Jenny and their help were holding the fort when a Chinese gentleman walked into the office. He told her that he was the owner of two barges at anchor in the bay, loaded with two hundred tons of cloves, destined for Batavia. He wanted to know the lowest freight rate by KPM steamer to Batavia. If acceptable, he then could return the empty barges, which were not in good condition, to Singapore for repairs.

"Two hundred tons of cloves? That is a lot," exclaimed Jenny. "Yes, and quite valuable. Did you smell when people smoke a self-rolled cigarette?" he asked, noticing Jenny's surprise. Yes, she knew that special sweet aroma. "Well, when they roll a cigarette, they put one clove in it for taste." He said he was in a hurry and wanted to leave late that afternoon, so would like to have a quote before, and left.

What do I do now, Jenny thought, and called Pheng Hui's assistant. "Where do cloves come from?" she asked him.

"From the Moluccas, in the eastern part of the Indies. If they come from there, I don't understand how they arrived here. We are far from a direct course between the Moluccas and Batavia." Jenny had learned that for merchandise a direct route is not always followed, and who knew where it originated from. She ran over to the post office and sent an urgent telegram to the KPM Singapore office for a freight rate with reply needed in four hours. Sitting on pins and needles while waiting, she thought of little else, and sent the oppas to the post office, telling him to stay there and bring the message as soon as it arrived. The answer came before the owner of the cloves returned and when she read the total freight amount, she whistled unladylike. She realized that their agency would get a full commission because this wasn't government cargo.

As promised, the Chinese returned. Jenny offered tea and after a proper time, he asked for the requested information. Now or never, Jenny thought, and gave him the rate. He studied it for, what seemed to her, a long time, and the silence grew thick. Then he looked up, smiled, and remarked that the rate was stiff, apparently ready to bargain. But he found a determined woman opposite him; no haggling. Her message was clear. "When could we ship from here?" he asked. Her assistant had told her that in two-days time the KPM vessel, now discharging, would be back from Singapore, bound for Batavia.

"In two days," she said, and in a daring move, added, "Your barges have to be repaired. They may be leaking, so part of your valuable cargo may be spoiled if you wait too long." It was a stab in the dark and she could not read his face as to how it was received. To smooth the waters and not lose the initiative, she added charmingly, "And since you have to leave later for Singapore, I offer you a cabin on the vessel tonight, so you are there tomorrow morning and need not sit on a slow-moving local craft all night. On the house, of course."

He looked at her in amazement. "The only thing missing is that you haven't offered to repair the barges at your shipyard." In the rush and excitement that was, indeed, overlooked. "My husband will return tomorrow, and I am sure he can make you a good offer for the repairs. No need to go to a shipyard in Singapore; we can do better." The shipper accepted the rate, a firm booking note was signed, and Jenny sent the oppas to the port office, asking for the launch to bring a passenger to the ship. A complimentary ticket was issued with a personal note from Jenny to the captain. When the Chinese was leaving, he looked at her, opened his briefcase, and put a number of expensive-looking wristwatches on her desk.

"What is that for?" Jenny asked, not knowing what to think. "A security that I'll be back to pay the freight." He was clearly enjoying himself. "Your husband better be aware what a tough businesswoman he married."

When Ian returned the next evening, they sat together and he talked about his trip and asked how the children were. Meagen was growing up just great, with all kinds of stories from school. But Jenny was concerned about Peter. Normally full of energy, running around and starting to babble, she had noticed that lately there was something bothering him.

"How can you tell?"

"Well, I can't explain, but he is slowing down. And his appetite is not what it was before."

"Maybe it would be a good idea to have Dr. Sie check him."

They went to bed, and half asleep, she murmured something that sounded like earning extra money, which made Ian sit upright.

"Do I hear you talking about extra money? You want a raise?" Jenny chuckled. "I made extra money for us yesterday." She told him about the cloves and the watches and the repairs to the barges. "If you are a business person as good as I am, you can make a deal with our Chinaman," she teased.

Ian felt mighty proud of his wife and responded in the same tone. "I better stay away from the office and let you seduce customers!"

She threw her pillow at him. "Don't dare stay away from me, you . . ." She couldn't finish. Ian stopped her by smothering her with kisses.

Dr. Sie Swie Dong could not find anything wrong with Peter, and suggested he should check him again if the symptoms remained or were getting worse. Jenny made it a point to feed Peter special foods he liked and this seemed to improve his appetite.

Chapter Twenty-Nine

In the United Nations, the pressure on The Netherlands increased to such a point that the world body threatened to apply sanctions if it continued to refuse to give the Dutch East Indies its independence. Warnings by the Dutch government that a change of sovereignty too soon would result in chaos and rapid economic decline went unheeded. The governmental committee formed to deal with the matter did not put up much of a fight due to lack of sufficient support from the home front.

Although all signs pointed to the fact that one day the colony would be independent, the official declaration of independence in August 1949, came to many as a shock. The cry, "Merdeka," meaning freedom, had a triumphant ring to it, and the official name of the new state became Indonesia.

Nobody knew what would happen to the ties between motherland and colony that had been established for more than 300 years. Would they be severed on short notice or was there still a chance for an orderly change? Intriguing questions for all of Dutch descent residing in Indonesia came up and there were no answers. How long would the Dutch military stay?

What would happen with the KNIL, with jurisdiction, Dutch interests, and many other matters?

The Rhio Archipelago had never been as much involved in the guerrilla actions as were other areas, and for its Dutch population, Merdeka struck like a thunderbolt from a blue sky. Everybody expected and knew deep down that something was going to happen, but when and how was too difficult to judge. It was a time of uncertainty when it was preferable to tiptoe through daily life.

When the news of independence was made public, Ian and Jenny looked aghast at each other. The same thought came up: what will become of us? What can we do? "Stay calm, panic will only make things worse," one of their friends advised. Luckily there were no repercussions against the Dutch in the Rhio Archipelago, and in the weeks following the declaration nothing tangible happened.

There were some surprises forthcoming. The personnel of the Rhio Lighterage and Stevedoring company came to the office and the spokesman told Andries and Ian that they didn't need to work anymore.

"Oh? Why not?" the two men asked.

"Our president gave a radio speech, telling us that it is now our own country and everything is ours."

That was quite a revelation, albeit a misguided one, and their employers tried to explain that there would be no manna coming from heaven. But it was to no avail, and the troop marched out without any trace of enmity but very determined.

"What do we do now?" asked Andries. "There isn't anybody to watch the tug and the barges."

"I'll try to get some Chinese; maybe they know better." It wasn't too difficult to find watchmen for the small fleet laying at anchor in the bay. Ian worried about what to do when a ship was calling, but Andries told him that the crews would soon be back when they found out that you still needed money to buy food. He was right, and since they had acted in good faith, they were signed on again.

The other surprise was that you had to cut all rupiah banknotes in half, meaning that from one day to another your money was worth only half its value. On top of that, the rate of exchange, rupiah to guilder, had been at par, but that day was three to one. Consequently, values of merchandise and property in Indonesia tumbled to one-sixth in one day. The effect of those measures threw the entire population of one hundred million into turmoil, with everybody trying to cope. Naturally the majority of the UN countries were jubilant, including some industrial nations who figured that a potential market for their products would open up. Whether the population at large had the capability to purchase was another matter. Providing monetary aid as a tool to improve the economy and thus create the desired market proved to be a long road full of pot holes.

As the Rhio Archipelago found itself in the favorable position of having the Singapore dollar as legal currency, it was not directly exposed. However, being part of Indonesia, there were strong ties with the country and many held rupiah accounts. One question much discussed was whether the new government would allow Rhio to maintain its dollar status. Other than the higher government positions, nothing much changed during the first months after independence day. As expected, the Dutch military began to return home and were gradually replaced by the previously underground army. The police force was kept intact to avoid a vacuum in the administration of justice.

In the midst of all the commotion there was one thing that worried Ian and Jenny most. Peter's health was not improving. Feeding him became a daily struggle and he was rapidly losing weight. It became so bad that they had to lay the little boy on the dressing commode, wrapped in a towel. Even then Ian had his hands full keeping Peter on the commode. He struggled with astounding force against being spoon fed, and each time after that ordeal both parents were exhausted. Jenny unwrapped the screaming boy and put him upright, and always he returned the food, which had become very dark in such a short time.

Again they went to the doctor, who could not find out what was wrong. Medication and soft food were prescribed, but to no avail.

One morning Jenny decided to turn the mattress of Peter's bed over, in the hope that it might be of help and give more comfort to their son. When she pulled the mattress up, she noticed that there was something under it, covered under a piece of cloth. Lifting it up, she stared in horror at what she saw—seven dried spiders, seven nail heads, and a knot of hair. She screamed, not knowing what it meant, but intuitively feeling that it was something evil. Fia heard her scream and came running to her. Speechless, Jenny pointed to the collection. Fia looked and was suddenly taken aback, obviously in shock. She called Anjoeng and the two started excitedly talking in Javanese. Not understanding that language, Jenny became impatient. "Stop it! Talk Malay or Dutch! Tell me, what does this mean, and who put it there?"

The servant couple were so agitated that they didn't hear Jenny, who became frustrated and stamped with her foot. At the top of her lungs she yelled, "Listen to me. What is this?" Peter, in his playpen, started to cry and this brought them to their senses. Anjoeng went to Peter in the living room and Fia turned her shocked face to Jenny.

"Oh, missus, Anjoeng and I think it is goena-goena, a sort of black magic. We don't know what these articles mean, but somebody tries to do harm to Peter and thus to you all."

In Holland, Jenny would have laughed at such an explanation, but in the tropics you don't take goena-goena lightly. She took Peter on her arm and went into the office. Ian was probably on the pier and she told the oppas to go and fetch him, lekas, lekas. The last words made it clear to the oppas that there was no time for gossip on his way to get the master.

When Ian arrived he listened to what Jenny told him, looked at the items she had found, and understood that it wasn't just a joke. During his more than three years in the Indies he had heard many stories about black magic. "Leave these things where you found them, close the door to the children's bedroom, and don't let Meagen or Peter in. I'll try to find out what is going on."

He went to the servants' quarters and called Anjoeng. "I know what it means in general, but I don't know how strong the curse is. Do you know a medicine man here who can neutralize the magic?"

Anjoeng at first was reluctant but when Ian pressed him it came out that Anjoeng knew such a man. "Go and ask him to come as soon as he can," Ian said, and Anjoeng left, returning shortly thereafter with a man dressed in typical Moslem garb.

They greeted each other solemnly and Ian led him into the bedroom and showed him the pieces in Peter's bed, which were still untouched. The medicine man asked Ian to be left alone for a while, remaining in the bedroom. Ian went to Jenny, who was still holding Peter as if to protect him. "What did he say? Can he do something?"

"He is inside and we have to wait."

While they were waiting anxiously, Meagen came home from school. She looked at her family, and young as she was, felt that something was amiss. At that moment the medicine man came out of the bedroom, and Meagen gaped at him. He smiled at the two children and said he wanted to talk to the two parents. Fia took both children to the yard, out of earshot. They sat together and the doekoen told them that the curse was too strong for him to neutralize.

"I haven't seen it for a long time, and it is not from this area. Obviously one or more persons foster a hatred against you through your son." He assured them that it was only Peter chosen as the victim and having heard from Anjoeng about the serious problem of feeding the boy, he suggested that the only way the spell could be broken would be when Peter left the area over water.

"You should go to the police; maybe they can find the suspect. Do you have enemies who could do something like this?" Ian shook his head. "I have no idea."

Ready to leave, the doekoen remarked, "Why don't you take your son to Singapore to see a British doctor who specializes in tropical phenomena? It may be worthwhile."

They thanked him and arranged his remuneration for the visit. Ian and Jenny looked at each other, digesting the discouraging news.

"I'll go to the police chief right now, and then we should go with Peter to Singapore as soon as possible." He crossed the street to the police station and asked for the chief. The chief was available and Ian told him what had happened.

"Any idea who it could be? Did you fire anybody lately?" Ian could not think of anybody; the only problem he had was with the crews of the tug and barges, and he told the chief about the misunderstanding at independence.

The chief smiled. "We had some similarities of that nature, but it was all settled. After all, many were misled by unjust information." He suddenly got an idea. "While you were in the coast guard you captured several smuggling boats. As you know, the boats are confiscated and the skippers sentenced. The crews remain hanging around for some time before they find employment again and have little or no money. I bet you that somebody from that crowd is taking it out on you personally. And a little boy has no resistance against a strong goena-goena." He promised to make a search and meanwhile would keep an eye on their house.

From friends they got the name of a doctor in Singapore and two days later took a boat going there, taking Meagen with them to make it less traumatic for Peter. The doctor examined Peter and looked at the mysterious spiders, nail heads, and hair. He did not take it lightly or wave it as being ridiculous. "The doekoen was correct by saying that your son should be taken away over water. But I am sure that the distance between

Tandjoeng Pinang and Singapore is not sufficient. I strongly urge you to go back to Holland soon. That will break the spell."

He added that, until they could make arrangements for the voyage, Jenny should try feeding Peter as if he was a six-month-old baby. In conclusion, he suggested, "Shall I dispose of the wicked items?"

"Please do, but first will you take a photo of the items? I'd like to give it to the police back home."

They stayed the night in Singapore, and when the children were asleep, discussed what they were going to do. Both agreed that there was little time to lose if they wanted to save their son's life, about which there was no doubt in their mind. Jenny suggested she fly with Peter and leave Meagen with Ian so he could take care of her and their business, but Ian wouldn't hear of it. "I love you and our children, and appreciate what you say, but we'll go together."

Jenny cried and he took her in his arms. "You and I are together, and that is the way it will be. Tomorrow I will go to KLM and tell them I will be away for maybe two weeks. I'll ask Frans to take over the agency as his office has done before, for a short time." Also he would make a booking for them to go to Holland. Thereafter he would visit the KPM office, informing them about the situation, and since the work with this agency was more involved than for KLM, he would ask whether they could send Max Dront, who had indoctrinated them in the beginning, to take over temporarily.

The managers of both companies understood Ian's dilemma and were cooperative. It had taken longer than anticipated and they stayed another night in the hotel. This enabled them to take the plane to Tandjoeng Pinang the next morning.

Jenny had a good idea. "We can send a telegram to my sister and her family in Amsterdam and ask to stay with her. She was a nurse there and no doubt will know a pediatrician for Peter." Then a second thought came to her. "You said two weeks staying in Holland. Do you think Peter will be better so soon?"

"That would be a miracle. No, but I reckoned that in two weeks you may be settled with your sister and can start visiting the specialist."

Each time Ian saw Peter he got a shock when he looked at his emaciated appearance, and his heart ached. He admired Jenny, who had to deal with it every moment of the day without obvious despair, or at least she controlled it. An answering telegram from Jenny's sister, Trudi, told them that they were welcome. The KLM booking was confirmed, and Frans was willing to take care of the agency for the weekly schedule. Max arrived and they were ready to go.

Uncertain when Jenny and the children would return, there were many good-byes. They became part of an exodus of people, most of them top officials and the military, all of them being replaced. The middle and lower ranks of the Dutch East Indies government were asked to stay on for the time being, and most did, not sure what to do otherwise.

The last evening before they were leaving for Singapore and then on to Amsterdam, they sat together. It was quiet, the children asleep, and Jenny looked around, wondering if she ever would come back. She and Ian had put so much energy in their work; would it all have been in vain? Ian looked at her, understanding what she was going through at that moment.

"We took a risk and now it is a big question how things will develop. We have no control over it, and will continue to work on our future, wherever that may be." Both knew that they had to take one day at a time, and that recovery of their son came first.

The next day they flew to Singapore; the plane for Holland would depart two days later. It was shortly before New Year's and they all needed warm clothing, which they could not find in Tandjoeng Pinang but was plentiful in Singapore. The one who enjoyed it most was Meagen, who asked hundreds of questions about cold, snow, and family. Shopping finished, they were ready to return to their homeland after four years.

Chapter Thirty

At the end of 1949, there were still monetary restrictions on currency transfers between countries, and this especially was the case between Indonesia and The Netherlands. Since they had no source of income in Holland, Ian had withdrawn dollars in large denominations from his bank account in Singapore and exchanged these into Dutch guilders at a non-official street office. For the time being they were covered.

When airborne, Ian discovered that the dentist couple from Tandjoeng Pinang were also on board. He said hello and noticed a certain strain between the two. The dentist got up from his seat and followed Ian to a small open area in the rear of the plane. There he whispered to Ian that he had Dutch money but wasn't sure where to hide it; maybe Ian knew of a very special hiding place? Ian was not inclined to get involved and told him that everybody was on his or her own on that frivolous matter. The dentist wandered off miserably.

Upon returning to his seat, he told Jenny about the dentist's predicament. Jenny listened and then asked point-blank, "Where are you going to put ours?" That was a blow, and Ian could not answer.

"Okay, give it to me. I'll take care of it and don't ask until we are at my sister's."

The first night stop was in Karachi where the passengers stayed in a hotel close to the airport. The next morning in the departure hall Jenny bought a doll for Meagen, who looked surprised. She never had played with dolls, but Jenny was insistent that in Holland girls played with dolls.

At the end of the second day, when the plane was over the Mediterranean, the captain announced an unscheduled stop would be made that night in Rome. Bad weather in Western Europe had caused airports to close, but probably not for long. Again, all the passengers were taken to a hotel, this time a specimen from old glorious times. Their rooms were larger than at home, with marble everywhere, crystal chandeliers, and huge mirrors in gilt frames. Even Peter found energy to run through the rooms, sharing his excitement with his sister.

There was a knock on the door and when Ian opened it, he saw seven people in the corridor. In rapid Italian, the spokesman made introductions of the personnel. Ian smiled and said, "Si, si," and they entered the sitting room and the story was repeated.

"I get it," Jenny said to Ian. "These two men are going to do something with our dinner; the other man will look after your suit and shoes; one woman will do the same for me; another will bathe the kids; and it beats me what the two remaining women will do, but I'm sure they will find something. Oh, I love Rome!" And in her excitement she exclaimed, "Viva Roma!" This met with loud approval from the hotel people, who started laughing and talking until the spokesman got them under control and started pointing to their tasks.

Meagen declared that she would like to live in a big house in Italy, to which Jenny reacted by stating that she was a spoiled brat. The next morning word came that Schiphol airport was open, and the passengers trooped into buses to the airport. On arrival there, Mrs. Halls was called over the intercom and requested to come to the KLM counter. She left the children with Ian and went, wondering why she was called. At the counter there was a ground stewardess. "Oh, Mrs. Halls, we found your daughter's doll. Another stewardess knew it was yours."

"Thank you very much. I appreciate it, and my daughter will be glad to have it back." That last part was bending the truth somewhat; Meagen had not the slightest interest.

"What was it?" asked Ian when she returned looking pale. "Oh, they found Meagen's doll, which she had lost."

Ian looked at her, thinking there must be more to it, but did not pursue it further.

In the waiting area the dentist couple came by and joined them. The lady, in a soft voice, told them she was going nuts because of her husband. "That stupid money. At least ten times during the flight he disappears and comes back and each time I must guess where he had hidden it, and always I was right because he is so nervous and obvious." Turning to her husband, she said, "You give it to me and stop being so uptight."

Ian and Jenny exchanged glances and both smiled. The rest of the trip was bumpy over the Alps but then the flat country came into sight and they landed in the snow. The children were dumbfounded seeing the white stuff for the first time and Meagen told her brother that Holland was one big refrigerator. The boy looked with admiration at his big sister: she knew so much!

The family disembarked, shivering as they walked over the tarmac, and entered the hall. The dentist couple was ahead of them, and of course, he was picked out by a customs officer and led into an office. Jenny noticed and told Ian, "See what I meant?" Their family was waiting behind a barricade and a lot of waving was going on. Construction in the arrivals hall was still unfinished and arriving passengers could call their families and friends, which caused a lot of hilarity on both sides. Jenny told Meagen, "See, there are granny and grandpa, remember from the photos?" Meagen wasn't sure but thought so. Jenny turned to a supervising customs officer. "Sir, may I send my two children to their grandparents? They haven't seen my girl for years and my son never before." The official looked at the children. "All right, but you must stay here."

Promptly Meagen, with doll under her arm and Peter by the hand, was gently shoved to the waiting family. The two kids were smothered by their next of kin and Ian and Jenny passed through customs check, and then it was their turn to greet their loved ones, including Trudi and her husband.

When they arrived at Trudi's house and settled in after the first commotion, Ian turned to Jenny. "You rascal, you hid the roll of banknotes in the doll; that's why you had Meagen go to the family. I'll be damned." She laughed. "I got a shock in Rome when they found it. I had forgotten all about it."

The first days in Amsterdam were devoted to getting used to each other, especially the children. The first nights Meagen and Peter had trouble sleeping without a mosquito net over their bed and no yard to play in. And it was always cold and rainy! In addition, the food was so different.

An appointment with the physician was made, and Trudi took Jenny and the children. Jenny and Peter entered his office. The doctor was an elderly gentleman who had been in the tropics before, so when he looked at Peter, he turned to Jenny. "So another mother from the Far East who was too busy with parties and playing bridge to look after her child!"

At first, Jenny was dumbfounded hearing these words, but quickly recovered. "Just a minute, doctor." And she left the office, returning with Meagen. "This is my daughter." The pediatrician looked at the roly-poly girl, cleared his throat, and apologized.

"All right, doctor, let us get to the problem with my son." She told him Peter's story in detail and soon they were on common ground. From then on there was a good understanding between the physician and Jenny, the latter having full faith in him.

It was going to be a lengthy road to recovery and soon Ian's two weeks elapsed. He was flying back to the Rhio Archipelago with the certainty that his family was in good hands.

There was another farewell, again with questions in their minds. As before, there was no choice and Ian felt that once again he was being pushed into situations and decisions, although this time for the well-being of his son.

The trip went smoothly and in Singapore he took one day to visit the KPM and KLM offices, informing their representatives that he was ready to resume the agencies. They told him there had been no problems during his absence, but he could not avoid the impression of a wait-and-see atmosphere. The president of the Republic of Indonesia had studied in Holland before the war and was a graduate engineer, but also had been in communist countries.

Which way the tide would turn was the big question mark. The fact that in earlier years the president had been imprisoned by the Dutch because of overt communist sympathy and actions was reason enough that Dutch interests in the erstwhile colony could be on shaky grounds. To top that off, one of the president's wives was a Japanese princess and the wounds of the cruel warfare were still wide open.

Ian's choice on how to return to Tandjoeng Pinang proved to be rather limited; going by plane meant waiting for four days and he was eager to get there. The only alternative was a Chinese motor junk which would take the entire night. Having little trust in the haute cuisine on board, he bought food of his own taste before boarding.

As a result, Ian was not looking forward to going home. He sat on a wooden bench, unable to sleep. Enough is enough, he told himself. Stop being pessimistic and feeling sorry for yourself. He started paying attention to the other passengers around him, some Chinese families, a couple from India, and a Malay, or were they now called Indonesian? The man had been observing him and apparently sensed that Ian was no longer absorbed in his own thoughts.

He opened a discussion. "Excuse me, but I have seen you in Tandjoeng Pinang before and know that you have your business there."

"Yes, you are right. Do you live there too?"

"Only recently. I am from Sumatra." There was a moment of silence. Oh brother, Ian thought, who knows, maybe he was in the TNI, the national guerrilla forces, now the Indonesian army.

The next question caught him by surprise. "What do you think of the fact that now we are independent and have our freedom?"

This question was so contrary to the generally polite conversation with a stranger that it caught Ian off guard for a moment. An inner voice warned: beware, thin ice, be careful. He hesitated, but the Indonesian kept looking at him for an answer.

"I am not a politician, and can only say that the Dutch government has been concerned that independence too soon could result in chaos." Taking back the initiative, he added, "And what do you think?"

His adversary, at least that's how Ian now considered him, changed suddenly from Malay to Dutch. "I don't care whether there will be chaos or that we starve from hunger; if we die, we die in freedom." And with a shrewd expression on his face, he continued. "Didn't your country long ago wage eighty years of war against the Spanish conquerors for your freedom?"

Aha, Ian observed, speaks Dutch and knows history. Who on earth and what can this man be? Here we are on a slow-moving craft, we cannot avoid each other, and telling him that the war he mentioned was under different circumstances will develop into an endless yea-nay circus. We better come to terms with each other before it becomes really unpleasant. It is his territory now, and I am sort of a guest. And then he remembered that before they left Indonesia they had to apply for a re-entry permit, which had given them a shock of realization.

"Okay, let's put pretensions and skirmishing aside. We have to deal with the future. By the way, my name is Ian Halls." The other man nodded. "You are right. My name is Joesoef bin Mohamed. I am the secretary of the governor of the Rhio Archipelago. Your governor left last week and we are awaiting arrival of his Indonesian replacement."

That was another surprise to Ian. "My governor?" Gone already? He didn't know what to say. Things had moved fast during his two weeks absence. Would that be one of the reasons for the subdued attitude when he visited the offices in Singapore? Their talk continued, but now in a more civilized fashion. Ian learned that Mr. Joesoef was on this junk for the same reasons as Ian, namely to reach Tandjoeng Pinang with the earliest transportation. Also he knew Ian's name and position, having checked the passenger list of the junk. This is going to be really interesting, Ian thought. How much more does he know about me? That I was in the coast guard? And how long was he in Tandjoeng Pinang before emerging as the new governor's secretary?

It was with a feeling of relief when at dawn they entered the bay and docked at the pier. Passports and permits were checked and before leaving, Joesoef shook hands with Ian. "My pleasure to talk with you. I am sure we'll meet again soon." Whether that was a promise or just a phrase, Ian didn't know and he left it at that.

Strange, nobody was there to welcome him, so he took his luggage and walked ashore. When he passed the port office he said hello to Frans' secretary who asked how the missus and children were. No, the harbor master wasn't in yet but he would let him know that Mr. Halls had returned.

Ian went to the house and the first thing he saw was Anjoeng hoisting the Indonesian and the companies' flags. As before, the first question was about Jenny and the children. Was Peter already getting better? Fia heard his voice and was eager to hear the latest news, and Ian told them that he had the greatest trust in the doctor and that things would work out in time. Inside the house he found Max having breakfast and after the first greetings they soon talked shop.

Ian mentioned the impression he got at the KPM office that there was a certain tension. Max wasn't surprised. "For the Dutch government officials the situation is pretty clear: the top is replaced, and for the middle and lower ranking officials they can choose—either stay on if asked and eventually become Indonesian citizens or leave."

"Not much of a choice," was Ian's opinion. "But what about the private section with huge investments here?"

"Well, take the KPM for instance. The entire fleet of ninety-nine ships, large and small, are registered in Batavia, which is now called Jakarta. That represents a huge investment and the risk of nationalization exists and rumors are increasing."

Great, Ian thought, this is what you call a heartwarming welcome. And that was not all, because Max, as a true KPM employee, continued. "Of course, my company cannot move any of the many buildings throughout Indonesia, but ships can pull out. Then the economy will collapse. The KPM is the only reliable shipping company for inter-insular traffic. Sounds menacing."

Ian decided to pull himself out of the somber predicament. It was no use dwelling on what could happen, and moreover, what could he do? There was no turning of the tide; the best answer was to prepare for the worst and make the best of today. They moved into the office and together went through the paperwork of the past two weeks. There had been one call of the regular line ship with the usual general cargo and passengers. Ian's personnel arrived and soon it was business as usual. Max had done a good job, and Ian thanked him for his help.

"When are you planning to leave?"

"If it is all right with you, I'd like to take the plane in three days."

"No problem. I'll go and see Frans and then Andries."

Ian walked to the port office and saw Frans at his desk.

"Hi, old boy. Welcome back. Tell me all about Jenny and the kids, especially Peter." He called the oppas for coffee and the two friends sat together.

Ian gave him the story of their trip, the hidden money, and Jenny's experience with the doctor. Frans burst out in a roaring laugh. "I can see Jenny defending her cub; boy that must have been something. Pity we have no children, otherwise my wife could do the same with a doll when we leave."

Ian caught the last words. "Are you leaving?"

"Yes, like so many others. My replacement will arrive soon and I think we'll leave within a month."

"And then do what? Sit in a little house with slippers on, look at the rain, and listen to the howling wind? You'll both go nuts in no time!"

A broad smile lit Frans' face. "No siree, fat chance. We'll go to Holland first to see our folks. Then we plan to invite more distant family and friends to see us, all on one day. When that is done and over with, we'll sail to the Caribbean and settle there." And Frans looked at Ian, awaiting his reaction to that idea.

"On which island are you two going to upset the neighborhood?"

"Ah," exclaimed the almost-terminated harbor master. "Finally the man comes alive. As a matter of fact, that decision has not been made yet. We can choose between French, British, Danish, and Dutch influences." And then in a more serious tone he asked Ian to come over to their home that night for dinner. "We'll have to talk." Ian thanked him for taking care of the KLM agency during his absence.

"Glad to have been of service. As a matter of fact, your personnel did most of the job."

After this visit, he went to Andries, his partner in the lighterage and stevedoring activity. Andries and his Javanese wife were at home; she went to the kitchen to make coffee, leaving the men on the verandah. Again, there had not been any problems and Ian started to feel that he wasn't needed at all; everybody did fine without him! Andries asked him what his plans for the future were, now with his family in Europe. Ian told him that he had not made up his mind yet, but having built a business here, that's where he belonged.

"Well, let's see how the cookies crumble. In the meantime, I have the tugboat and lighters re-registered in Singapore."

"Well, I don't mind as long as they are available here." They discussed the operation in general, with emphasis on the decreasing tonnages now that the Dutch military presence had been decreasing rapidly. Again: wait and see.

To complete a busy day, Ian took his small boat to the remaining part of his kingdom, the shipyard on the little island. At a distance he could see that there was one fishing boat on the slip. Greeting his yard manager, he asked how things were proceeding. The man shrugged his shoulders. "Could be better. Boat owners aren't sure whether the new government will continue issuing annual certificates on the same basis as before."

"We will soon learn, won't we?" He looked around and noticed that the LCT was still firmly bedded and secured. "Is the winch operating all right?"

"No problem there, sir. What do you think will happen with the yard?"

Ian had heard the question in one form or another enough on that day. "Allah's will, my friend, Allah's will." It was a cheap shot, but well understood.

Ian went through the books and complimented his manager for a job well done, and then took off. After a while he shut off the outboard motor and let his boat drift on the current. Looking back at Bajan Island a sudden thought struck him. What if the Indonesian government would not recognize his ninety-nine-year lease on the island? Floating along the coastline of the land he had started to love as a second native country, he talked to himself. "Come on, you often have been in uncertain and unpredictable situations. Get yourself together and take one day at a time." Hearing his own words, he smiled, thinking that he was either becoming a second-rate philosopher or a fatalist.

Dinner at the Fransens that night was a delightful affair with intelligent conversation. Besides Ian, there were two other couples, Mr. and Mrs. Pelle, and to his surprise, the reverend and his wife.

After dinner, the men went to the porch while the ladies stayed inside "doing something about clothes," as Frans expressed. Relaxing and looking out from the hilltop over the bay, Ian asked the pastor if he was going to stay now that he was demilitarized.

"Yes, I plan to stay as long as there is a congregation here."

"Hear, hear," said Mr. Pelle, who was the local government's jurist.

"I am asked to stay on for the time being and that is what I will do."

Frans, as a good host, had been listening politely but couldn't remain silent any longer. "Well, gentlemen, so far it is three to one. Three who stay on as long as they can or are allowed to stay on for who knows how long, and one who is leaving."

"You have no choice, since you are a navy man," said Ian, but Frans didn't go for it.

"During three years of brutal war both sides lost thousands of lives. And for what? Our persistence that chaos would follow if independence was given too early. And what are you doing: you are undermining the very reasoning our government sought to delay that day, by hanging on. Has all that wretchedness been in vain? When India, Pakistan, and Ceylon wanted independence from British India, the British military and government went out in mass. Of course, chaos erupted, and the new nations had to ask the British to come back on their own terms and assist in establishing an orderly transition. Now you stay to do the same, not on your own terms, but on theirs. Your insight, experience, and what-not are the tools which give the new leaders the opportunity to show the world: 'see, the Dutch were wrong'!"

The three men were listening to Frans' tirade in growing astonishment. They all knew him well, but this outburst was very unusual for him. After a while, the clergyman responded. "Only history will show what was right or wrong. In the meantime, each of us has to live with his own decision."

The conversation went into calmer waters, touching on subjects like anecdotes of life in the Indies, before the war; the good humor was restored when the ladies joined them and they all had a memorable evening. When they bade their farewell, Frans asked Ian to stay for a moment.

"Sorry to touch on raw nerves, but I had to give my opinion. I invited you tonight so that you would get somewhat better acquainted with both men; they could become trustworthy friends in the near future, when you need friends. But what I would like to tell you is that people living in the Rhio Archipelago may soon no longer be permitted to maintain bank accounts abroad, including Singapore. You'll have to convert your dollars into Mickey Mouse rupiahs and what that means needs no explanation. The reason is obvious: the government is in urgent need of hard currency."

Ian swallowed hard. "You are full of surprises tonight. Do you think I have time to consider the consequences?"

"I don't know, but suggest you talk with one of your Chinese customers; they are used to situations like this and have learned the hard way."

"Thank you, Frans. You are a good friend and I hate to see you go."

On his way home Ian came to the conclusion that it had been quite a day with a lot of food for thought. Back home he went to bed, looked at the photo of his family on the nightstand, and fell asleep.

The following morning he asked Pheng Hui if he knew how to reach the Chinese gentleman 'with the cloves,' as they called him in the office. Pheng Hui said that the man did not live in Tandjoeng Pinang but occasionally appeared. "Let me know when he is in town, please. I would like to talk with him." He had remembered that Jenny had trusted the man by issuing a Bill of Lading before the goods had been loaded, so maybe that was a starting point on the monetary topic.

Max returned to the KPM Singapore office. Ian handed the KLM captain a sealed envelope with money to put into his account with the KLM. He had done this before, to have cash available when he was in the city. It went into the same envelope as the cash received from private passengers. Anyhow it was not a bank account, he figured.

Weeks went by and contrary to the first day of his return nothing spectacular happened. The letters he got from Jenny were upbeat; Peter was slowly gaining weight and Meagen wanted to know when they would see daddy. Jenny didn't ask the same, but Ian knew better. He had written her that Fia and Anjoeng had it easy with a one-man household, and added some local news, but did not dwell on the more questionable topics. No need to have her worried.

Chapter Thirty-One

One morning Pheng Hui announced that the 'clove gentleman' was in town and would come into the office that afternoon. Mr. Lin Po Tjin was his name, and after general pleasantries Ian cautiously touched on the topic of possible monetary restrictions. The man needed only a few hints to grasp Ian's dilemma. The Chinese was contemplating Ian's situation and had a few questions.

"You are a Dutch citizen?"

"Yes, I am."

"Are you considering becoming an Indonesian citizen?"

"No."

He nodded and for a few moments was lost in thought.

"You haven't asked, but I think you are looking for advice?" Ian liked his direct businesslike approach, and told him that he was looking for a safe haven for his money in Singapore, and to terminate his bank account there.

"Good. Before we go any further, I'll do two things. Tonight there is a meeting with several of my friends, and I would like to take you there. The other thing will follow thereafter. I'll pick you up at six, okay?"

That evening Lin Po Tjin led him to a room behind a Chinese restaurant and Ian was introduced to six Chinese men who were seated at a round table. He recognized two of them as shippers and airline passengers. When all were seated, the meeting began in one of the many Chinese languages, which was abracadabra for Ian. So he sat there observing the others. Within an hour everybody stood up, smiled at him, and left.

"Sit down, please. Would you like some tea?"

"Yes, thank you." Good heavens, Ian thought. What am I into? Tea was served and Lin Po Tjin waited until the waitress had left.

"You were just witness to the foundation of a trading company. Capital of two million dollars has been spoken for. Each member has his task in the company."

"But nobody took notes," said an astonished Ian.

Lin Po Tjin smiled. "A typical Western reaction. You people believe only in written contracts with signatures and lawyers. We handle it the way you just saw."

"But if one or more do not live up to the agreement?"

"Then such a person will be an outcast for the rest of his life and as a merchant be virtually dead. So, we trust each other." He gave Ian a moment to digest the meaning and continued. "When I had to flee China from Mao Tse Tung, I had to leave my family behind. Recently I returned under cover to smuggle my son out. I had to carry hard currency to bribe many persons. It was dangerous since you were not allowed to have foreign currency on you. If caught, you were put in a special prison. Nobody beat you, the guards were friendly, but you had to sit outside at day and inside at night. You pay a fixed small amount of the money they found on you for each day in confinement until you have used up the total amount. And meanwhile you do nothing, just nothing."

Knowing the Chinese, Ian could imagine what that meant.

"So, if we both trust each other, I am willing to help you. You give me your funds, and wherever you are and whenever you need part or all of it, you get it. No papers, just our handshake."

This was an approach Ian was not used to at all and it took him some time to make a decision. Then, considering the alternatives, he told Lin Po Tjin, "I accept your offer," and they shook hands. He got Lin's addresses in Singapore and in London, the latter a surprise to him. Arrangements were made, and they parted as friends.

Soon thereafter there were some special events taking place in town. The new harbor master arrived, and when meeting him, Ian wasn't sure whether the good relationship he had enjoyed with Frans would be continued. He never let first impressions rule but couldn't shake off an uncomfortable feeling. Time would tell.

Frans' departure thereafter culminated in a roaring good-bye party and when they had left, Ian felt lonely. There were so many other friends and acquaintances leaving that it looked like the European sector was vanishing almost completely. Then the new governor arrived. Ian received an invitation to attend the inauguration, followed by a reception. Guests lined up to greet the new official and when it was his turn he was introduced to the governor by Joesoef bin Mohamed, the so-called secretary he had met on the junk.

"Mr. Governor, this is Mr. Halls. The gentleman is acting as agent for the KPM and KLM, has a working arrangement with the owner of the local lighterage company, and holds a long-term lease with the Dutch East Indies government on the island Bajan." Smiles on both sides continued, but inwardly Ian was seething. The man was out of line to disclose his recent background for everybody to hear, and especially mention of the ex-government lease was not called for. Ian's feeling of isolation strengthened.

The next evening he went to Pelle's home and told him what happened during the reception. He asked the jurist if the Indonesian government would honor his lease on the island.

"Ian, I can only tell you that in some cases they do, but not always. The independence didn't come in a very friendly manner. It depends on two considerations: if it is to the government's advantage to uphold a contract for lack of a better short-term solution, or if it is based on a personal matter. The first case to declare a lease null and void will not apply to you, but for the other I am not so sure. Of course, I have heard about your encounter with Joesoef, who, by the way, is more of a lieutenant governor than a secretary. Apparently he doesn't like you for, to me, obscure reasons, and he could push to have your lease terminated."

"In that case, what can I do?"

"Nothing, I am afraid. But continue your activities as before. In the worst case, you will get a notice."

It didn't sound very encouraging and suddenly he was glad he had made a deal with Lin Po Tjin; at least that was one less burden, he hoped.

During the next months his determination to prepare for possible unpleasant surprises became stronger. He even made preparations for a sudden departure in the form of an emergency flight suitcase with papers and sheer necessities. One reason was that he received a circular from KLM, informing their agents that the Garuda Airlines, owned by the Indonesian government, had taken over all domestic flights. In the interim period, as yet undetermined, KLM would act as supervising body.

From the shipping company there was no word as yet, but something was bound to happen there also, although ships could rapidly be moved out of the country, as he remembered Max told him. So, if he had to leave on short notice, the Garuda people had to take care of their Tandjoeng Pinang business themselves, but with the KPM it was different. Then he remembered that his ex-colleague on the *Rian* had an apprentice on board, a young Eurasian whose fiancée lived in town. Since the future of the coast guard also was uncertain, maybe the young fellow was interested in becoming his assistant. Although the cargo was diminishing, the workload continued and Jenny's absence in the office was an extra burden on the others.

When the *Rian* was in port, Ian went on board and said hello to the commanding officer, a career coast guard man. "How are things nowadays?" Ian asked.

The other didn't respond right away, then shrugged fatalistically. "Who knows. So far only changes at the top, not down to the lower echelons. Many of us are just waiting for the ax to fall."

Ian decided to play an open card with the man. "I know you have an aspiring officer on board. As you know, my family is in Holland and my wife used to work in our office. Now that she isn't here, I am looking for an assistant. Would your second be interested?"

"I think he might be; he told me that they are going to be married and the future in the coast guard is not certain for Dutch nationals."

Ian asked whether he could talk with him.

"Go ahead, fine with me. I'll tell him to see you."

That evening somebody called at the door. It was Hein Ebbink, the apprentice. Ian asked him to come in, offered a beer, and soon broached the subject of becoming his assistant. "Your qualifications for this type of work are satisfactory; fluency in Dutch, Malay, and English, plus, most important, basic knowledge of the shipping industry."

Hein was clearly interested. "Sir, I think I'd like to accept your offer. However, there is one matter of concern. I plan to get married, and if I work for you, we cannot get government housing. Private housing for rent is non-existent."

Oh shit, Ian thought, that could be a problem. But . . . and then he got an idea. "You know what. As long as my family stays abroad, you two can live here. There is room enough and we can arrange it so that you two will have privacy. Think it over, talk with your bride-to-be, and let me know when you can start."

The next morning Hein came in, introduced his Eurasian fiancée and both were on cloud nine when the deal was closed. Ian was relieved with his, as he called it, 'negative progress,' so far, and he wrote Jenny a long letter about his assistant and the situation in general. After all, he mused, a good businessman plans ahead and that is what I am doing. If I can avoid being forced into situations, so much the better.

Although expected, the official notification came out of the blue. The government informed Mr. Halls that the lease on the island Bajan, as arranged with the former Dutch East Indies government, would not be honored by the Indonesian government. Therefore, Mr. Halls had to vacate the island and restore it to its original status within three months of the date of the notification. It was signed on account of the governor of the Rhio Archipelago by Joesoef bin Mohamed, secretary. Ian cursed the secretary under his breath. Less than three months! And he had to dismantle the yard, the office building, and what about the LCT with its machinery and stores? And all that at his expense! That was going to cost a small fortune, which he didn't have, and selling it as scrap would bring very little money. When he showed it to Mr. Pelle, there was little the jurist could say to find a way out for Ian.

He now had no options; begging the governor to change the verdict was against his character and would make him a spineless man. And having no close friends since Frans had left, there was nobody in town with whom he could talk. Well, anyhow he had more than two months to contemplate the next move. The shipyard remained the hot item and he noticed that the new harbor master did not have boats for inspection at the yard as often as before. When high tide was during the daytime, Ian had seen him sloshing through the spongy mud inspecting the boats. Lately Andries, the owner of the tugboat and lighters, had started talking about taking up residence in Singapore. When Ian asked him why, he got only evasive answers. They had worked together in good harmony, so Ian wondered what was really behind such talk.

Exchange of letters between Jenny and him were always light points in his life. Having been apart for three months made their longing for each other stronger and when taking his latest experiences into account he felt that his life was coming to a climax.

Because Tandjoeng Pinang was a small town, Ian was certain his moves were being followed, and more unsettling, too many people had information about the pending eviction of his boat yard. So, for the outside world, he made some statements about selling the works to somebody who could obtain a lease from the government. There was no reaction, not even a nibble.

Meanwhile the harbor master, with whom he maintained a rather cool relationship, was occasionally hinting that the Garuda Airlines was a national company, and that earlier the port management had acted as agent for KLM. Ian didn't like beating around the bush and one day he asked him, "Are you planning to take the agency away from me?"

The harbor master eyed him coolly. "I think that it is important to have one branch of government rendering services to another branch." The observation was clear; the airline and the port organization were both in the Department of Transportation. Moreover, it would mean more revenue for the port of Tandjoeng Pinang.

That did it for Ian. He went to Andries. "Where is your tug right now? And your lighters?" Andries knew that there was not a vessel calling for several days and looked at Ian searchingly.

"The lighters are in Singapore waiting for cargo at the refinery. The tug is here at anchor. If a KPM vessel is due, we can charter the harbor master's barges."

"Okay, Andries, we have worked together quite well. I need a favor from you; I want the tug for an urgent trip to Singapore, tonight."

A faint smile appeared on the old man's face. "I know what you want Ian. You want to get out of here and avoid paying big money out of your pocket to restore that little hump called Bajan. You can get the tug and leave her in Singapore. I'll tell the skipper to make ready. You are in command. Farewell, my boy."

Ian felt tears burning behind his eyes. "Thank you, Andries. I should have come to you earlier."

Well before dark Ian went in his motorboat to the tug, climbed on board and asked the skipper to put his little boat in tow. He placed his suitcase in the wheel house. The anchor was weighed and Ian cast a last glance at the town he was leaving surreptitiously. They passed near the governor's mansion but Ian didn't look. The tugboat wasn't the fastest in the world, but should make Singapore at daybreak. They were well underway when in the twilight Ian noticed a minesweeper coming up fast. He took a pair of binoculars and trained on the other vessel. Yes, it was the *Rian*, approaching at full speed.

Ian turned to the skipper. "I'll take over now. Can you increase speed?" The skipper went to the engine room and Ian felt that the vibration and the pitch had increased. "We are on maximum revs, sir," he announced.

"Thank you, skipper," Ian answered, looking again through his glasses at the *Rian*. Suddenly he gasped in surprise; on the bridge next to Jalim he saw Joesoef. No doubt they were after him to bring him back to Tandjoeng Pinang; somebody had gotten wind of his escape plan. Ian was back in his element; only this time he was the hunted. Scanning the chart, he said to the skipper, pointing at a narrow channel at starboard, "Did you ever take this shortcut?"

"Only in daytime, when there is enough water under the keel."

"Well, tell your helmsman to follow my orders without hesitation. We will go in the channel in five minutes."

The skipper looked at him with wide open eyes. "But it is almost dark."

With no time for explanation, Ian snapped, "No talk. Just look ahead." Ian had noticed that on the *Rian* they used the signal lamp to get his attention. They were closing in on the tugboat fast. At the very last moment he ordered "full starboard" and the tugboat listed heavily when it entered the barely visible narrows. Behind them the *Rian* was unable to follow the maneuver instantly and passed the entrance before turning around. At that time, Ian ordered "slow ahead" and placed a sailor in the bow as lookout. He knew that the *Rian* could not navigate the narrow channel, surely not in the dark without radar.

Slowly they proceeded. So far luck was with him; there was no sign of the *Rian*.

Thank you, Jalim, my good man. I know you are under pressure to do what you can, but I also know you won't follow me here, he thought.

Calling the skipper, who was on pins and needles, he switched on a little lamp on the chart table. "About three miles from here the channel splits; one northwest in the direction of Singapore harbor and the other northeast into the straits to the South China Sea. We take the northeast channel, which is wider than where we are now, and head for Singapore Island, entering, so to speak, at the back door." The skipper had regained his trust in the situation and observed Ian.

"You reckon the *Rian* will lay in wait at the other channel?"

"That's what I think, yes. Extinguish all lights and let's creep along." The lookout did a good job calling out when changing course. It was slow progress until finally they reached the fork and headed northeast. A late moon came up which, together with the wider channel, allowed better speed. Near daybreak they crossed the straits, heading due north to close to the coast of Singapore island, and finally reached the backwaters of Singapore city. Bleary eyed and exhausted but triumphant, Ian thanked the skipper, donated his motorboat to him and went to a hotel. He had made it!

After a refreshing sleep he went to Lin Po Tjin's address, told a young Chinese who he was and that he wanted a small sum of his money, if possible in Dutch currency. No questions were asked and within half an hour it was accomplished. Ian chuckled when he thought of the money-smuggling operation by Jenny; soon they would be together and laugh about it.

He did not go to the KPM and KLM/Garuda offices in order to avoid creating problems for them in Tandjoeng Pinang. Instead, he would send cables to them from Holland informing them of his return to Holland for family reasons, with promise to send explanatory letters. In the cables he would mention that for the time being their interests in Tandjoeng Pinang were well covered. He went to the BOAC Airways and booked a one-way ticket to London, and sent a telegram to Jenny, advising her of his date and time of arrival in London, leaving open when he would arrive in Amsterdam. Buying presents for his own and Trudi's families, he boarded the plane, and then he promptly dozed off.

Disembarking at Heathrow Airport, going to passport control and customs, he immediately saw his beloved Jenny. She was crying and rushed into his arms. After a long time, he held her away from his face. "And how are the children?"

"Fine. Trudi is taking care of them."

"Good. They unfortunately will have to wait two days."

"Oh?"

"Yes, my love. You and I are going underground in London for at least two days!"

With a glitter in her eyes, pretending to be surprised, she asked, "Are we going underground again? And only for two days?"

"Yes, among other things we have much to talk about, and come to think of it, two days may not be enough!"

Surely they had come a long way.